Praise for
Roland's Labyrinth

"*Roland's Labyrinth* is a marvelous historical novel filled with mystery and political intrigue. In the first few lines, Anne Echols pulls the reader into the sweeping story of a passionate young Spaniard learning about the art of surgery as well as love and life in fifteenth-century Provence."
—KRISTINE F. ANDERSON,
author of *Crooked Truth* and *Outside the Diamond*

"*Roland's Labyrinth* is a fascinating, delightful read and an engaging glimpse into life in the late medieval period, with all its complexities, drama, and medical advances."
—BEVERLY J. ARMENTO,
author of *Seeing Eye Girl: A Memoir of Madness, Resilience, and Hope*

"From love story to murder mystery, *Roland's Labyrinth* will guide you through the politics and medicine of fifteenth-century France enfolded in the person of Roland, a student of surgery. The twists and turns of this plot will keep you turning the pages and wanting more."
—LINDA ULLESEIT, author of *The River Remembers*

Roland's Labyrinth

Roland's Labyrinth

A Novel

ANNE ECHOLS

SWP
SHE WRITES PRESS

Copyright © 2025 Anne Echols

All rights reserved. No part of this publication may be reproduced, stored in a retrieval system, or transmitted in any form or by any means, electronic, mechanical, photocopying, recording, or otherwise, except for brief quotations in reviews, educational works, or other uses permitted by copyright law.

Published in 2025 by
She Writes Press, an imprint of The Stable Book Group

32 Court Street, Suite 2109
Brooklyn, NY 11201
https://shewritespress.com

Library of Congress Control Number: 2025909645
ISBN: 978-1-64742-954-6
eISBN: 978-1-64742-955-3

Interior Designer: Stacey Aaronson
Map is courtesy of Carson Evans

Printed in the United States

This is a work of fiction. Names, characters, places, and incidents are either products of the author's imagination or are used fictitiously. Any resemblance to actual persons, living or dead, is purely coincidental. No part of this publication may be used to train generative artificial intelligence (AI) models. The publisher and author reserve all rights related to the use of this content in machine learning.

All company and product names mentioned in this book may be trademarks or registered trademarks of their respective owners. They are used for identification purposes only and do not imply endorsement or affiliation.

*In memory of Russ Echols,
my beloved life partner, 1950–2025.*

Table of Contents

SOUTHERN FRANCE AND PROVENCE
IN THE FIFTEENTH CENTURY . . . *i*

CHAPTER 1 . . . 1
CHAPTER 2 . . . 21
CHAPTER 3 . . . 33
CHAPTER 4 . . . 53
CHAPTER 5 . . . 79
CHAPTER 6 . . . 91
CHAPTER 7 . . . 115
CHAPTER 8 . . . 137
CHAPTER 9 . . . 161
CHAPTER 10 . . . 173
CHAPTER 11 . . . 195
CHAPTER 12 . . . 217
CHAPTER 13 . . . 245
CHAPTER 14 . . . 257
EPILOGUE 269

AUTHOR'S NOTE . . . *275*
SELECTED SOURCES . . . *276*
DISCUSSION QUESTIONS . . . *279*
ACKNOWLEDGMENTS . . . *281*
ABOUT THE AUTHOR . . . *283*

Southern France and Provence in the Fifteenth Century

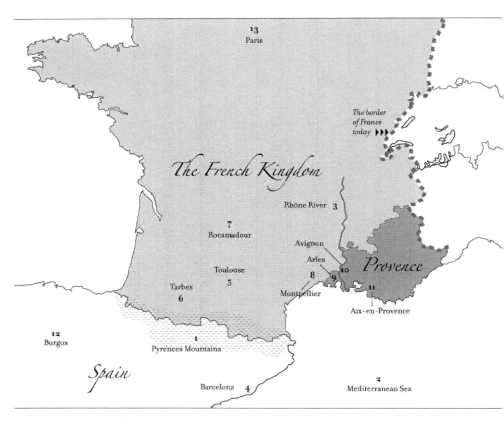

1. Pyrenees Mountains
2. Mediterranean Sea
3. Rhône River
4. Barcelona — The city where Roland was born.
5. Toulouse — The judicial capital of southern France.
6. Tarbes — A city on the pilgrimage route between France and Spain.
7. Rocamadour — An important pilgrimage destination in the Middle Ages.
8. Montpellier — The city where Roland attends the university. Its medical school was renowned in the Middle Ages.
9. Arles — The city where Roland works as an apprentice surgeon.
10. Avignon — Roland lives briefly in this city.
11. Aix-en-Provence — Roland visits this city.
12. Burgos — The city in Spain where Roland's brother Carlos lives.
13. Paris

One

"Humanity, take a good look at yourself.
Inside, you've got heaven and earth, and all of creation.
You're a world—everything is hidden in you."

—Twelfth-century Abbess Hildegard of Bingen,
from her book *Causes and Cures*

Montpellier, France
Septembre, 1477

The body, covered with a blanket, lay on a table in the courtyard. Despite his thick wool cloak, Roland shivered, not from dread or the autumn chill but from anticipation. Today he would see with his own eyes the parts within a dead man and begin to discover the inner workings of the body.

The medical students gathered around the table grew quiet as a servant uncovered the body. Roland averted his gaze and a sick feeling settled in the pit of his belly. This man was a murderer who had been hanged in the church square the previous day. Roland had been in the library when he heard the drum rolls and the crowd cheering at the moment of his death. He should have guessed that this man's body would be the one chosen for dissection. Once again looking at the cadaver, his question of the previous day, one that would haunt him forever, returned: *How does a man come to take the life of another?*

On the dead man's chest and belly was a line of red paint with three shorter red lines crossing it. A servant handed a long knife with a sharp, crescent-shaped blade to Thomas of Arles, the surgeon performing the dissection. He was solidly built, like many of the people from this part of France, with light brown hair and eyes. As he rolled up the sleeves of his shirt, Roland saw that his arms were muscular from his labor as a surgeon.

"Follow the lines of incision," intoned the professor from his podium overlooking the courtyard. His name was de Guy, and he was one of the most renowned professors of medicine in all of Europe. Dressed in a rich brocade robe, he was reading from a text by the ancient Greek doctor Galen of Pergammon. De Guy was so far away that he would barely be able to see what lay inside the body, Roland suspected, but maybe he had observed so many others that he knew where every inner part was.

Thomas thrust the tip of the knife into the top point of the vertical red line. He grunted as he cut into the man's chest. There was the sound of flesh and sinew ripping. Clotted blood pooled inside the wound. Roland's chess companion, Matthieu, stumbled away from the group and vomited. Roland hoped his friend would soon get used to the sight of blood.

Thomas cut into the first red cross line, then the second and third. He took a rag from the servant and wiped away blood.

"Pull apart the ribs and crack them to expose the innards," de Guy continued, but Thomas was already doing so. At the loud snap of breaking bones, several students recoiled.

The man's body had stiffened in death, and only with great effort was Thomas able to open the incision wide enough to expose the parts that lay beneath the rib cage. He hammered nails into the flesh to hold it down, thus creating a large, oval-shaped opening.

Thomas spooned the clotted blood into a pewter basin so that the man's innards were visible. Some were roundish and others flattened or shaped like coils, but all were various shades of reddish brown. These innards were packed together inside his chest and belly, more closely than those of the animals Roland had dissected.

As de Guy recited from the list of body parts in Galen's book, an assistant professor used a stick to point to that part in the body.

"The liver is on the right side when looking down at the body," de Guy proclaimed.

Roland frowned. De Guy's text was wrong. The liver was clearly on the left side but the assistant pointed to a smaller organ on the right, as he was instructed. De Guy next read about the pancreas, a part whose purpose, Galen wrote, was to cushion a netting of blood vessels that lay beneath it. But the shape of the organ, as Galen described it, was inverted from the way it was positioned in this man.

"Small intestine . . . large intestine," de Guy continued, reading the location and position of these body parts. But again Galen's description was not correct; Roland could see with his own eyes that the larger tubing encircled the smaller one.

As soon as Thomas covered the body, servants came to take it away for burial in unhallowed ground. Everyone left except for Roland, who stood rooted to his spot as Thomas of Arles wrapped his tools of dissection in cloth.

The surgeon glanced his way. "Why are you still here?" he demanded.

Galen's text was wrong. But Roland kept that reply to himself, and merely pointed to the dissection instruments. "Could I help you clean those?"

"Yes." The surgeon gave Roland an appraising look. "You were watching the dissection very closely. If you were shorter, I would surely have felt your breath on my neck. I wager what you really want is to ask me questions. Follow me with my instruments."

Roland usually stooped so that he wouldn't be conspicuous among the people of Montpellier, but today he had been so eager to see the dissection that he had forgotten to do so.

Roland followed Thomas into the lecture hall and down the stairs inside to a small, dimly lit room. Thomas poured water into a basin and cleaned the instruments with a fresh rag, bidding Roland to dry them with another rag.

"I suppose you came from Spain to study medicine?" the surgeon asked.

"Yes." Roland was relieved that Thomas merely nodded instead of insulting him for his Spanish blood or shunning him as some of the students did.

"I am a surgeon in Arles and travel to Montpellier every few months to assist in dissections." Thomas said. "What do you want to know?"

Roland laid a knife that he had dried on the table. "I mean no heresy, but the parts within the dead man did not correspond to Galen's description. Is that because our bodies do not all look the same inside?"

Thomas shook his head. "All the men I have cut into resemble each other on the inside," he said. "But at the university, the purpose of cutting into the body is not to heal it or to observe what lies within but simply to illustrate Galen's text, which I believe shows the inside of a pig."

Roland shook his head slightly. This made no sense.

"It would be best not to mention our conversation to the professors or students," Thomas advised. "I heard rumors at the tavern that de Guy warned you about something heretical you recently said in the lecture hall. I do not wish to be seen as your ally, nor do I want him or the other professors to remind me of my lowly place as a surgeon."

In one of his first lectures, de Guy had repeated something that Roland had already heard about surgery—that it was a bloody craft done with the hands and learned through apprenticeship. A doctor's work was superior, de Guy asserted, for it was done with the mind and learned by attending a university. That did not make sense, of course. Both surgeons and doctors had to use their minds and their hands.

Roland and Thomas finished cleaning and drying the tools in silence.

"*Merci*," said Roland as he handed over the last instrument. "Could I help you again and ask you more questions?"

"Certainly, but here, not in public," Thomas said. "Now, I have a question for you: What did you say in the lecture hall that the professor deemed heretical?"

"De Guy claimed that, according to Galen, a woman's womb can travel around the body. Sometimes it lodges onto a body part such as the heart or liver. When the womb attaches itself, it can cause the woman to suffer from hysteria, melancholia, or mania. When I questioned Galen's idea, my professor warned me against heresy."

Thomas snorted. "You saw today with your own eyes how the parts within the body are very close together. It would be impossible for the womb to wander."

NOVEMBRE, 1477

Thomas leaned over the table, examining Roland's handiwork in dissecting a dog found dead on the streets of Montpellier. The surgeon straightened his back and grinned at Roland. "In less than two moons, you have learned how to use my surgical tools quickly and with much skill."

Roland smiled. "*Merci*, Thomas. You are a good teacher." He grew thoughtful. "One day I hope to understand the nature of diseases and how the parts within might cause them."

Thomas raised an eyebrow. "That is an ambitious task."

"I know, but maybe surgery would give me some of the answers," Roland mused. "I might find answers to other questions in ancient texts. Maybe there were doctors of long ago who knew more about the body than the authors of the texts I am required to read."

"I doubt that," Thomas said, covering the dog's body with a ragged blanket. "And though any surgeon would be pleased to have you as an apprentice, I would advise you against that path. As a doctor, you will be held in higher regard than you would as a surgeon. As a doctor, your patients will be wealthy men who will pay you well. And lastly, your work will be far easier than that of a surgeon's."

As they walked out of the dissection room into the twilight, Thomas added, "It seems to me that you wish to pursue the path of both a doctor *and* a surgeon."

Roland smiled. "I had not thought of it that way, but yes, I suppose I do."

They came to a square with a fountain and public oven in the center. No one else was out walking now, but tomorrow morning the square would be teeming with people buying fresh bread at the oven and filling earthen vessels with water.

"There is the house where I am lodging," Thomas said, pointing to a half-timbered two-story house with sconces illuminating the great room. The house surprised Roland; he had expected that Thomas's lodging place would be a room at an inn.

"It is the home of . . . a friend of mine," Thomas said as the front door opened and a woman of around five-and-twenty emerged. She smiled broadly at Thomas as she came to stand close to him.

Thomas returned her smile and his visage softened. "Lucienne, this is one of my students, Roland of Barcelona. He is very eager to learn about the parts within the body."

Roland bowed to Lucienne, suddenly at a loss for words. Who was this comely young woman, and how had Thomas befriended her when he only traveled to Montpellier every few months or so?

Lucienne was craning her neck, gazing at the darkening sky. "Ah, Thomas, there are no clouds tonight and only a crescent moon, so we will be able to see many stars."

"Yes," Thomas said, pointing to a star shining in the eastern sky. "There is our first one."

They stood so close to one another that their bodies almost touched. Roland felt an invisible thread binding them together while he stood alone. It made him feel awkward. Like a trespasser.

"Farewell," he bade them. "May you see many stars."

"Yes," Thomas said, looking down from the sky, "until tomorrow, Roland."

As Roland walked down the hill to the room he rented, he was overcome with a feeling of loneliness. He could seek out a prostitute, as he did from time to time, and he would take pleasure in the woman's body—but afterward he would long for something more than she had to offer, something that eluded him and which he had no knowledge of how to obtain. He sensed that Thomas had found this closeness to a woman, both in body and spirit, with Lucienne... but how?

Unlike the many questions about the body that he asked Thomas, this was a question that Roland doubted he would ever ask the surgeon.

Arles, France

1 JUILLET, 1478

"Be quick and heat the cautery iron," Hubert, the master surgeon, commanded.

Hubert was Thomas's father-in-law. In April, Thomas had told Roland that Hubert needed another apprentice at his shop. Roland had quickly decided that he would work there for the summer.

Hubert pressed a cloth against a gaping knife wound in the man's shoulder. The cloth was quickly soaked in blood.

Roland strode to the table where all the surgical tools were laid out and grabbed the cautery iron. He thrust it in the fire until it glowed red. By the time he returned to Hubert's side, a pile of blood-drenched cloths were heaped in a basin.

The surgeon added the latest bloody cloth, grabbed the iron, and pressed it to the wound. At once, the man's screams and the stench of his burning flesh filled the surgery shop—and were seared into Roland's mind forever.

Still, he forced himself to look at the iron pressing against the wound. Within moments, the instrument had done its cruel but necessary work: it had staunched the flow of blood.

At the tavern, Roland collapsed into a chair at a corner table and propped his throbbing feet on the empty chair across from his. He arched his shoulders backwards to coax the taut muscles into slackening. His hands ached from all the intricate and precise movements they had performed this day, as well as the five other days of that week.

He flattened his hands and stretched his fingers wide apart. Alternating hands, he massaged the sides of his fingers, especially around the knuckles. He smiled, knowing that his pain was a worthwhile exchange for everything he'd learned that day.

Hélène, the innkeeper's wife, bustled over to his table. Her face was flushed from standing over the oven, her stringy hair coming loose from her coif. Not for the first time, he wondered how such a slender woman did not grow fat from partaking of the delicious meals she prepared day in and day out.

"*Bon soir*, Roland," she greeted him. "What will you have for supper?"

"*Bon soir*, Madame Hélène." he said. "By any chance is there any cassoulet left over?"

She grinned, revealing the gap from the missing tooth he had helped Hubert extract a month ago. It had been abscessed and caused her much pain, but now her mouth was healing well. "I saved some for you," she replied. "Would you like wine while I warm it in the oven?"

He nodded. "*Merci.*"

"Will you come for another cooking lesson soon?"

"Yes, in a few days," he said. "What dish will we make?"

"I will buy geese at the market. We will roast them and also make goose liver pâté."

"*Bon.*" His mouth watered at her mention of this savory dish, which she served in a flaky pastry that he had been wanting to learn how to make.

Hélène jostled her way through a throng of men and women dancing to the merry music of tabors, lutes, and drums. It was a Saturday night, and the tavern was quickly becoming crowded. In the far corner, people cheered for their favorite rooster in a cockfight, and throughout the room prostitutes wearing yellow knots of fabric sewn onto the shoulders of their bodices sat in men's laps with arms around their necks, enticing them with their low-cut bodices.

A serving girl brought Roland wine. He took a sip, drew out a sheaf of paper, quill, and ink pot from his satchel, and began to draw one of the surgeries Hubert had done after cauterizing the knife wound that day.

The surgery had been performed on a patient suffering from a sour stomach. In a fortnight's time, despite Hubert's regimen of bloodletting, the man's discomfort had intensified into a searing pain. Upon kneading the man's belly like bread dough, Hubert had detected a hard lump. He'd bidden Roland to find the lump too—a difficult process with all the layers of fat, but he'd eventually managed.

During the surgery, Roland's tasks had been to make sure that the patient remained in the deep sleep induced by the alcohol sponge and to hold back the four flaps of skin where Hubert had made an x-shaped cut in the man's belly.

Roland drew two vertical lines down a sheaf of paper, creating three columns. In the first, he sketched Hubert using scissors to snip the tumor off at its base, careful not to cut into the man's stomach. In the middle column, he drew the surgeon clamping the forceps around the tumor and pulling it out. In the third column, he made a detailed picture of the tumor, its surface covered with ridges and bumps. Its appearance had surprised him and made him curious about its nature. Below that drawing, he wrote his questions about tumors. When—if— he returned to university, he would search the library for a text on them.

As he put his drawing away, Roland marveled that he had seen inside a living body today as a surgeon removed a part that was causing the patient great pain. Roland smiled, a warm glow spreading within him. This was why he had come to Arles.

The serving girl appeared with Roland's meal, apologizing for the delay.

"I understand—it is very crowded in here," he shouted over the music and loud voices.

The cassoulet, a dish of sausage, pork, and beans, was even more flavorful as a leftover, and the creamy goat cheese and bread were perfect accompaniments. The wine, meanwhile, soothed his aching muscles. He opened his satchel again and pulled out the book of Lucretius. He was very tired, but he would read for a while before walking to the house where he rented a room.

He had found the book a few weeks earlier at a bookshop in Arles. Lucretius wondered if there were tiny particles that lay within human bodies and within plants and animals. Roland paused, staring at the page. The ancient Roman philosopher wondered about the same idea that he did.

As he turned to the next page, someone slammed into his table, tipping his cup of wine over. It spilled onto the page, the ruby-colored liquid mingling with the black ink.

"You fool," he growled at the careless person as he frantically blotted the sheaf of parchment with his napkin, only to see the words on the sheaf disappear into the wine.

Scowling, he glanced up and was surprised to see a young woman backing unsteadily away from him. She had dark, curly hair parted in the middle, a mud-streaked face, and deep shadows under her brown eyes.

"I am sorry. Here . . . buy a new book," she slurred, swaying as she looked down at her belt. "My purse is gone," she mumbled, lurching precariously forward.

Roland jumped to his feet and turned the empty chair to face her. "Sit here."

She shook her head as she clutched the table to steady herself and squinted into the room. "I was playing chess . . ."

She set out again, stumbling through the crowd. He followed her, and when she pitched forward, he grabbed her by the arm. He felt awkward doing so, but there was no other way to keep her upright.

Her clothes were muddy and rumpled but made of fine green wool and devoid of yellow knots. Nor did she wear a wedding band. Her shoes were muddy too, but made of fine leather. She seemed a high-born young woman—but how had she escaped her father's house? Maybe she was a prostitute after all but of a higher class than the others at this inn, and as such more desirable to the rich men of Arles.

He scanned the crowded tavern and, near the fire, found a chess table with an empty seat. A young man, cheeks flushed from drink, clapped to the beat of the drum.

When he saw Roland and the young woman approaching, he scowled at her and rose to his feet. "You said you were going to find the privy, not another man," he said sharply.

Roland tried to explain, but the young man ignored him as he grabbed the young woman's arm and sat her down across from him.

"It is your turn," he said, pointing to his knight. "I moved here."

Roland backed away from the table but his height allowed him to see the position of the pieces. The young woman and man were fairly well matched except that she had more control of the center of the board, a position that boded well. They made several more moves, all the while quaffing wine. The young woman and the man moved their pieces in a bolder manner than Roland and his brother, Carlos, did, but their moves were clever nonetheless.

He knew he should return to his table, but he could not pull his eyes away from the intricate game.

The young woman slid a bishop halfway across the board and Roland leaned forward, astounded by her daring choice, which put a chink in her king's defenses. Somehow she had thought of the best move, even in her drunken state.

"*En garde*," she announced with a jubilant grin.

Men crowded around the table.

"By God's teeth, Giraud, the whore has your queen in a stranglehold. She is a better player than you are," a red-headed man teased, clapping her opponent on the back.

Giraud guzzled wine, then slammed his cup against the table. "The game is not over yet." He scanned the board and, straightening his back, smiled as he moved his rook to protect his queen but also to threaten her king and her rook. "Check," he said.

She drank a long measure and stared intently at the board. Roland, looking over her shoulder, became very still. She could block his attack and checkmate his king all in one move.

Only a moment later, that is what she did. The men gathered around the table fell silent as she knocked Giraud's king over.

"For shame, losing to a woman," the red-haired man said playfully.

Giraud's face darkened and he jumped to his feet. Unsheathing his knife, he thrust it close to the woman's heart. Roland moved forward, about to pull her out of the way, while the red-haired man grabbed Giraud by the arm that held the knife. "I was joking, my friend," he soothed. "You are the better player. She just had Lady Fortuna on her side tonight. Besides if you kill her, you won't have the pleasure of bedding her."

Breathing heavily, Giraud stared at his friend. The woman slowly backed away from the men as if a sudden sense of danger had pierced through the fog of drink surrounding her.

Giraud laughed as he sheathed his knife. "I will pierce her with a different weapon—my 'lance.' We all will. We will teach her never to beat a man at chess again."

The men cheered loudly, boasting about which of them would pierce her the deepest. They did not notice her creeping away until she was well behind Roland.

"She is fleeing," one of the men shouted.

A cry rose up and Giraud jumped to his feet. "Seize her!"

Like a pack of dogs, they surged forward.

Without thinking, Roland stepped into their path. Tables blocked them from going around him, and they skidded to a stop. He usually hunched over to make himself look shorter, but now he drew himself to his full height and towered over them, his arms crossed against his chest, trying to look strong. He was annoyed that the muscles around his mouth kept twitching.

"Let us pass, filthy Spaniard," Giraud commanded.

Roland felt his face turn red but ignored the insult and stood his ground.

"Get out of our way!" the red-haired man shouted.

Roland still did not move, searching for a way to stop them without getting hurt himself. As he was thinking, Giraud shoved him with such force that Roland had to grab hold of a table to keep his balance.

As the men swept past him, an idea came to him.

"Stop!" he shouted. "Pursue her and her terrible disease will eat away your manly parts! There is no cure for it."

The men, already almost to the door, stopped short and faced Roland.

"What do you mean?" Giraud growled.

"My friend took her to bed once," Roland lied, his voice shaking, "and she gave him the pox."

The men and other people close by recoiled from Roland.

"My God," the red-haired man cried out, "she could have spread it to all of us."

"Begone, Spaniard, and never approach us again," Giraud shouted as he and his companions backed away from the door.

"Wait, are you not Hubert the Surgeon's apprentice?" a man called out from the back of the crowd.

Roland did not answer as he strode to his table and grabbed his book and satchel. With great effort, he controlled his shaking. What a fool he was to have put himself in such grave danger for a woman he didn't even know. Those men could have killed him.

Without acknowledging everyone's stares, he fled to the square. The sun was just beginning to set, and he had to find the young woman before other men tried to harm her.

She was not there.

He ran down each street that fanned from the square and found her at last, sprawled in the shadows. Letting out a breath of relief, he lifted her into his arms and carried her into the fading sunlight.

After walking a ways, Roland laid the young woman down again and saw that she had fallen into a deep stupor. He quickly felt her neck for a heartbeat. Her flesh was sweaty but cool, her heart beating faintly. Leaning over her still body, he could barely detect a shallow breath.

He had heard tales of very drunk people never awakening. He could not leave her here to die. He lifted her into his arms again and turned toward his room, intending to revive her there with a wet cloth to her face.

The farther he walked, the heavier she became.

He passed the Jewish quarter as men were leaving the temple, only a stone's throw away from him. Made of light stone, it had high, arched windows and was taller than the rest of the crudely built houses and shops that crowded the square. But the most prominent building in the quarter was a stone fortress not far from the temple. One day when Thomas and Roland were walking on this street, the surgeon had told Roland that the king of Provence had given the Jews of Arles permission to build the fortress in order to defend themselves from attacks by Christians.

All of the Jewish men wore circular badges, half red and half white, sewn onto the front of their cloaks. Some of them cast curious glances at the woman in Roland's arms, but only a round-faced man with a short beard stepped forward.

After looking around to make sure that no Christian was watching, careful to keep the prescribed distance between himself and Roland, the man said in a thick Hebrew accent, "I am a doctor. Do you need help?"

In Barcelona, the Jews had more privileges and freedoms than they had in Montpellier. The Christians' treatment of the Jews in Arles seemed to fall somewhere between those two other cities. Although in Arles Jews could serve as doctors and purveyors of used clothes and a few other items, they could not work on the Sabbath or use Christian bathhouses. At curfew, they had to return to their quarter or else be punished severely. Worst of all, as the fortress indicated, Jews in this area of France were often the victims of bloody attacks by Christians.

As darkness fell, Roland stood rooted to his spot on the boundary of the two parts of the city. Hubert might well censure him for consorting with a Jew, or even dismiss him for such a breach of judgment. But the young woman was hardly breathing . . . he could not simply let her die.

He turned toward the streets where Christians lived and worked. He could hear lively music in the distance, but no Christians were walking on this street lined with ragsellers' shops and decrepit houses, their shutters all closed for the night. He turned back to the Jewish doctor and nodded.

The doctor pointed to the rear of the temple and hurried in that direction.

Roland darted across the street and into the shadows of the temple. There he found several Jews speaking harshly in Hebrew to the doctor, likely warning him not to offer help to a Christian, but he waved them off. There was a final barrage of warnings, and then everyone but the doctor left.

Roland laid the young woman on the unpaved street and the doctor pressed a finger to her neck.

"Her heartbeat is very faint." He leaned over her to listen for her breath. "So is her breathing. We must get her to my shop quickly."

Roland picked her up and kept pace beside the doctor, keeping to the shadows as much as possible.

"Tell me how you came to help her," the doctor said.

A lamplighter was lighting a few oil lamps along the narrow street, and Roland could now see his new acquaintance more closely. He appeared to be around ten years older than Roland, with even features and a kindly manner. In Barcelona, Roland had heard stories of Jewish doctors who performed wondrous surgeries on their patients, especially on their eyes and skulls. Although he had never spoken to a Jew before, something about this doctor made it easy for him to tell him what had happened at the tavern.

"You took a risk, but you did your best to help her," the doctor said when he'd heard the whole tale. "Not everyone would do as much for a stranger."

"Yes . . . that is right," Roland said. "Just as you are helping a stranger."

They both fell silent. Was the bond between them as unsettling to the doctor as it was to him?

Along the narrow, winding street, the houses were built so close together that their walls were almost touching. And in many places it seemed that the upper stories were actually separate houses with stone stairs leading to the street below. Roland guessed that this crowding of houses was necessary since the quarter was only a small section of the sprawling city of Arles. At many of the houses, the shutters were open to the warm night air and the aroma of roasting meat drifted outside. Roland caught glimpses here and there of girls in black veils playing lyres or harps by candlelight.

He and the doctor remained in the shadows, and no one took notice of them. Finally, they stopped at a house on the street level and the doctor chose a large key from several that hung from his belt. He opened the door and motioned for Roland to follow him inside.

As they entered a narrow hallway, a woman holding a candle walked toward them. She stared at Roland and the young woman in his arms. "Isaac, what have you done?" she asked in alarm. "You could be punished for bringing these Christians into the quarter!"

The doctor replied in brisk Hebrew. Whatever he said seemed to calm her. She nodded and left the anteroom, only to return seconds later with a cup of water. She handed the cup and candle to her husband as two small girls looked on, clutching the door frame but remaining in the room to the right of the hallway, staring at the strangers with wide eyes.

Roland followed the doctor into his shop, which was on the left side of the hallway. The shop was quite large, with a table that held many instruments. "Let her rest there," the doctor said, pointing to a bed in the corner.

The woman did not stir as Roland laid her down, and the doctor set the candle and water on a side table. Her face was pale, and she took shallow breaths through her mouth. The doctor felt her wrist. "Her heart is beating a little faster," he said. "I do not believe that she will die."

"*Bon*," Roland murmured, exhaling deeply.

"I could give her a drink made of ginger and juniper berries to help her recover from an excess of drink," the doctor said, "but I am not certain if she is drunk."

"But she drank a large quantity of wine," Roland insisted.

"I know," the Jew said. "Even so, we must observe a patient carefully before reaching a conclusion about the cause of the problem and the best remedy."

Roland's face grew hot. He had made the same mistake as his professors at the university, who taught their students to provide useless remedies without even observing the patient or asking him to describe the pain or injury. "Maybe you are right," he conceded.

"Even though she could hardly walk, she somehow had the wits to play chess with great skill."

The doctor nodded, his gaze on the young woman. "For now, let us simply keep watch over her. If she awakens with a headache and great thirst, I will give her the remedy for excessive drink."

"But what else could cause her to seem drunk?" Roland asked.

"A lack of sleep or a disease of the spirit," the doctor replied.

"Madness?"

The doctor nodded. "Some healers would call it that. I prefer *maladie de l'esprit.*"

"Do you believe that an imbalance of the humors is the cause of Magali's disease of the mind?"

"We do not know, but some of the ancient authors like Galen believed that such diseases are caused by an excess of one of the four humors or too little of one of them . . ."

The two little girls appeared at the door to the shop. "Abba, supper is ready," the older child announced.

"I am coming," the doctor replied with a smile. He turned to Roland. "I will return after supper. Call me if her breathing becomes shallower. My name is Isaac ben Abraham."

"And I am Roland of Barcelona." There was no need to hide his Spanish blood from a Jew, so Roland straightened his back to his full height as he introduced himself. "I am studying medicine at the university of Montpellier, but this summer I am an apprentice to a surgeon in Arles."

"Ah, that explains your interest in her illness." Isaac checked the woman's breathing and heartbeat again before leaving. "Still unchanged," he announced. "Keep good watch while I'm away."

As soon as he left, Roland stood by her bed, watching her chest rise and fall with each breath. Shifting his gaze to her mud-streaked face, he noticed her comely features—rounded cheeks and thick eyelashes. Again, he wondered who she was.

He crossed the room to look at Isaac's supplies. Many of them were familiar but some were new. Isaac also had a shelf containing dozens of books. Roland pulled one out and opened it, only to find that it was written in Hebrew. He put the book back on the shelf.

When Isaac returned, the woman was still in a deep stupor, with the same slow heartbeat and breathing. "My wife made a pallet for you in the great room," he said. "Try to sleep a short while before checking on the young woman again. My chamber is just beyond the great room. If you need me, you can knock on the door."

"And what will I do with her in the morning?"

"You must leave my house with her before first light," Isaac said, his kind eyes on the young woman. "Seek those who search for her."

Roland nodded, but inside he was discomfited to learn that he would soon have sole responsibility for her care. As Isaac turned to leave, he remembered he had questions for the doctor. He felt he could learn from him and was grateful for his help. "Please, before you go—I wanted to ask if you are a surgeon as well as a doctor?"

"Yes."

"I noticed that you don't have any cautery irons. Why not?"

"They are very dangerous and painful tools," Isaac said simply.

"I know." Roland shuddered. "My master had to use one this morning."

Isaac crossed the room to a shelf, picked up a pottery crock, and brought it to Roland. He took off the lid to reveal an amber paste smelling of turpentine. "When a patient has a deep cut or wound, my apprentice holds the two sides together while I seal the cut with this paste. Even if blood is still spurting, the paste soon creates a seal over the wound. Then the two sides of flesh can be stitched together."

"That is wondrous!" Roland exclaimed.

"You may keep this remedy," Isaac said, "but do not tell your master or anyone else that you got it from a Jew."

"Never." Roland would be in as much trouble as Isaac if a Christian found out. After sealing the crock tightly and putting it into his satchel, he pointed to the bookshelf. "I see that you have many medical texts."

"Yes," Isaac replied, "they belonged to my father, who acquired them when my grandfather died. In one of those texts my grandfather found the recipe for that salve. He believed that ancient texts are buried in university libraries throughout France and contain other effective remedies for diseases of the body and the spirit."

Curiosity sparked within Roland. "Including Montpellier?"

"Especially there." Isaac nodded. "There is knowledge to be gleaned from Greek, Arabic, and Jewish doctors . . . maybe even ancient texts from the Far East written in languages we do not know. My grandfather's dream, then my father's, now mine, was to translate all those tomes, observe which remedies are truly effective, and compile only those to share with other doctors."

Isaac's words echoed in his candlelit shop as the flesh of Roland's arms prickled with excitement.

Lying down on his pallet in the great room, he gazed at moonlight spilling in from a round window. How strange it was to be in a Jewish doctor's quiet house, with a young woman who might or might not be a prostitute asleep in a bed close by.

Two

" . . . certain people talked of a peculiar case of *frenesis magna,* the great frenzy of the brain. Others, however, believed that [the patient] to be possessed by evil spirits."
—LATE FIFTEENTH-CENTURY ACCOUNT OF MENTAL ILLNESS

Arles, France
2 JUILLET, 1478

A faint noise awoke Roland and his eyes popped open. Where was he . . .

Then he remembered. He sat up on the pallet and peered through the open door into the doctor's shop. Illuminated by moonlight, the young woman knelt on the floor. She had taken Roland's satchel from beside him and scattered its contents around her, along with her bodice and skirt. Heat rose to his face. He could at least be thankful that her body, covered only by a light-colored shift, was in the shadows.

She did not seem to notice him as she sang, "To the sea, to the sea, I must ride to the sea."

"Is that where you live?" he called to her as he rose to his feet.

She stood abruptly and strode into the hallway, passing the doorway to the great room before he could reach her. He went quickly to the shop, where he thrust his belongings into his satchel and picked up her bodice and skirt, and then strode to the hallway. The young woman was halfway to the front door, swaying back and forth to her song.

Roland ran into the great room, which was faintly lit by glowing embers in the fireplace, and knocked on the door to the doctor's chamber.

Isaac emerged at once—like Roland, still dressed in his clothes. The young woman was now banging on the front door and shouting, "Let me go!"

"It is locked from the inside and I have the key," Isaac whispered to Roland. "I did not tell you last night, but I know who she is; her mother sent word to me. We will take this young woman to her now. I must be very cautious so that no one sees me. I feared that you would leave my house last night, but I need your help to remain hidden from the Christians. That is why I did not tell you then."

Relief washed through Roland that he would no longer have to care for this young woman after tonight, but that relief was quickly replaced by alarm. What if someone saw him and told Hubert that he was in the company of a Jew?

He followed Isaac to the door.

"Take me to the sea!" the young woman cried, pounding her fist on the door.

"We will," Isaac soothed her as he led her to a bench, "but first you must sit down and drink some wine that my wife is preparing for you."

To Roland's surprise, she sat down. Isaac's wife walked toward them holding a candle and a cup of wine. In the candlelight, Roland caught a glimpse of the young woman's breasts through the thin silk of her shift. Blushing, he quickly turned away and distracted himself by breathing in the scent permeating the hall. It was cinnamon mixed with something bitter and wood-scented—maybe from an herb that would calm the young woman, he speculated.

She took the cup and gulped the wine down. When she had emptied her cup, Isaac's wife helped her to don her clothes and shoes. "Be careful, *mon mari*," she warned her husband as he unlocked the door.

"I will." He led the young woman outside, Roland following them.

It was still dark in the street, but in the faint moonlight, the young woman stared at a post used for tethering horses. "Where is Belle? I left her here."

Isaac and Roland exchanged a glance. Last night, Roland had not seen a horse anywhere near the tavern.

"Belle is gone," she moaned.

"We will find her," Isaac reassured her, taking her by the arm.

Roland walked on her other side as they made their way along the Jewish side of the street forming the boundary between the two parts of the city. It was Sunday, he remembered, and no one would be walking to work. Since there was only a faint lightening of the sky, it was also too early for Christians to walk to Mass. Still, he remained alert to any sound or movement as they moved through town.

He wanted to ask Isaac how he knew the young woman's mother, but he kept that question to himself. At least her mother had not abandoned her like the family of the mad beggar wandering the streets of Barcelona.

They walked a long way through the Jewish quarter; the smell of fish grew stronger as they got closer to the river. The young woman closed her eyes and her body became so heavy that both Roland and Isaac had to work to hold her upright.

"We will wait here," Isaac bade Roland as they approached the dock.

In the gray light of dawn, they saw a watchman holding a lantern and walking toward them. Roland hoped he was too far away to see Isaac. A nod of understanding passed between the doctor and Roland, and then Isaac ducked onto a side street. Summoning his strength, Roland continued toward the dock with the young woman.

To his dismay, the watchman approached him directly. "Why are you walking the streets at this early hour?" the man asked, frowning. "And who was the man with you?"

Roland's mind raced to devise a story. "The owner of a brothel," he said. "My sister didn't pay him his just due—spent it on drink. I just paid him."

"Well be quick and take her home," the watchman snarled. "She is forbidden to work today. Tomorrow she must wear the yellow knot so that we righteous Christians know of her grievous sins."

Roland bowed subserviently and waited for the watchman to disappear onto the next street before helping his charge the short remaining distance to the dock. He stood there watching, supporting the young woman with both arms, as a large boat drew closer, its sail billowing in the wind. It came from north of the city, and at its helm stood a woman wearing a hooded mantle. Even in the gray light of dawn, Roland could see her curly black hair, dark eyes, and round cheeks, so like those of the young woman in his arms. This woman had to be her mother, although she looked so young she could be taken for her older sister. Several men, wearing tunics bearing a green and white livery, were aboard, some steering the sailboat and others guarding her, their weapons drawn.

By this time Isaac had emerged from his hiding place. After glancing around to make certain that no one was about, he waved his arms to get the woman's attention.

"Magali!" she cried out as the boat reached the dock and two of her men helped her to step down onto the walkway.

"Lay the young woman down here," Isaac said to Roland, gesturing to a stone bench.

The older woman rushed to her daughter's side and, falling to her knees, wrapped her arms around her.

"She is in a deep sleep, Lady Beatrice," Isaac said. "She was very distraught and determined to go to the sea, so I gave her a remedy. She will likely sleep most of the day."

"Thank you, Isaac." Lady Beatrice wept as she stroked her daughter's hair. "If you please, could you board my boat and tell me what has come to pass?"

Isaac nodded toward Roland. "This young man can give you a better accounting than I."

"I cannot," Roland said hastily. "I must go." The sky was brightening. He could not risk being seen in the Jewish quarter. With a nod of thanks to Isaac, he walked quickly away from the mother and her daughter, wishing he had time to sleep before joining Hubert and his family at Mass.

He had only gone a short way when he heard brisk footsteps behind him. The two men, who helped Lady Beatrice descend from the sailboat, had followed him.

"Lady Beatrice wishes to speak with you!" shouted one of the men.

"I am not free to attend her," Roland replied and kept walking. Soon, Hubert would be waiting for him at Mass.

"Lady Beatrice commands you to come to her," the man's voice rang out again, this time from close behind Roland.

He stopped and turned. Panting to catch their breath, the two men were less than an arm's length behind him. The taller of the two was a thick-lipped man of middle years, while his companion was a stocky man not much older than Roland.

"I have done nothing wrong," Roland protested. "I simply helped Lady Beatrice's daughter."

"Come with us," the older man insisted, "or else we must take you to the countess by force."

Already a group of Christians had gathered along the street to watch the exchange.

Reluctantly, Roland followed the men back to the dock, where servants were lifting Magali onto the boat. Isaac was gone.

Lady Beatrice stood close to the sailboat, glaring at Roland. "Did you harm my daughter?"

"No, milady, I swear to you I did not," he said quickly.

"As soon as we return home, the village midwife will examine her." Lady Beatrice's voice rose. "You will be punished severely if you laid a hand on her."

What if another man had harmed her before Roland came to her rescue? What a fool he had been for helping her. His stomach knotted.

"Tell me everything that happened from the moment you met her," Lady Beatrice commanded.

He did so, his cheeks growing hot when he remembered Magali's breasts showing through her shift.

The countess's eyes bored into him and she squared her arms against her chest. "Your account does not convince me of your innocence. I need proof that you did not harm Magali and that you did not steal her horse and purse."

Once again, he felt he was in the throes of a strange and frightening dream. "Milady, please believe me," he pleaded. "I repeat that I did not hurt your daughter. I saved her from men who wanted to do so. Last night, when I helped her, she had neither purse nor horse. You have my word that I have never stolen in my life. I have no need of money, for I inherited a great sum of it from my father. As proof of my innocence, your servants may search my person and my room for the purse, and the stables in Arles for your horse."

"So it shall be," Beatrice said with a nod to her men.

If the horse was found, another man could easily accuse Roland of stealing it in order to protect himself. The punishment for horse thievery was death by hanging. His heartbeat quickened.

Beatrice once again fell to her knees beside Magali, who lay on a pile of blankets in the ship's hull, and gently touched her mud-streaked forehead. No cuts or bruises, no blood, only a torn skirt and sleeve. Beatrice collapsed onto the hull, facing her daughter and stroking her cheek. "Blessed Virgin," she whispered. "Help her to heal . . . help her to be whole."

Noises assaulted her from all directions, her men untethering the ship, turning it to catch the wind. The sails billowing and snapping taut. Voices rose from the shore: "I was there at the tavern . . . I took her for a whore, not the countess's daughter . . . Marie Magdalene only knows where she spent the night . . . pleasuring the surgeon's apprentice, no doubt . . ."

Beatrice shivered and drew a blanket over Magali and her. It offered a little protection against the cold, damp air but not the onslaught of hateful words: "Let us hope that the girl is spoiled . . . the French king won't be able to wed her to one of his men . . . Arles will remain free of the French crown . . . forever!"

Arrest them . . . throw them into my dungeon! The command rose to Beatrice's lips, but she stifled it. "I have no power over these people," she said softly. "Dear Virgin, help us to sail away quickly."

She drew closer to Magali and wrapped her arms around her stiff shoulders. "I am losing my power over you too. I can no longer protect you from your illness or from the dangers that will come—" Her voice broke.

At last, the ship began to sail—slowly at first, so slowly that she could still hear the crowd on the dock. And then, in an instant, the sound of the wind against the sail and river water slapping against the hull silenced the townspeople. With tears streaming down her face, Beatrice ran her fingers through her daughter's matted hair and felt the coldness of her cheek. The wooden deck pressed into her body and the cold wind made her teeth chatter. "At least I can keep us both warm," she whispered in Magali's ear. Then, turning her head away from her sleeping daughter, she shouted, "More blankets!"

Her men obeyed at once. Beatrice hoisted herself onto the makeshift pallet, warming Magali's body with the blankets and her own body, holding her as once she'd held her as a swaddled newborn.

Roland's landlord and his wife watched with curiosity as Lady Beatrice's servants accompanied him up the stairs to his room so small that it could only fit a narrow bed and a desk. The younger of the two men untied the pouch from Roland's belt and opened it wide. "My

God, Denis, look at all of these coins," he said, squinting at Roland. "You must have taken Lady Magali's money and thrown her purse away."

"I swear I did not," Roland insisted. "This is my own money."

The men ignored him as they patted their hands up and down his body, looking for a hidden cache. His cheeks flushed in humiliation but he forced himself to remain still. Then he remembered Carlos's letter. "Can either of you read?" he asked.

"I can," Denis replied.

"Read that," Roland said, pointing to a scroll on his desk that had been set apart from the others.

Denis snatched it up and began to read. "Ah, your brother holds your inheritance in trust and explains how it will be allotted to you. By God's fingers, you are rich."

"As I tried to tell Lady Beatrice. I have no need of her money or her horse," Roland muttered wearily, looking longingly at his bed. "Will you release me?"

"No. Lady Beatrice bade us to take you with us to look for Belle."

The bells of Saint Trophime rang for Sunday Mass as they began their search. Roland sighed. Hubert would be displeased that he had not joined his family at church.

At the fourth stable they found the horse, a chestnut brown mare with a white diamond marking on her forehead.

"I am here to claim this mare for the Countess of Provence," Denis informed the ostler.

The man frowned. "Giraud, the magistrate's son, brought that mare to be stabled here. He is no horse thief."

Giraud? Roland's eyes widened. That was the name of the young man playing chess with Magali.

"But the mare belongs to the Countess of Provence," Denis argued as he drew out a scroll and presented the countess's seal.

"Lady Beatrice only rules the countryside and has no power over me or the city of Arles," the ostler declared. "The magistrate rules here. He will decide what will be done with this mare. You must go to him at Saint Trophime."

Roland and the countess's men waited in the church square for the bells announcing the end of Mass. Townspeople swarmed out of the arched doorway of Saint Trophime, Giraud among them. His pale face and somber manner contrasted sharply with his wildness of the previous night. He also appeared younger in the light of day. Beside him was a man with gray hair and a square jaw much like his.

The magistrate frowned as the countess's men, gripping Roland's arms, approached him. Just then, someone in the crowd shouted, "Vincent, I need a word with you."

The voice was Hubert's. Roland fought an urge to flee.

"Come here, Hubert," Vincent shouted.

Hubert and his family came forward. They all glanced with disdain at Roland—except for Thomas, who gave him a warning look that clearly meant *be careful*.

Denis extended a parchment scroll to the magistrate. "Lady Beatrice, Countess of Provence, has a message for you," he announced ceremoniously.

Roland heard a wax seal being broken and parchment crinkling as the magistrate read the message.

Vincent shifted his gaze to Denis, his eyes narrowed. "What concern is this horse to me?" he demanded.

Denis cleared his throat. "The ostler says your son brought it to his stable last night."

Roland glanced up and saw Vincent scowling at his son. "What say you, Giraud?"

"The horse had been stolen by a whore," Giraud replied. "I was only going to find the rightful owner."

"Not a whore, you fool!" Vincent shouted. "You were too drunk to recognize the countess's daughter?"

Giraud shook his head as if to dispel the fog of wine and turned to Roland. "You told my friends and me that she was a whore and that she had a terrible disease."

"I-I believed she was," Roland stammered. "I lied about the disease because I thought you and your companions would harm her."

"Liar—you wanted her for yourself!" Giraud surged forward and seized Roland's arm with both hands, squeezing it and twisting the skin in opposite directions.

Roland howled at the searing pain and struggled to pull away.

The young man suddenly released his hold. Clutching his stomach and gagging, he stumbled to the side of the road and vomited profusely. Roland rubbed his aching arm.

"Vincent, this Spaniard is my apprentice," Hubert said as he stepped forward.

"You are right then. We must speak privately," the magistrate said.

It was strange to witness Hubert, who commanded everyone at his shop and home, meekly following Vincent as they walked to the graveyard of Saint Trophime and were soon hidden from view by a large tombstone.

A short time elapsed and the magistrate returned. "Go to your master," he bade Roland.

Roland reluctantly joined Hubert behind the tombstone.

"I knew something was wrong when you did not attend Mass this morning." The surgeon's voice was low and terse. "Tell me what really happened last night."

Roland squeezed his hands together behind his back and met Hubert's gaze. As Roland feared, it was as sharp as his knife, poised to extract the truths and falsehoods of his story. He tried to imitate Hubert's and the magistrate's impassive expressions. *Omit Isaac.*

After Roland briefly recounted the events of the previous night, Hubert stroked his beard down to the point. He often made this gesture in the surgery shop as he decided how to cut into the patient. In this case, Roland hoped it was a sign that he accepted his account.

"Vincent thought to banish you from Arles but I convinced him otherwise," Hubert said. "You are far too skilled at your work for me to lose you. But I must have your reassurance that you will be more careful in the future. Protecting young women in danger of being attacked is noble indeed, but not at the risk of harming your reputation. Do you understand?"

"I do now," Roland replied.

"There are several other important matters that I must make clear to you. First, never enter a tavern where Giraud is drinking. If he comes in after you, leave at once. That will show him you are no threat and are even willing to submit to him, and that you respect his rank as the magistrate's son."

"Yes, *monsieur*."

"As for the Countess of Provence and her daughter, they have no reason to seek you out again, nor do you have any reason to approach them. They are nobles, and there are rumors that the king of France is planning to arrange a marriage for the daughter to one of his kinsmen. As a Spaniard, you must avoid being caught in the web of the Spider King, as the French king is called for good reason. Is that understood?"

Ah, that explained the angry tone of the townspeople toward the countess. "I understand, *monsieur*."

"You are free to rest this afternoon," the surgeon said, his gruffness softening. "I will see you tomorrow morning."

"Thank you, *monsieur*." A bowl of stew and bed . . .

They walked side by side back to the square, where the crowd had thinned. Giraud was propped against a stone wall, his face ashen.

Hubert conferred with Vincent briefly, then the magistrate turned to the crowd. "All is well," he announced. "Hubert has reprimanded his apprentice for his deceit. The guild master of the surgeons will not dismiss the Spaniard, who is a very skilled surgeon himself. As for my son, he is no horse thief—he only intended to keep the horse safe until he could find the owner. He and I will go forthwith to the stable to see that the countess's horse is returned to her. Go to your homes at once."

Three

> " ... You will have other teachers ... but not anyone like me, your mother, whose heart burns on your behalf."
> —FROM DHOUDA'S (A NINTH-CENTURY NOBLEWOMAN'S) ADVICE MANUAL TO HER SON

Lady Beatrice's Château

5 JUILLET, 1478

Thank you, Blessed Virgin, for protecting her from harm during her flight to Arles! Thank you for sending the young student of medicine, who I now know did not harm her, to watch over her and for guiding him to the doctor who has knowledge of how to treat those suffering from madness.

Dear Mother Mary, shine your blessings on this new remedy as you shone your blessings upon the doctor's father's remedy, which saved my mother's life. I beg of you, Mother Mary, to intercede with your Son on my behalf and urge him to heal my daughter.

The village church bells rang the midnight hour as Beatrice put her secret book back into a small wooden chest. Even though she kept it locked within, she dared not mention Isaac by name. Taking her candle, she rose from her writing desk and walked from her chamber to Magali's, her keys jangling at her waist.

Her housekeeper, Alienor, awoke with a start and sat up on the pallet in the hall where she'd spent the night, rubbing her eyes. "Milady," she said, "you have not slept in two days. I beg of you to return to your chamber."

Beatrice shook her head. "I cannot sleep. Go to your bed and I will keep watch over Magali."

"But milady—"

"Not another word," Beatrice interjected. "Now go."

With a sigh, Alienor rose to her bare feet and walked to her chamber. Beatrice chose a key hanging from her belt and unlocked the door to Magali's room. The candlelight cast shadows over her sleeping daughter as she crept to the bed and sat down on the edge.

Magali did not stir. Isaac's medicine thrust her into a deep sleep for many hours—until the mania returned and it was necessary to repeat the remedy. It took Beatrice and three servants to accomplish that task.

Beatrice set the candle down on the bedside table and leaned over to comb her fingers through Magali's dark curls, loose and tangled like her own. Beatrice's eyelids were heavy from lack of sleep, her mind clouded as if filled with a thick fog. The seed of hope she had just planted in her secret book, in her prayers to the Virgin, withered.

Her confessor, Father Etienne, was wrong. God had not sent a demon to possess Magali. In sending her illness, He was punishing Beatrice for her sin of pride that she, a mere woman, had managed her lands without her deceased husband's guidance for fifteen years. That she reaped great riches from selling the fruits of her olive groves and vineyards and gave generously to Saint Trophime. That Renè, king of Provence, valued her counsel and entrusted her to forge treaties and marriages among the counts and countesses of his kingdom. That for the time being, she had kept Magali free from a betrothal to Provençal and French suitors.

She collapsed onto the bed next to Magali, her tears flowing onto her daughter's hair.

9 JUILLET

Holding a torch, Lady Beatrice emerged from the olive grove. Her face was hollow and tear-stained, her gray bodice and skirt rumpled.

Isaac's horse whinnied as he dismounted, a dimly lit lantern in hand. Yet again, he looked toward the road to Arles and listened. No one had followed him.

After tying the horse to a sapling, he removed his cloak with the badge sewn onto it and threw it aside with great relief. He approached Lady Beatrice and bowed to her. "I can only remain here a short while, milady, and I cannot risk attending you again."

"Thank you for agreeing to come at least this once." She drew in a deep breath, clearly fighting tears.

"Tell me about your daughter's disease of the spirit," Isaac gently bade her.

She took a moment to compose herself before telling him everything. How more than a year ago, it was as if a wheel within Magali had begun to roll, causing her to act in ways that Lady Beatrice had never seen before. At first, Magali had not slept for days on end. A wild spirit had possessed her for the next week or so, during which she'd wandered about the château writing notes on scraps of parchment all night long or drinking wine, singing, and dancing in the olive groves. Then it was if a black pall had settled over her, and she had not left her bed for another week. For a few days afterward, she'd returned to being her Magali of yore—strong-willed and quick-witted, reading her books and winning at chess against every opponent. She'd been happy on those days, and Beatrice had been at peace. Following that time of respite, however, the wheel had begun to turn again. The sleeplessness had returned, the wildness, and then the blackness, in an unending circle.

But lately, it had worsened. She'd been more frenzied than usual during the wild parts of her cycle, and several times she'd managed to flee secretly and ride Belle into the forest. But her foray two days earlier was the first time that she'd traveled to Arles and disappeared for an entire night.

"I thought she was dead," Lady Beatrice concluded in a trembling voice.

"And what has she been like since I last saw her?" Isaac asked.

"She remained beset with mania for a few days. But now the blackness of melancholia is upon her. It robs her of sleep."

"Is she still taking the remedy?" he asked.

"She refused it the last two nights and I did not have the heart to force her to take it," Lady Beatrice replied. "She is angry at me and claims I am holding her captive, but I am only trying to keep her from running away again—keep her safe."

Isaac nodded. "I have seen such anger in those suffering from a *maladie de l'esprit*. With sleep and medicine, she may stop thinking of you as her captor. Tell me, Lady Beatrice, have *you* been sleeping?"

"What does that matter?" she asked, her eyes brimming with tears. "My only child suffers, and I must do whatever I can to help her."

"You will only be able to do so if you are rested," he said, untying a satchel from his belt. "Here is more valerian for you and Magali. I have also given you a smaller portion of an herb called St. John's wort, which I hope will lift her spirits."

The countess took the pouches with a trembling hand, and Isaac instructed her on the preparation of the remedies.

"May they return Magali to the way she once was," she murmured.

"Remember, milady, what I told you at the river," he warned. "I can make no promise that she will ever be as she once was. For now, as long as she takes large doses of the two remedies at bedtime for a week, she will find sleep. And in sleep, she may be restored at least for a short time."

"Could you try to convince her to take the medicine willingly?" Lady Beatrice pleaded. "It pains me greatly to resort to force."

Isaac thought of refusing, but his heart would not let him. "I will try, milady. I have a dose of it already prepared in a vial. But I must go soon."

She led him through the grove to a clearing. A stone's throw away, Magali sat on the bed of a horse-drawn cart, looking at the ground, while a woman held her hand and talked softly to her. Startled, Isaac abruptly turned around and started to walk back to his horse before the woman could see him.

"Do not fear," the countess whispered. "She is Lady Alienor, my housekeeper. As a young woman, she was a lady-in-waiting to my mother. She remembers how your father saved my mother's life. She has proven her loyalty to me, and she knows that I would dismiss her if she were to reveal your presence here to anyone."

He stopped but kept his body turned away from the servant. He trusted Lady Beatrice because she needed him to help her daughter, but he could not risk trusting another Christian. Too often, that trust led to betrayal. "Milady, I must think of my family's safety. I can allow only your daughter to see me."

"*D'accord*," the countess said. "I will bring her to you."

His wide-brimmed hat would cast shadows on his features, Isaac reassured himself. And in her melancholia, Magali would probably not notice that he was a Jew, just as she had not noticed in her mania a couple of days earlier.

When Lady Beatrice presented Magali to him, Isaac was struck by the change in her visage. Her eyes were deeply shadowed and her lips were pursed together in a tight line. It was as if the life had been drained from her, leaving only the shell of her body.

"*Ma chère*," Lady Beatrice said to her daughter, "this is the doctor who found you on the streets of Arles and returned you to me."

Magali frowned at Isaac. "I do not remember you. Besides, I do not need a doctor. I am not sick."

Lady Beatrice sighed. "*Ma fille—*"

"Lady Magali," Isaac interrupted, "would you like to ride your horse?"

She lifted her head abruptly, her eyes widening and her lips curving into a faint smile. "Yes . . ." Her hopeful look faded as her gaze shifted to Lady Beatrice. "But my mother has forbidden me from riding."

"Because you want to ride by yourself to the sea," the countess explained. "It is not safe."

Magali's lips were clenched in a tight line. "Yes, it *is* safe!" she shouted. "You just want to imprison me here."

"Hush, *ma chère*, that is not true." Beatrice turned to Isaac, a silent plea for his help etched across her face.

He stepped closer to her daughter. "Lady Magali," he said, "there is a way for you to ride to the sea."

"How?" she demanded.

"You must agree to take the remedies for a week," he said. "They will help you sleep. Then you will be able to ride to the sea if you allow someone to accompany you."

"But—"

"Agree to these two things," Isaac said, his voice low but firm, "and very soon you will be astride your horse, riding to the sea."

Magali stared at him for a long moment before shrugging and saying, "You force me to agree."

"*Bon*," he said as he took out a vial from his satchel. "It will not taste good, but it may help you enjoy your days a bit more."

Magali gulped the remedy down quickly and shuddered in disgust.

"Tomorrow evening, when you have the next dose, mix it with honey," Isaac advised.

"Please, wait here while I take my daughter back to the cart. I will make haste."

Lady Beatrice's words were a plea, not a command, and Isaac nodded.

She soon returned. "Magali is already yawning."

"Good. May she find sleep soon."

"How I wish that you could continue to attend Magali, but I understand why you cannot." Lady Beatrice's voice broke and she paused to recover it. "It is just that your knowledge of her illness is so much deeper than that of our physic. He only knows to bleed her, a treatment that does her more harm than good. Is there any other doctor who might agree to attend my daughter?"

Isaac shook his head. "The only advice that I have is to continue giving her the remedy until she is more settled. I must warn you that I do not know how long it will be effective. But until doctors learn more about diseases of the mind, it is the best medicine we have available to us."

"And how would doctors learn more about such diseases?" Lady Beatrice asked.

"Most of them do not wish to do so," he replied. "What I have learned, both about diseases of the mind and of the body, is from what my father taught me and from searching ancient texts and observing if remedies contained in them help my patients. But I have so many patients that I have little time to read the texts that I own." He frowned. "And I am not permitted in the libraries of Christian universities."

Lady Beatrice began to pace back and forth, her torch flickering in the breeze. "I have determined that the Spaniard Roland, who helped Magali, neither harmed her nor stole her horse. My men tell me that he is a skilled apprentice surgeon. What else do you know of him, Isaac?"

"He is also a student of medicine at Montpellier," Isaac shared. "In the short time I conversed with him, he seemed most eager to learn about all manner of diseases of the body and spirit."

Lady Beatrice stopped pacing and turned to him with a look of resolve. "I have an idea. Though Roland does not have your knowledge of diseases of the mind, he can help me to observe Magali. Could he secretly send word to you about how she fares and receive instructions on how to proceed?"

"I can do little more for her than what I am doing now," Isaac replied somberly, "but yes, he could send me secret messages through a beggar, as you and I have done."

He remembered the look of excitement on Roland's face when he learned about the trove of knowledge and remedies recorded by doctors of long ago. He shared the young man's anticipation of what might be unearthed.

"I believe that Roland is interested in reading ancient texts," he said. "If we were to pursue this plan, he could also send me any remedies that he finds in Christian libraries, both for diseases of the body and of the mind, and I could observe whether or not they help my patients."

"Would you trust this young man to do as you instruct him?" Lady Beatrice asked.

Isaac considered for a moment. "Yes."

"Do you believe he would comport himself in a chaste manner with my daughter?"

"All I can say is that his intentions were good when he took care of her the night she ran away."

She nodded slightly and untied a pouch from her belt. "I will try this plan for a short while to see if it works. I will pay him, of course." She stared at the grove of olive trees. "I do hope he agrees to it. Just as I dislike forcing Magali to take her remedy, I do not wish to force this young man into serving me. But Magali's health is far more important to me than his freedom to choose." She handed the pouch to Isaac. It was very heavy with coins. "Here is a small token for all that you have done for Magali and the risks you have taken. Do you want my men to accompany you back to Arles?"

He shook his head as he put his cloak back on and made sure that his knife was still hanging from his belt. "It is not far to the gate that Jews are allowed to use, and I will be wary of thieves. Farewell, Lady Beatrice."

She bowed her head. "It saddens me to think that you cannot attend Magali at the château as your father attended my mother—that in fact I may never see you again. Farewell, Isaac."

9 JUILLET

Here are your 500 livres de tournois for the summer. I will send no more until you return to university. It has never been my way as your brother to command you, but in the matter of you considering the path of a surgeon, I must. We are rich and powerful men who learn our art at a university and use our minds, Roland, not men who learn a trade through apprenticeship and work with our hands. You must continue the study of medicine, and when you have completed your studies, I can help you secure a position as a physician at court.

I beg of you, return to Spain and enroll at the university of Salamanca rather than returning to Montpellier. Perhaps I should have forced you to attend school in Spain last fall, but again, I do not want to command you in all matters; I simply must intervene in important cases, such as deterring you from becoming a surgeon.

Your letters have become less frequent since your journey to Arles. I miss hearing word of how you fare, brother, but more importantly, I miss being in your company. I cannot come to Arles, for I have much work at court. But I hope that you will travel to Burgos for Christmastide. Better yet, I beg you once again to attend university in Spain. There, we could see each other far more than once a year . . .

Love and anger waged a war in Roland's heart as he traced his brother's signature, the "C" large and thick while the rest of his name was written in a smaller and fainter hand. "I miss seeing you too, Carlos," he said as he rolled up the parchment, "but you cannot make choices for me. And I can make no promises to you."

Roland rose to his feet in his small room and paced back and forth from the bed to the window. In his letters, he had not been completely truthful with Carlos, the brother who'd become more than a brother ever since their mother had died many years earlier. The brother who'd clasped his shoulder during her funeral and promised to take care of him, just as she had taken care of both of them. The brother who'd helped him accept their father, an aloof man who had always either been away at sea or buried in his ledgers.

It had not been his intention to draw away from Carlos and yet he had, first by leaving Spain to attend the university in Montpellier and now by exploring the craft of surgery in Arles. For nearly a year he had been under the tutelage of his professors at that renowned school of medicine. But now that he knew many of their teachings harmed rather than healed their patients, he was drawn to follow the path of a surgeon. As a surgeon, he felt, he had a better chance of healing the body and could pursue his understanding of its inner workings.

He contemplated this decision as he washed in cold water and dressed in his finest tunic of deep blue wool. In an hour he was to join Hubert and his family at Mass, followed by dinner with them for the first time. He would have preferred to spend his day of rest reading and drawing, but he knew it was important to spend as much time as he could in the company of others, for it helped keep his loneliness at bay.

He took care with trimming his beard, as he had since he started his apprenticeship. (The beard had been Carlos's idea, to make him look older than his nineteen years.) Holding a looking glass he'd borrowed from his landlord, he stroked his short, dark beard, which also helped to make his narrow face appear rounder. His hair was cut short, framing his high forehead and large dark brown eyes. True, he was not as handsome as Carlos, but his brother had always said there was something about him that drew the attention of others. "Use that to your advantage," he'd advised Roland more than once. In the mirror, Roland saw a young man of Spanish blood with an intensity to his eyes —maybe that was the intangible quality that Carlos observed.

As the bells rang for morning Mass, Roland reached the Church of Saint Trophime. The surgeon and his family knelt on the right side, close to the altar. Roland made his way there and knelt at the end of the family's row. Thomas, who sat at the end, nodded a greeting. Roland wished that he were dining alone with Thomas so they could be free to discuss the surgeries of the week. In truth, they had only spoken a little since their journey to Arles in May.

Throughout the long service, Roland feigned reverence and joined everyone else in receiving the sacrament of the Holy Eucharist, all the while knowing that such a miracle was impossible. It was not the body and blood of Christ but simply a morsel of bread, dry and tasteless, and a sip of sour wine.

At last he was released from Mass and the dark nave. Outside, in the bright sunshine, Hubert bade him to walk with him and his wife, Perronelle. She was a plump woman with pale skin and sharp features. She kept her eyes cast down as she fingered the pearls on her alms purse.

As they passed an ancient Roman amphitheater, Hubert pointed to it and asked Roland, "What do you think of it?"

"The Romans interest me because they used the power of their minds to build edifices that would last many hundreds of years," Roland said.

"Ah," Hubert said with satisfaction, "then this afternoon you will accompany us to Alyscamps, another Roman building."

The surgeon proceeded to ask questions about Roland's father's shipping business and Carlos. Roland tried his best to be vague in his replies; his brother had always advised him to keep their wealth to himself. He could not grasp why Hubert was so interested in him.

Maybe the surgeon simply took pleasure in knowing such details about people.

At the dinner table, Roland was seated between Hubert, at the head of the table, and his youngest daughter, Hubertine, whom everyone called Bertine. She had the same slender body as her father, as well as his light blue eyes. Roland guessed her to be around seventeen.

Across the table from them was Perronelle; Marie, the oldest sister; her husband, François; and their two sons and daughter. Thomas, his wife, the middle sister Clare, and their two sons were seated at the other end of the table.

Clare bore a strong resemblance to her mother, with sharp features that contrasted with her round body. She looked nothing like the dark-haired woman Roland had seen with Thomas in Montpellier the previous November.

Thomas spoke in a low voice to Clare. How could he pretend so easily to be a faithful and courteous husband? Thomas was an honest person—blunt, even—but surely he kept his lover secret from his wife.

Roland tried to settle himself by observing Thomas and Clare's shared devotion to their sons. As they waited for the meal to be served, Thomas advised them on war tactics and weaponry as they pretended to be Crusaders preparing to do battle against the infidels. When the younger boy, Arnaud, pretended to be wounded by an arrow, Clare played the role of a battlefield healer who pulled it out.

"Thank you, kind lady." The little boy smiled at his mother as she pretended to dress the wound.

"Daughter, that is your husband's work, not yours," Hubert chided her from across the table.

His tone was light, maybe even playful—Roland could not tell for certain—but his words made Clare's eyes flash with anger. "You—" she began, but stopped abruptly. There was an awkward silence as she turned to Thomas, pleading for something, maybe for his support. He shook his head slightly before resuming the game with his boys. Tears welled up in Clare's eyes, and she took a long swallow of wine.

Roland felt a twinge of pity for her. He was glad that Solange, the light-haired servant who always called the surgeons to the midday meal, chose that moment to carry a tureen to the table. She lifted the lid and ladled out the soup, a rich broth scented with garlic and flecked with the beans that were served in cassoulet.

Separate conversations rose around the table as everyone partook of the delicious soup.

"Tell me, Monsieur Roland," Bertine ventured, "do you enjoy our Provençal food?"

"Yes," he replied, "although the spices, like this rosemary, are different from the ones I am accustomed to in Barcelona."

"If you please, tell me about the dishes that are served in your city."

"Since Barcelona is on the sea, we have many recipes with fish..." He told her about some of them, and added, "I am learning how to cook these dishes."

"Maybe Papa would let you help our cook," she suggested eagerly.

"No, there is no need to ask him," he said quickly.

They talked throughout the soup course, turning from food to Roland's courses at the university. "I have a tutor," Bertine said proudly. "He is teaching me Latin and Italian."

Hubert gazed fondly at her. "*Ma chère*, even though you are but a woman, you have the workings of a man's wit."

Once the soup bowls were cleared, Hubert rose to his feet. He smiled as he looked around the table. "*Ma famille*," he began, "we are most fortunate to prosper both in riches and in good health. And my goodwife and I are blessed by God to have five thriving grandchildren."

Roland was a bit suspicious that Hubert's intent was self-serving. Yet everyone else at the table except the children listened attentively, or at least gave the appearance of doing so.

Turning to his oldest son-in-law, Hubert raised his cup of wine.

"François," he said, "you have increased your father's wine trade and you sell your wares throughout Provence. One day, I wager, your wine will even be poured at the table of the king of France."

"May God allow Provence to remain separate from the Crown," Perronelle said softly and made the sign of the cross.

"Goodwife, as I have told you many times, we must accept whatever comes to pass," Hubert scolded her. "To François—may you profit from selling your wares to the French if they do come to rule over our lands."

Hubert took a sip of wine and everyone, including the children with their watery wine, joined him. Marie leaned closer to her husband and smiled proudly. "François's vintages are the best in all of Provence."

"If one employs restraint in imbibing them," Hubert cautioned, his expression growing serious. There was a faint sigh from the other end of the table and the sound of clothes rustling as people shifted their positions. Roland could tell that this was not the first time the family had heard what was to come.

"Forgive me, *ma famille*, while I tell our guest my story," Hubert went on. "As a young man, I vowed that my life would be different from my father's. He drank wine far to excess, and continued to do so even after he killed a patient with his own knife. The news of his misdeed spread, and the people of Arles sought other surgeons to tend to their ailments."

A sober look spread over Hubert's face. Around the table, several people sipped their wine. Roland saw Clare's eyes drift to the open window and the courtyard garden beyond.

"When my father died," Hubert continued, pride entering his voice, "I took charge of his surgery shop and worked hard to restore its reputation. Soon my father's patients returned, as well as many new ones. You see, I learned from him to be moderate in drink. Other surgeons in Arles may take wine with their midday dinner, but I do not permit my surgeons or myself to do so. It is for this reason that our hands are steady as we work."

Hubert turned to Thomas, who was looking down at his hands. "Thomas, your skill rivals mine, and because of you there is an alliance between my surgery shop and the great school of medicine at Montpellier." He shifted his gaze to Roland. "You have also brought me a gift in this promising and skilled apprentice. To Thomas and his student, Roland of Barcelona."

Roland flushed as everyone raised their cups first to Thomas and then to him.

"Now," Hubert continued as he held Roland's gaze, "it is of utmost importance that all of us do our best to promote this young man's reputation . . . especially in light of the unfortunate incident that happened to him last Sunday." He returned his attention to his family. "Some people of Arles—especially the older ones, who remember when the king of Aragon invaded Provence—will mistrust Roland because of his Spanish blood. As a family, when we hear such talk, we must put an end to it by praising him for his skill and his sharp wit. My goodwife and daughters, I know how much women enjoy gossip. Make certain that you contradict any rumors that might threaten Roland's reputation."

"Our daughters and I will do our best," Perronelle said dutifully.

"Roland, you must take more care in your appearance," Hubert advised. "Even on workdays your clothes must befit a man of your status and wealth. Tomorrow morning, before you come to my shop, my wife will help you find the best tailor and bootmaker in Arles."

"As you wish, monsieur," Roland said, "but I will only be in Arles for a few months."

Hubert gave him a knowing look. "That remains to be seen."

After dinner Hubert announced that the family would ride to Alyscamps, a Roman cemetery.

"*Mon mari*, my headaches have returned," Perronelle said meekly. "Please, may I stay home and rest?"

Roland expected his master to say no, but instead Hubert held his wife's eyes for a long, silent moment. Roland knew not what passed between them, but he was relieved when Hubert nodded.

"I am sorry, Father," Marie said in her high-pitched voice, "but François and I have been invited to go sailing with our neighbor Raymond and his family."

"You always find an excuse not to spend time with your family, don't you, Marie?" Hubert chided her.

His oldest daughter's face reddened.

He turned to Thomas and Clare. "Will you come with us to Alyscamps?"

Staring at the table, Thomas and Clare sat like statues on either side of their sons, who were still playing and not aware of the sudden tension at the table. Roland tried his best to catch Thomas's gaze, but to no avail.

Her lips pursed together, Clare clasped her younger son's shoulders.

"Yes, monsieur, we will," Thomas said. "Nicholas and Arnaud will enjoy climbing on the stones."

Bertine ran to embrace her father. "Thank you, Papa, for letting us go to the Alyscamps," she said. "May I recite my poems there?"

"Certainly, *ma chère*, but just to our family and Roland." Hubert smiled and returned her embrace.

"How fitting that I wrote my poems in Latin and we are going to the Roman ruins," Bertine exclaimed.

Thomas had told him that Clare and Bertine often recited poetry after Sunday dinner. Roland was curious to hear her original poem and was certain that it would mirror the enthusiasm he'd enjoyed about her company today.

A servant was dispatched to secure Hubert's carriage and horses from the stable, and soon afterward they set out. Bertine sat with Clare and her boys while Hubert, Thomas, and Roland sat on the opposite bench. The horses made too much noise for them to talk so Roland was free to look out the window at the countryside with its rolling hills of vineyards and fields of lavender. The sweet-scented wind on his face refreshed him . . . exhilarated him. Despite his hard work, he felt free this summer—free to learn so many things about the body. He had made the right choice in coming to Arles.

When they arrived at the Alyscamps, they found other families already enjoying the cemetery on the warm summer day. Thomas's boys scampered off the carriage to climb on the ruins. Roland wanted very much to explore the graveyard as freely as they were, but instead he waited in his seat while Hubert and Thomas helped Clare and Bertine descend. How beautiful were the ruins outside the carriage window, the stone arches intricately made and yet solid.

"Are you going to sit on the carriage for the rest of the afternoon?" Hubert joked.

Roland laughed at himself and made haste to descend.

Thomas had gone ahead and was calling for his sons, who had disappeared behind the rocks. One of their patients, an elderly man with a goiter, was talking to Hubert so Roland went ahead to join Clare and Bertine, who were strolling toward a low-lying pile of chalky white stones, their arms linked together. These two women seemed to be in harmony with one another, in contrast to the discord Roland sensed between their parents.

By the time he reached Bertine, Clare had walked ahead to a large stone, where she sat to rest and wipe sweat from her face with an embroidered cloth. Thomas had told him that Clare was more like a mother to Bertine than a sister; seeing Clare's watchful gaze upon her, Roland sensed that the surgeon was right.

"Monsieur Roland," Bertine said when he joined her, "I am sorry you had to endure what happened last Sunday. Is everything settled between you and Giraud?"

"Thank you for your concern," he said, feeling pleased that she had been thinking of him. "No, the matter between us is not resolved, but I have been able to avoid him."

"*Très bien.*" She curtsied and walked swiftly to join her sister.

Hubert, who had finished his conversation, called to Roland. They walked together to an arched stone doorway.

The surgeon traced his finger along one of the stones. "My wife never wants to come here."

"I thought she was ill."

"Those headaches of hers always occur whenever she wishes to avoid something unpleasant," he said. "I wager that she is on her knees as we speak, praying for his eternal rest."

"Whose eternal rest, monsieur?" Roland asked.

Hubert drew in a deep breath and exhaled slowly. "Many years ago, before Clare was born, I stood in this very spot, marveling at how precisely these stones were cut. On the meadow over there, Perronelle was chasing after Marie, who was two years old at the time. I heard a horse approaching and turned to see my servant Antoine, looking most distraught, dismount and run toward me. My not-yet-six-month-old son, he informed me, lay dead in his crib." The surgeon bowed his head. "To this day, I know not why a healthy baby like my son Hubert was alive and well one moment and dead the next. I will never understand why God punished me so."

Roland looked down at the rocky earth. This was not how he had expected the afternoon to unfold. "I am sorry to hear that you lost your son, monsieur."

"His death took place twenty-eight years ago," Hubert replied, "and I no longer grieve for him. I hoped that François or Thomas would be as a son to me, but that has not come to pass. Still, I have not lost hope that the future husband of my youngest daughter would be like a son."

Hubert paused and Roland kept his eyes on the ground.

"I would ask you to consider marrying Bertine," the older man said. "She is clever and pretty. I believe you enjoy conversing with her."

"But monsieur, I am not ready to be married—"

"You do not need to make any decisions now. I just wanted to let you know that I would be quite pleased to have you as my son-in-law. Come, let us go and listen to Bertine's poems."

Four

> "A physician is bound, inasmuch as he is a physician, to present with a beneficial regimen ... the patient is endowed with the freedom to choose whether to follow or not. If [the physician] fails to mention everything that may be helpful ... he is guilty of acting dishonestly, for he did not offer trustworthy advice."
> —From a letter by twelfth-century physician Maimonides about the treatment of depression

Arles, France
13 Juillet, 1478

It was the end of the workday; Hubert had just gone home, and Roland was with the other apprentices, folding blankets and putting surgical instruments back in their places.

Ever since he'd come to Arles, everything had happened so quickly: Hubert suggesting that Roland marry Bertine one day; Bertine seeking a moment alone with him to express her concern about Giraud; her voice rising and falling in melodious waves as she recited her lovely poem about roses to the family. Her verses had been neither childish nor shallow, and he wanted to hear the poem again to grasp its meaning more fully. And yesterday at dinner and at the cemetery, she made him feel at ease, skillfully steering the conversation to topics that interested him.

Still, he was not ready to wed anyone, and when he did, the

woman would be someone of his choosing, not Hubert's. Surely Bertine would want to do likewise, although she would have to comply with her father's choice of a husband. But if she could choose for herself, was it possible that she might choose him? That one day, he might also choose her?

"Walk home with me," said Thomas as he and Roland left the shop together. They had taken off their aprons and wore only their shirts and breeches on this hot afternoon. "We have hardly had a chance to speak privately since we came to Arles."

"I miss talking with you and hearing about your surgeries," Roland said.

"They are not as interesting as Hubert's," Thomas said bluntly. "Tell me, how are you faring under his tutelage?"

"Very well," Roland said. "I am learning so much every day. I will never forget helping Hubert break apart a thin, upper layer of a man's eyes that blurred his vision. In some ways it is a good thing that he made me his apprentice."

"That is what I guessed," Thomas said. "What do you think of Hubert's family? You can speak freely; I will keep whatever you say to myself."

Roland thought for a moment before answering. "Marie and her husband boast too much about their wealth, and Perronelle, though pious, seems distant from the rest of the family. It also seems that Hubert has more affection for Bertine than he does for his other daughters."

"You are right," Thomas said, "especially about how Hubert dotes on Bertine."

"Are the other sisters jealous of her?"

"Marie is, but not Clare. She and Bertine are very close. When my sons were little, Bertine was still a child and would come play at our house with her nephews. It was as if Clare had three children instead of two. Now that the boys attend school, Clare spends many hours of the day with Bertine. Clare is just as clever as her sister, and they enjoy reading and tending the garden together. Tell me, do you enjoy talking to Bertine?"

"Yes," Roland replied, his face reddening. "Thomas, I need your advice. Yesterday at Alyscamps, Hubert said he would be pleased if I were to wed Bertine one day."

Thomas stopped walking and looked at Roland intently. "Listen well," he said in a low voice. "Hubert is like unto a puppet master who seeks to control people instead of puppets. I fear that he is beginning to take away your freedom, just as he took away mine when he arranged for me to wed Clare. Try to remain free of him; remind him that you are returning to the university in September."

Was he? He was learning so much more as Hubert's apprentice than he had from attending lectures at Montpellier.

They had now reached the grammar school, where Thomas's two sons awaited their father. Thomas tousled their hair and asked what they had learned that day. They eagerly told him about their lesson in adding sums of Roman numbers.

They continued walking to Thomas's house, where they found Clare picking herbs in a small side garden. It was well tended and had many of the medicinal plants—mint, betony, and lavender—that had been in Roland's mother's garden.

The boys ran to greet their mother and she hugged them before inspecting their hands. "Filthy," she pronounced. "Go and wash them. Supper will be ready soon."

"Good, I am very hungry," Nicholas said.

"Me too," Arnaud agreed, and they ran inside, slamming the door behind them.

Clare greeted her husband and Roland with a curtsy. He had never before stood so close to her, and for the first time he noticed the fine wrinkles on her face.

"Roland, would you care to sup with us?" Thomas asked.

A frown crossed Clare's face. She started to say something but stopped herself.

Roland quickly thought of an excuse. "I have much studying to do tonight," he said. "But I thank you for the invitation."

"Farewell until I see you again, then," Thomas said. "I will journey to Montpellier tomorrow."

"Farewell." Roland turned to leave.

He had only gone a short way when he overheard Clare say softly, "Thomas, you did not tell me you were going away. I hoped we could take the boys sailing on the river."

"Soon, goodwife," Thomas soothed her. "Come, let us sup."

Overhearing this snippet of their conversation unsettled Roland, and he quickened his pace. He felt a twinge of pity for Clare. For the first time, he understood a little of what she, or any woman whose husband was unfaithful, might feel. As an intelligent woman, maybe she had an inkling of the deceit. It was possible that Thomas thought of himself as kinder than husbands who flaunted their mistresses in front of their wives, but maybe she sensed that he had a lover and resented his treating her like a child by attempting to protect her from that knowledge.

Thomas was usually forthright and direct. Roland could talk freely with him about the inner workings of the body without fearing that his friend would accuse him of heresy. But Roland doubted that Thomas and he would ever speak freely about his wife and mistress.

The next day, as Roland descended the stairs for the day's work, his landlord called to him from the great room. A beggar boy had just come with a message for him: A doctor wanted to speak with Roland at his shop, tonight, at the same hour as they'd met a fortnight earlier. The message must be from Isaac. Would his tidings concern the countess's daughter? Roland was curious to find out and knew it would be a long day until darkness fell.

Roland thanked the landlord and set out for the surgery shop, the morning sun on his back. As he did every morning, he watched for chamber pots being emptied onto the street from upper-story windows and for excrement left by dogs and pigs wandering along the streets. He was grateful when he reached the square with the public oven, and the scent of fresh bread drifted toward him on a warm breeze.

Roland passed the morning treating common ailments like boils that needed lancing and rotten teeth that needed to be pulled. Just as the bells were tolling the noon hour, the time when the surgeons and apprentices took their midday meal, a carpenter's apprentice staggered into the shop, moaning in pain. He was no more than twelve, but with arms already made strong from wielding a hammer and sawing wood.

The boy had a thick splinter of wood driven deeply into his palm.

"Trying to imitate Our Lord at his crucifixion?" Hubert joked but the apprentice only moaned louder, his round face so pale that his freckles looked even more pronounced.

How had this injury come to pass? Roland wondered this as he ran to fetch the forceps. Upon returning to Hubert's surgery table, he poured the boy a large cup of wine, which he quickly drank.

"Pulling out the splinter will be quick work," Roland reassured the boy as he rolled up a cloth for him to clench between his teeth. He then tied the apprentice's arms and legs to four straps positioned on the bed posts.

After Roland pinned the injured hand to the bed, Hubert placed the forceps on either side of the splinter and gently twisted it from side to side. "Never pull," he warned Roland. "That would tear the flesh and muscles."

Hubert's movement gradually loosened the splinter and he was able to remove it. He motioned for Roland to follow him across the shop. "I didn't want the boy to overhear me telling you how important it is that you lean very close to the bloody hole and use my tweezers to remove the smaller splinters," he instructed Roland in a low voice. "If you do not take care, those remaining splinters will fester and we will have to amputate the hand."

Hubert left to partake of the midday meal, and the other surgeons and apprentices in the shop gradually left to join him. This quiet hour alone in the surgery shop was usually when Roland drew what he had seen of the body that morning. This dinner hour, however, he took his time inspecting the boy's wound. Little bits of wood still dotted the bloody hole, and he picked off as many as he could find.

"How did this splinter come to be driven into your palm?" he asked the boy.

"My master bade me to fetch his horse from the stable," he replied. "On the way back to the shop, the horse shied and bolted. To steady myself, I clutched hold of a wooden railing, but the horse was so strong that my hand was dragged along the railing, and the splinter pierced my flesh."

"Ah." Roland had noticed that was the way most accidents occurred; in the blink of an eye, great damage was often done. He soaked a cloth in vinegar. "This will sting," he warned the apprentice, "but it will help keep pus from the wound."

The boy whimpered as Roland applied the vinegar and then wrapped a bandage around his hand. "Put vinegar on it day and night," he instructed him, "and wrap a clean cloth around your hand. If it still hurts in a week's time, return here."

"Will he cut off my hand?" the boy asked, his voice wavering.

"I do not think so," Roland replied as he untied the straps. He wondered if some mysterious inner parts of the body were already working to heal the boy's wound.

After the day's work was done, Roland remembered that Isaac had summoned him to his shop. He wondered again about the doctor's purpose in inviting him. To help pass the time until the late hour of the meeting, he went to a bookshop, where he bought a new sketchbook to replace his other one, which was completely filled with drawings of animals and surgeries.

As usual, his favorite inn was very crowded—townspeople and

pilgrims alike came to partake of the delicious food prepared by Hélène, the innkeeper's wife who was teaching him Provençal recipes. Unable to find any place to sit, Roland almost gave up and went somewhere else, but just as he turned to leave, a gray-haired man waved his arms and pointed to a vacant chair at his table.

A woman with a streak of gray in her dark hair was also seated there. She did not greet Roland, for she was holding a little girl who was crying loudly for her mother.

The elderly woman rocked the girl back and forth, murmuring words that Roland could not hear in the noisy tavern. Despite the merriment all around them, he sensed a deep sadness on the drawn faces of the elderly man and woman. He wanted to do something to help them or to comfort the child. As he sat down, an idea came to him.

Loosening the drawstring of his satchel, he reached inside and found his used sketchbook. He took out a sketch of a turtle he had once seen laying eggs on the beach. "Would the child like to have this sketch?" he asked the man.

The man nodded gratefully and tapped the little girl on the shoulder. "Look, Jeannine, I have a surprise for you."

At once the child lifted her head and looked at the sketch. "A turtle." She sniffled, tracing the curve of its shell with her finger.

"Yes," Roland said. "I saw her crawl out of the ocean onto the sand. She dug a hole in it with her back legs and laid her eggs in it."

The child's eyes grew wide. "Did you see the baby turtles?"

Roland shook his head. "When I returned to the beach a few weeks later, the eggs had already hatched and the babies had crawled back into the ocean."

"Do you want to draw the babies?" the old woman asked the child.

"Yes, Grandmère." The little girl wiped her tears while her grandmother took a quill and an ink pot out of her satchel. The task occupied Jeannine until the serving girl brought Hélène's fish and lentil stew to the table.

"My name is Georges," the man introduced himself in the French of the North. "This is my wife, Felise, and our granddaughter, Jeannine. We own a bookshop in Tarbes, a town on the pilgrimage route between France and Spain."

"I am Roland, a student of medicine and surgery," Roland said.

As they supped, Jeannine settled back into Felise's arms and grew still. Very soon, she was fast asleep.

"What brings you to Arles?" Roland asked, careful to speak softly enough not to wake the child.

"We are on a pilgrimage to Rome," Georges replied. "Our son's wife died and we are going with him to pray for her soul."

Ah, that was the source of the couple's sadness.

"You are studying medicine, so you may have observed how sorrow affects the body," Georges said. "Our son's is so great that he cannot rise from his bed. A physic advised that Henri take a remedy of St. John's wort to help release the excess of black humor from his spirits. He is sleeping now, and we must return to him soon." He frowned. "I have never understood the humors. Do they truly exist?"

"Black bile, yellow bile, phlegm, and blood," Roland replied. "In addition to being one of the humors, the blood is the vessel that carries the other humors throughout the body. According to the ancient Greek doctor Galen, they must be kept in balance for the body to be hale. My professors at Montpellier lectured about them, but like you, I have wondered if they do exist," he admitted. "In my first month at the university, I pricked my finger and inspected a drop of my blood while wearing a pair of spectacles. I saw nothing, but maybe the humors are too small to see even with spectacles." Roland remembered the remedy Isaac had given the countess's daughter. "Yet the St. John's wort that the physic gave to your son is one that other skilled doctors use to treat diseases of the mind."

"*Merci*," the elderly man said with a grateful smile. "You have helped me to understand."

During the meal Roland tried to distract the couple from their sorrow by asking questions about the northern part of France where they had once lived, for he had never been there. They told him about the cities and the countryside, as well as about the war between France and England that lasted nearly a hundred years.

"You helped battlefield surgeons?" Roland's voice lifted in surprise as he stared at the elderly Felise, in vain trying to imagine her as a fifteen-year-old assisting with amputations and tending to terrible burns as cannons boomed and soldiers screamed in pain.

"Yes," she said quietly. "It was the most difficult work I have ever done. It also opened my eyes to the horror of war." She turned to her husband. "Georges and I realized that war is never worth the suffering it causes and we moved far away from where the battles raged."

"I have not lived through a war and hope that I never will," Roland said quietly.

They finished the meal in silence. Felise took a bowl from her satchel and spooned the rest of the fish and lentils into it. She also wrapped the remaining bread in a napkin.

"I hope that our son takes some supper too," she mused aloud. "He has eaten very little on our journey." Georges took the sleeping child from her lap and she rose from her seat. "Thank you for the sketch. You knew how to release Jeannine from her sorrow, at least for a short time. You distracted us too and were truly interested to hear our story."

"Yes, I was," Roland said. He had never before had such a meaningful conversation with strangers.

The couple inclined their heads in farewell and left him alone at the table.

He had been around the same age as Jeannine when his mother died. He remembered sobbing on the floor beneath the table that held her coffin, the scent of beeswax candles surrounding him when he heard his uncle's voice say, "Roland, look what I brought you." Lifting his head, he'd seen his uncle kneeling on the floor, pushing a basket toward him. In it was an orange kitten who lay sleeping. *Naranja*.

He hadn't thought of the kitten in years. A new thought came to him: Did the mind have a secret room where memories were hidden until one day, the door mysteriously opened? He would ask Isaac that question.

As he reached for his satchel on the floor, he saw a book lying under the chair where Felise had been seated. He quickly left the inn and spotted the elderly couple crossing the square. He strode toward them, calling their names. "I think this is yours, Madame Felise," he said, extending the book to her.

She smiled. "You may keep it, in exchange for the gift of the turtle sketch and your companionship during supper," she said. "You also seemed quite interested in the war and the battlefield surgeons. This book is an account of my girlhood during that war—not one that I merely copied from another writer, but one written by my own hand."

"Thank you," he said, trying to hide his amazement. Never before had he heard of a woman writing her own book, but maybe more women had done so, like Felise, without signing their names.

After it was fully dark, Roland crept through back streets, as furtive as the rats rustling at his feet. He reached the street that bordered the Jewish quarter and listened for footsteps. Silence.

After making certain that no Christian was nearby, he darted across the street.

At this late hour, no one was walking in the Jewish quarter either. An oil lamp shone outside Isaac's shop, however, and when Roland knocked on the door, Isaac immediately opened it and motioned for Roland to follow him inside.

Candles set in sconces illuminated the shop, which smelled of cinnamon and garlic, just as it had the last time.

Isaac set another chair by his desk and they both sat down.

"It is very important for both of us to keep our meeting secret," the doctor began.

"Yes, I know," Roland said with a nod.

"A few nights ago, I secretly met with Lady Beatrice..."

When Isaac finished telling him what had happened in the olive grove, Roland sat very still, staring at the shuttered window. "I find it quite unexpected that the countess would want me to take your place in attending her daughter," he said. "I know nothing about diseases of the spirit."

"But is it not true that you are eager to learn about them?"

"Yes."

"I cannot attend to Magali in person or be your teacher, but I could advise you in our secret messages back and forth. You would also glean what you could about these maladies, as well as diseases of the body, from ancient texts and share those ideas with me."

"I will not be able to go to Montpellier and search in the treatises kept there until the fall, when lectures resume." *If I return there at all*, Roland added silently.

"Until that time I can loan you the few texts I own that have been translated into Latin," Isaac offered.

Roland's excitement about discovering effective remedies returned in full measure. And he would be paid for his service to Lady Beatrice and her daughter. If Carlos stopped sending him his allowance, he would need the money.

But if he agreed to this proposal, he would attend Magali a few hours every Sunday morning. He would not only be entangled in Hubert's designs for him but also in Lady Beatrice's. Hubert's warning against becoming involved with the countess and her daughter echoed in his mind, mingling with Thomas's warnings about Hubert.

And then there was Magali's wildness, her unpredictable nature, to which he was unaccustomed.

All of these considerations swirled within him like a fog blinding him to the path he should choose. "I do not know," he said at last.

"I understand," Isaac said. "Would you like to hear my counsel?"

"Yes."

"Lady Beatrice wants to try this arrangement for a month. Let it also be a trial for you. But in the end, it is for the countess to decide whether or not to keep you in her employ."

Roland would be taking a risk in accepting Lady Beatrice's proposal, but his curiosity overcame his fear. "I will do as you advise," he said.

Isaac walked over to the bookcase and Roland followed him. Pulling a book from the shelf, the doctor handed it to Roland. "Here is one that I have not read. It has been translated into Latin and might contain some passages about maladies of the spirit and their remedies."

Roland eagerly took the book. "If I discover something, I will send word to you."

Isaac nodded. "Employ a beggar boy, as I did this morning when I sent you a message. Tell him there is a tree on the boundary of the Jewish quarter near the temple that has thick, leafy branches where he can hide the message. Now, you must go. Make certain that none of your people see you leaving the quarter."

"Of course." Roland's heart beat quickly as he walked to the door, hiding the book under his cloak.

16 JUILLET

A few days later, Roland hired a driver and a carriage to take him a short way along the road north of Arles. As the carriage passed olive groves and orchards, Roland saw the tower of the château that Isaac described as Lady Beatrice's. "Stop!" he called out to his driver.

The carriage rolled to a stop, and Roland dismounted.

"Wait here," he bade the driver after paying him generously. "I will return in time for you to take me to Mass at Saint Trophime."

The day was dawning as he walked past olive groves and vineyards before reaching the courtyard in front of the château, a massive structure built of a light-colored stone.

A manservant opened the front door and led Roland through a foyer to the great room. Servants were already beginning the day's work, opening the shutters to tall windows and lighting a fire in the huge stone fireplace. It was so inviting and Roland so tired at this very early hour that he could have easily collapsed onto the thick, green carpet spread before it. Bookcases lined the walls on the other side of the fireplace. Hundreds of books stood within them, but they were too far away for Roland to read their titles.

The servant bade Roland to sit at a long oak table in the great room. Lady Beatrice soon joined him, accompanied by her lady-in-waiting. The countess seemed more at ease than she had been when he'd last seen her. Still, he was wary of her.

She nodded a greeting. "Thank you for agreeing to help my daughter," she said. "You may tell Isaac that she remained in her chamber for the past three days, barely waking to take a little food before tumbling back into a deep slumber. But last night, following his advice, I gave her a lesser dose." She smiled. "She slept well, and when she awoke, she said that she felt she had been asleep for a long time. She will soon come to break her fast and I will introduce you to her."

"Good," Roland said, wondering how Magali would receive him.

A few moments later, Magali, carrying a thick book, walked to the table with a maid. Trying not to stare, Roland noticed that the color had returned to her cheeks, rendering her freckles less visible, and the dark circles beneath her eyes had faded. These changes, as well as the neatness of her hair, which was pinned precisely beneath her coif, lent her a composure quite different from that of the wild spirit he'd met only a short time ago.

She took a seat across from Roland and frowned at him. "Who are you?"

Isaac had warned him that she would probably not remember her night in Arles.

"Roland is a student at the university in Montpellier," Lady Beatrice answered for him.

"You look too young," Magali said bluntly. "How old are you?"

His face flushed. "Nineteen," he muttered. "How old are you?"

"Twenty." She turned to her mother. "Why is he here?"

"He is the messenger between your new doctor and me—"

"I do not need a doctor."

"Yes, you do," Lady Beatrice gently countered. "Do you feel well-rested this morn?"

"Yes—"

"Your new doctor gave you a different remedy that helped you to sleep," Lady Beatrice interrupted her. "Remember how you dreaded when your other doctor drew blood from you?"

Magali nodded.

"Your new doctor assured me that he will not do so."

Magali stretched her arms overhead. "I do feel better this morning," she admitted, "and I am very hungry."

Servants brought a plate of food for Magali but only a cup of water for Lady Beatrice, her lady-in-waiting, and Roland, since they were obliged to fast until Holy Communion. His stomach growled as he watched Magali pull off a large hunk of bread and spread soft cheese on it.

She took a big bite and opened her book.

"What are you reading?" he asked.

"Tales of the Greeks. This one is the story of the Amazons."

"What is an Amazon?" he asked.

She gaped at him. "You do not know the stories of the Greeks?"

He shook his head. "Only what they wrote about philosophy and medicine." Some of which also appeared to be stories instead of the truth.

She smiled, her lips parting to reveal even teeth, except for one on the top row that was smaller than the rest. "I will tell it to you."

She showed him the miniature that illustrated the tale. It was a woman dressed in a white tunic with a rope belt. She was teaching a girl, who was similarly clad, how to use a bow and arrow. Magali recited the entire tale from memory.

"You must have read this story many times to know it so well," Roland said when she was finished.

"Yes. I can see the words in my mind."

He stared at her in wonderment. He too could picture pages from his treatises, but he had never met another man, much less a woman, who could do so.

"Did you enjoy that story?" she asked.

"Yes," he lied, not wanting to upset her, "but it was very different from the books about philosophy and medicine that I usually read."

"Do you want to read some more tales?"

Roland glanced over at Lady Beatrice to see if the time had come for him to leave. Tears of joy were streaming down her face. "You have come back to me, *ma chère*," she murmured.

"But I have not taken a journey," Magali insisted.

"Only a few more tales," her mother said, wiping her tears with a handkerchief that her lady-in-waiting gave her.

Magali recited the next tale, which was about a winged horse named Pegasus. The tale after that was illustrated with a miniature of a bear. "*The Tale of Callisto*," she cried, springing to her feet. "Roland, help me act out this story. I have enjoyed putting stories into plays since I was a child."

Roland barely stifled a groan. Like Carlos, he believed that religious plays were means for priests to have power over their parishioners, and farces about cuckold husbands and devious wives were frivolous and overplayed. But he would be far worse at acting than those players were, for he would underplay his role, and Lady Beatrice and the servants would witness him making a fool of himself. He wished to be anywhere else but here.

"Lady Magali, I have never acted before, and besides I do not know the story," he pleaded. "Perhaps your maid could help you?"

Magali laughed as she pointed toward a short young woman. "Tell me, does Nina resemble Zeus, King of the Gods?"

How could he avoid this role? But Isaac had instructed him to be her loyal servant and do as she bade him unless it was dangerous. He bowed his head. "As you wish, milady."

She sprang to her feet and set to work teaching him his part. Everyone's eyes on him made him feel unsettled. He said his lines quickly, desiring only to finish the ordeal as quickly as possible. The servants tried to hide their smiles but Roland noticed anyway. Never had he been so embarrassed, especially when he learned that Zeus was dallying with the nymph Callisto, played by Magali. Nina was not particularly convincing as Zeus's jealous wife, Hera, who found out about Callisto and transformed her into a bear. Magali, on the other hand, was vibrant in the role of the nymph, especially when her beloved son mortally wounded her in her bear form. Roland's discomfort as an actor eased as he realized how important it was for Magali to play a part so different from her ordinary life.

When the performance was over, Lady Beatrice rose to her feet. "Magali, are you feeling well enough to attend Holy Mass with me?"

"Yes," she said. "It seems as if it has been a long time since I did so."

"It has been two weeks," her mother said quietly. "Père Etienne assures me that you committed no mortal sin, for you were ill."

"I do not remember being ill," Magali said again. "Roland, I will tell you more tales of the Greeks on the way to Mass."

Lady Beatrice touched her daughter's arm. "Magali, he cannot come with us. He is from Spain and a stranger to the villagers. Some of the older ones may fear him because they remember the war that the king of Aragon waged against us."

"But I want to tell him more stories, Mama," she insisted.

"On the next Sabbath, he will return. Go with Nina and dress quickly, *ma chère*."

As soon as Magali and Nina left the great room, Roland handed Lady Beatrice more of the remedies that Isaac wanted Magali to continue taking. "You should continue to follow the instructions that Isaac gave you, lowering the dose if your daughter enjoys several nights of restful sleep."

She nodded, looking at him thoughtfully. "You helped her today," she said with a note of surprise. "Tell me, did you really enjoy those tales of the Greeks as much as Magali does?"

"I am studying to be a doctor, not a writer of tales or an actor," he admitted. "But that matters not. I am here to help your daughter."

Lady Beatrice handed him a pouch of coins. "Thank you, and when you write to Isaac, please thank him for me."

What the past few weeks must have been like for her to watch her daughter descend into madness, and what relief she must feel that the illness had passed. Even so, he should remind her of Isaac's warning that she could not be certain of what her daughter would be like from day to day—shouldn't he? *No*, he decided, *not today*. He would grant Lady Beatrice a brief respite from her worries.

He bowed in farewell and walked toward the door.

"Wait," she called out.

He turned around. "Yes, milady?"

"The Feast of Saint James is in a week's time. Will the surgery shop be closed for a few days?"

"Yes." Hubert would be away with Perronelle and Bertine, attending his nephew's wedding. Clare and her boys would attend the wedding too, while Thomas would be in Montpellier . . . with his lover.

"I must attend the Mass and feast in the village, but I believe partaking in all the festivities would disrupt Magali's health. On the eve of the feast, will you come here and spend a night or two? There is a room for you in the tower. My housekeeper, Lady Alienor, will remain here with you, and you will be able to observe Magali during the feast day. But I believe that you can do more than simply bear witness to the turnings of her mind; you can be a companion to Magali, someone who can read and converse with her. I would have you ask Isaac if I am right to believe your company could help her spirits to remain in balance."

He hid his surprise as best he could. "I would be honored, milady."

As he accepted her invitation, however, Hubert's warning echoed in his mind: *Have no more dealings with the countess or her daughter.*

24 JUILLET

On the eve of the Feast of Saint James, Roland followed a young servant—yet another one in Lady Beatrice's vast household—to the tower, which was a separate building across the courtyard from the château. Inside, a stained-glass window depicting the birth of Jesus caught the bright afternoon sunlight. On the long worktable lay a smaller, unfinished window featuring a horse. It was crudely rendered but somehow captured the spirit of the animal.

He himself had never drawn a horse nor attempted to form one from pieces of glass. It would be an intriguing puzzle to solve, he thought, but for now he followed the servant up the stairs.

"Your chamber," the young man said when they reached the second floor.

It was a large round room with four small windows, neatly appointed with a bed, a desk, and a chair—all that Roland needed.

After setting his satchels down, he followed the servant around the exterior of the château to another large, paved area where supper was to be served. Just beyond this patio was an expansive garden and farther in the distance, vineyards terraced up rocky hills.

Lady Beatrice sat at the head of a stone table, watching Magali walk along the garden pathways and gather herbs in a basket. Her back was to the courtyard, and she lowered her head now and then to smell a flower. Seeing her tranquility, Roland felt at ease.

When he greeted Lady Beatrice, she smiled. She seemed calmer today as well.

"Magali slept well this week, even with taking less of the remedy than she did last week," she said. "She was so calm that I allowed Nina and my lady-in-waiting, Catherine, to return to their families tonight for the Feast of Saint James."

"Isaac will be pleased that your daughter continues to sleep well," Roland said, handing her a pouch. "He instructed me to give you these remedies for the coming week. The dose of St. John's wort and valerian is slightly less than it was last week. There is valerian for you as well, should you have trouble sleeping."

"I am much more rested now." The countess tied the pouch to her belt and made the sign of the cross. "I thank Our Lord and His Holy Mother every day for Magali's return to health."

"Isaac asked me to remind you that nothing is certain about your daughter's illness," Roland said, wishing he did not have to do so. "If her mania and melancholia returns, her remedies will need to be increased again."

"I know," she said quietly, "but I do not wish to consider the future. Let me simply enjoy her company on this beautiful evening."

"Yes, milady."

In the morning, Roland broke his fast with Magali in the dining hall. Lady Beatrice had already taken a carriage to the village and Lady Alienor sat across the table from them, writing in a thick ledger. All around them, servants went about the morning tasks of bringing in water from the well, fresh milk from the barn, and logs for the day's fire. Through the arched doorway to the kitchen, scullery maids set loaves of freshly baked bread to cool on racks. Roland could only see part of the vast room; he longed to enter it so he could watch the cooks at work.

"Your candle was lit until late into the night yesterday evening," Magali remarked as she spread a thick layer of freshly churned butter on her bread.

"Yes, I was reading a treatise on medicine," he said. "Could you not sleep?"

"Not until the village church rang Prime. I sat by the window, watching the full moon."

They'd supped outside as the sun set and the full moon rose the previous evening. Never had Roland witnessed such a beautiful sight. Yet now he worried that the full moon had been so bright it had kept Magali awake.

"I probably would have fallen asleep more easily if I were reading your treatise," she said, a touch of mischief in her tone. "Such a dull book, with no stories, would certainly have put me to sleep."

"Actually, there *is* a story in it," he said. "The story of the body and how all of its parts work together. They are like the soldiers in an army fighting against evil warriors, such as diseases and wounds."

"A story without people." She wrinkled her nose. "I doubt I would find it interesting."

"I think you might," he said. "How the parts of the body act in concert is a puzzle that I am trying to solve."

"I like puzzles too, but when I read, I like stories about people." She rose from her chair. "Come, I will show you our library."

Lady Alienor followed the two young people into the great room.

"Other than in the library at Montpellier, I have never seen so many books in one place," Roland said as Magali and he stood in front of the bookcases.

She pointed to three intricately carved wooden chests in the corner. "There are even more locked away in there. Those books are bound in jewels."

"How did your family come to acquire all of these books?" he asked.

"They came mostly from my grandmother," she replied. "She was my father's mother and died before I was born. Her name was Marguerite and I am her namesake. When I was a child, I could not pronounce my own name and called myself Magali. Ever since, that has been my name." She moved her gaze from the books to Roland's face. "Tell me how you got your name."

"Rolando was my uncle, my mother's only brother," he explained. "He died a few years ago."

"Are your mother and father still alive?"

He shook his head, remembering again the candles that flickered around her coffin, the stone floor that was rough and cold on his cheek, and the sleeping kitten that Uncle Rolando gave him. "My mother died when I was young, and my father died when I was fourteen. My mother would have enjoyed this library, for she loved to read, and I loved listening to her stories."

Magali smiled wistfully. "My father read stories to me," she said. "Like your mother, he died when I was young."

Roland's own father never read to him, hardly ever took notice of him. But he kept that thought to himself as he noticed small squares of parchment glued to the shelves, marking different sections of books—travel logs, saints' tales, encyclopedias, and Greek tales, of course. There were also many books of instruction and manners. He pulled one from the shelf and saw from the miniature paintings that the book was intended to teach noblewomen how to be good wives.

"Those are boring." Magali took the book from him and replaced it on the shelf. "Let us try some of these puzzles instead." She took a thick book from another section.

Looking over her shoulder, Roland saw that the book contained a variety of puzzles, including some in words and some in a combination of words and pictures.

"I have not tried to solve these since I was a child," she said. "They were too hard for me then—but maybe, with your help, we can solve some of them now." She opened it and read, "What is the sister of the sun, though made for the night? The fire causes her tears to fall, and when she is near dying they cut off her head."

Roland was intrigued. "The first part sounds like the moon, but not the second part."

"This riddle must have something to do with fire," Magali mused. "The word 'tears' is what puzzles me. How is something watery connected to something composed of fire?"

Maybe it is not truly made of water but something liquid, thought Roland—and suddenly, the answer came to him. "I know what it is! Do you want me to tell you, or do you want to keep trying to solve the riddle?"

"I want to keep thinking about it," she said and began to pace. "Something that flows like water but is not water..."

She asked Roland some questions about its color, size, and shape, seeking to clarify what the substance looked like. Then, suddenly, she stopped pacing and turned to him with a triumphant look on her face. "It is a candle!"

"Yes!" He beamed, impressed she had figured it out.

An hour later, they had solved several more riddles and were searching for a new book in the vast collection.

"You have no books about philosophy and medicine," Roland commented.

"Are they interesting?"

"To me they are."

Pursing her lips together, Magali studied him closely. "Are you interested in the books I have been reading to you?"

"Yes," he replied, not wanting to unsettle her, "and I want to keep reading them. Yet in order to become a doctor, I must continue reading medical texts and on my own, I enjoy reading books of philosophy. Would you consider taking turns choosing what we read together?"

She crossed her arms against her chest. "Yes, on one condition. If I judge your books to be tedious, I will not read them. You may do the same."

They returned to the great room and Roland opened his satchel, considering what might interest Magali the most. Certainly not books about surgeries or ingredients for remedies; they might bore her—or, even worse, disturb her.

He saw the spine of the Lucretius book peeking out and smiled. A few days after Magali had spilled wine on it, he'd found another copy of the text at a bookshop and hired a scribe to make a copy of the ruined page. He had read it many times and always found it to be a wondrous passage.

Book in hand, he joined Magali in front of the fireplace and settled into the barrel-shaped chair next to hers. Before them, a fire blazed and logs crackled. He read aloud:

Anything made out of destructible matter
Infinite time would have devoured before.
But if the particles that make and replenish the world
Have endured through the immense span of the past
Their natures are immortal—that is clear.
Never can things revert to nothingness.

He read these words slowly and with expression.

Magali listened intently, her small hands resting on her lap. "Tiny particles, inside of us and inside the rocks, the sea—everything . . ." she mused, her voice far away. "Do you believe, as this writer does, that they have always existed and will always exist?"

"I have often pondered that question and still do not know the answer," he admitted. "And how did Lucretius, who lived almost two thousand years ago, arrive at his ideas?"

She nodded. "I often wonder the same thing about the ancient Greek storytellers. I wish it were possible to go on a journey back to ancient times and see for myself how their stories came to be."

Her words echoed in the great room. This was the first time another person had shared Roland's idea aloud.

That afternoon, Magali and Roland planned to go riding with Lady Alienor while Lady Beatrice was still in attendance at the feast, but it was raining steadily. Magali was disappointed, and Roland tried to think of a way to restore her spirits.

As they finished their noon meal, he noticed a bowl of ripe plums on the side table. Earlier, he'd overheard Lady Alienor telling the servants that the supper would simply be leftover pork along with bread and cheese. This meant he and Magali would not be in their way in the kitchen.

He asked Lady Alienor's permission to make a plum pie.

"Yes," she replied, looking out the window at the rain. "A pie will at least bring us some cheer."

"Yes," Magali agreed as she rose from the table, eager to begin. "I did not know that you liked to cook."

"I have enjoyed cooking ever since I was a child," Roland shared. "At my favorite tavern in Arles, the innkeeper's wife is teaching me how to prepare some of her recipes. She just showed me how to make the pastry we will make today."

"Maybe you should become a cook and not a surgeon," Magali said.

He shook his head. "Healing is my work, and cooking is merely a pastime. But in some ways, they are alike. Learning how to use knives in the kitchen has helped me as an apprentice surgeon."

"Cooking and surgery." She laughed. "I have never before thought of their kinship."

While servants washed the dishes, a scullery maid showed Roland and Magali where they could work and where to find the things they would need. First they combined flour, butter, and water for the crust. Roland then showed Magali how to use the rolling pin. Soon, her hands were covered with flour.

Next they peeled the plums using a method Roland's housekeeper in Barcelona had taught him: first they made a small X at the bottom of each fruit, then they submerged it in boiling water for a short while.

"The color is even a deeper red now," Magali exclaimed. "I wonder why."

"I have never thought of that," Roland said thoughtfully. "I do not know."

The next step was to cut the skinned plums into juicy slices. Magali worked too quickly, and Roland feared that she would cut herself with the knife.

"Be careful," he warned her. "The plums are slippery."

He showed her how to hold the fruit with her hand like a claw, keeping her fingers away from the knife. He was relieved that she quickly learned this method.

"Let us decide what spices we would like to add," he suggested after the plums were sliced and sprinkled with sugar.

They walked over to a shelf that contained all manner of spices, labeled in a neat hand and stored in pottery crocks with fitted lids. They took turns opening the crocks and lifting them so they both could smell the contents.

"In the book about Marco Polo's travels, the author wrote about the gardens of China and India where these spices are grown," Magali murmured as she smelled the cinnamon. "How I would love to go there one day."

"I would too," Roland agreed.

Cinnamon, nutmeg, and ginger—just a half spoonful of each—were their final choices for the plums. Magali sighed in pleasure at the mingled scents. "I think our spicing is just right," she murmured.

"One thing I have learned about cooking," Roland said as he set the pie in the oven, "is not to put too much of any ingredient into a dish, for it overwhelms the other flavors."

"You are very precise," she said quietly. "I believe you are just as precise in your work as an apprentice surgeon."

"Now I am a precise cook, but I was not always that way," he said, smiling. "Once for my brother Carlos's birthday, I made him an octopus dish with so much raw garlic that our breath and even the palms of our hands reeked of it for days."

"Did he ever let you cook for him again?" Magali laughed.

"Only if he watched me prepare the dish." Roland laughed too, remembering Carlos's exaggerated wariness.

Nearly an hour later, the pair opened the oven to check on the pie. The plums were bubbling and the crust was a golden brown.

"It's ready!" Roland proclaimed. Using scraps of cloth to protect his hands, he removed the pie from the oven and set it on a stone table to cool.

"It is beautiful and it smells delicious!" Magali exclaimed.

Roland felt content as he always did when he cooked. This time, however, he was even more pleased than usual, because he was sharing that enjoyment with Magali, just as she had shared her enjoyment of the Greek tales with him.

Five

> "A surgeon who does not know his anatomy is like
> a blind man carving a log."
> —From the writings of fourteenth-century
> surgeon/physician Gui de Chauliac

Arles, France

1 AOÛT, 1478

On the first day of August, Roland saw his first patient die. The man, Julian, was a childhood friend of Hubert's and had been bitten by a snake while hunting. Hubert and Roland had done everything they knew to do, making an X-shaped incision and drawing out the venom. But it was too late.

Roland watched as the man took his last breath, his eyes wide open as if startled by his untimely demise. Had his humors left him with that last breath? Roland stared at his face, amazed that life could depart from a body so quietly. Despair came over Roland, despair that Hubert and he had failed, as the surgeon covered his friend's face with a blanket.

At the end of the day, Roland was usually alone in the shop, washing the last of Hubert's surgical instruments by the fading daylight. Today he was so distraught he could barely make his arms and hands do this familiar task, so he was grateful that Hubert stayed to help him.

"I can tell that Julian's death weighs on you," the surgeon said. "It weighs on me too. Know that you did everything you could for him and worked quickly to ready him for my knife. And I, too, did everything I could. But we surgeons cannot always stop a patient from dying. Nothing in this life is certain. One day, you will come to accept this truth."

11 AOÛT

"Holy Virgin, save my boy!" a woman shouted as she rushed into the surgery shop carrying a small child. Blood soaked the blanket that covered his lower body.

Thomas and Roland put down the surgical tools they were cleaning and strode toward her. Seeing his condition—his eyes closed, his face pale—Roland surmised that along with his blood, the boy's life was surely draining from him.

Thomas yanked off the blanket. Blood gushed from a deep, curved cut in the boy's thigh.

"His own brother cut him with a scythe," the woman wailed.

Thomas pressed the two flaps of skin together but blood continued to gush. "Prepare the cautery iron," he bade Roland.

A sick feeling came over Roland as he imagined the smell of the boy's burning flesh. He forced himself to cross the room and set the cautery iron to heat in the fire while the mother carried her son to Thomas's table.

"Save him," she wailed again as Thomas continued to press the two sides of the wound together.

"I will try my best," Thomas said grimly.

The iron was almost ready; the queasy feeling returned to the pit of Roland's stomach. He suddenly remembered the crock of ointment that Isaac had given him, the one capable of sealing wounds completely. He had carried it with him like a talisman in his satchel since that night.

"Thomas, I brought a remedy from Barcelona," Roland shouted across the room. "It is said to seal wounds without using a cautery iron."

Thomas did not look up from staunching the wound. "Let us try it before we resort to the iron," he said. "Bring it here at once."

Roland grabbed it from his satchel and brought it over as the mother prayed at the foot of the bed. He opened the crock and smeared the ointment on a clean rag. The smell of turpentine made him cough as he applied the remedy to the wound.

"Look at that," Thomas exclaimed, bending closer to it. "It is sealing the two sides together."

The mother abruptly stopped her prayers and came to see. "A miracle," she murmured and made the sign of the cross.

Thomas wiped blood from around the sealed wound. "I don't know if there is more blood pooling below the seal that would cause it to burst open," he said, "but the ointment is so greasy that we won't be able to stitch the wound. We will have to wait until tomorrow."

Roland stared at the seal that had formed over the wound—a seemingly impenetrable barrier. He did not believe in miracles but there it was, a miracle wrought from a remedy found in an ancient text.

Hubert strode to the table, scowling at Thomas and Roland. "You fools, what are you doing with turpentine?" He jostled between them and peered down at the boy's wound. "My God," he whispered, "where did you get this remedy?"

"I brought it with me from Barcelona," Roland lied.

Hubert nodded at him in approval. "We will observe the wound tonight and if it is still sealed, we will close the wound with stitches on the morrow."

Roland spent the night in the surgery shop, examining the boy's wound every hour or so. To his great relief, the seal held. The next morning, Hubert stitched the two flaps of skin together with thread made of a pig's belly. Throughout the day, Roland checked on the boy's stitches; each time, he was pleased to find that no blood was seeping through. At mid-afternoon, Hubert bade the woman to take the boy home but to return on the morrow so he could inspect the wound.

Roland was folding blankets when Hubert came over to him and clasped his shoulder. "You have made a wondrous discovery," he said, grinning broadly. "You will come to my study after the day's work is done."

Alone in the shop cleaning the surgical tools that evening, Roland dreaded facing Hubert, not wanting to reveal that he had gotten the salve from a Jewish doctor. He took his time cleaning the last knife before forcing himself to walk to the door connecting the shop to Hubert's house. *Do not mention Isaac,* he silently reminded himself before knocking.

Solange answered his knock and led him to Hubert's study. It was a large room partitioned from the great room by an elaborately carved wooden screen. Hubert sat at an oak desk, stacking the coins that he and his surgeons had earned that day. He motioned for Roland to sit across from him and took a sip of wine from a silver goblet.

Something was different about Hubert; his face and arms were distended—swollen, even. Did he have dropsy? Roland had just found a remedy for this disease, which caused fluid to collect in the body, in the treatise that Isaac had loaned him.

It seemed to take a long time for the surgeon to count the money. "A good day," he said at last. He opened a ledger, recorded the amount, and put the coins into a wooden chest, which he locked with one of the many keys hanging from his belt. Then, leaning back in his chair and stroking his beard to the point, he said, "Now, tell me about that salve."

Roland straightened his back as he quickly thought of a lie. "In Barcelona, Christians often seek help from Jewish doctors. My mother, who tended the poor of my city, bought the salve from a Jewish doctor and used it on a beggar who had a deep wound from a dog bite. Just as you saw today, it completely sealed the wound and there was no need for cauterizing it. Before coming to Montpellier, I bought a crock of the salve from that doctor."

Hubert smiled, making Roland feel even more uneasy. "How fortunate that you brought it here. You will secure more of it for me —say, a dozen crocks."

Roland stared at the table. "That will be difficult unless I return to Barcelona," he lied.

"Purchase it from a Jew in Provence."

Roland kept his head down. "Is that permitted?"

"Not as much as it was when I was a boy and Jewish doctors could serve Christian patients, but as long as there is a gain to be had from the exchange, we Provençal look the other way," Hubert said. "Still, we will be cautious, just as the Jews are in their dealings with Christians—especially now, as the French king seeks to add our land to his kingdom. There are even rumors that he plans to expel the Jews." He tapped a finger on his desk. "Instead of purchasing the salve in Arles, go to Aix-en-Provence. It is not far away and the Jews have more freedom there than they do here. To protect ourselves, we will let it be known that you purchased the salve from a Christian doctor in Barcelona."

"But the Jewish doctors in Aix-en-Provence may not know about this remedy," Roland said.

"I wager they do," Hubert asserted. "The Jews are a tribe, after all; even though they are scattered all over Europe and the lands around the Mediterranean, they have many books about medicine—written in Hebrew, of course—which their doctors share with one another. Now, secure the salve for me."

Roland rose to his feet. "I will try my best, but it may be that I can only obtain the recipe."

"That will suffice, but I would prefer the salve. See that you secure one or the other as quickly as possible." Hubert smiled as he looked out the small lattice window, open to allow a summer breeze. "It will save my patients from the pain of the cautery iron, and for that, both they and I will be most grateful. Furthermore, I will make much money from this salve, for patients will flock to me when they hear of this remedy. My reputation will be further elevated when I share it with the guild of surgeons. And yours will be elevated, too, when I tell them that you brought it to me."

Reputation . . . that was what mattered most to Hubert. Or was it? Thomas would say yes, but clearly Hubert was also concerned about providing his patients with the best care possible.

"I will try to find this remedy for you, Monsieur Hubert." Roland rose from his seat and turned toward the door, eager to escape.

"Before you leave," Hubert said, "I have a question. Have you given any more thought to marrying my daughter?"

Roland was glad that he had his back turned to the surgeon. The past two Sundays, Bertine had sat very close to him while they read. He enjoyed her attention, quick wit, and beauty, and she seemed to enjoy his company too. The most recent Sunday, he'd caught Clare looking at her sister as they read. As always, her gaze had been affectionate—but this time it had seemed wistful as well. Did Bertine's older sister know about her father's plan for his youngest daughter?

"I do enjoy talking and reading with Bertine, monsieur," he said, slowly pivoting to face Hubert. "But I do not understand why you want me to wed her. I am a Spaniard. Would not a wealthy townsman like Giraud, the magistrate's son, be a better choice?"

Hubert shook his head. "You know full well the young man's quickness to anger, and I want a gentler husband for my Bertine. It matters not that you are from Spain. Other than your lapse in judgment regarding the countess's daughter, you have been proving each day that you are an excellent match for Bertine. Not only are you skilled at surgery, but you are also quite wealthy, judging from what you have told me about your family's worth. You seem a trustworthy young man, but I had to make certain that you were telling me the truth about your wealth. I asked my childhood friend Father Etienne to write to the bishop of Barcelona about your family. Your father's shipping business was indeed very profitable, and you and your brother inherited his wealth."

Roland's cheeks burned. He had tried his best to follow Carlos's advice and keep his wealth a secret, but he also could not be rude to the man who was teaching him so much about surgery. And now to find out that Hubert had secretly probed into Roland's family's wealth? Thomas was right about Hubert's desire for control.

"But I am only nineteen and not ready to be wed," Roland stammered.

Hubert smiled fondly at him. "Everything in its own time."

13 AOÛT

Roland eagerly read the latest message from Isaac:

I am happy that the salve spared your young patient from the cauterizing iron. I am also pleased to hear that the master surgeon wants to use the salve with other patients. Even if he simply wants wealth and fame from them, many lives might be saved through his knowledge and yours. To protect my family and me, tell him that you found the recipe in a Jewish text in Avignon. Here is the recipe . . .

Sitting at his desk in his room, Roland copied the recipe from Isaac's letter onto another piece of parchment. Turpentine, rose oil, and egg yolks; how could a paste so simple have such a wondrous effect, and how had the Jews discovered it?

Many thanks for sending me the remedy you found for dropsy. I purchased a plant called foxglove from an apothecary in the quarter and will make the recipe for my patients who suffer from this disease. If the remedy works, I will notify you so that you may share it with your master.

In your last letter, you asked to borrow more of my treatises that have been translated into Latin, but I have already loaned you all of them. You will find many other Latin manuscripts at the library of the university in Montpellier, the city where my family lived for hundreds of years. My great-grandfather and other Jewish doctors once lectured in medicine at the university. Our doctors treated Jews and Christians alike and doctors of both faiths shared remedies and techniques. At that time, the teaching of medicine at the university was based on carefully chosen texts that contained true observations about the body.

In the past few years, the cities of Provence have begun to enact laws against us—likely because of the uncertainty about whether the French king will take control of Provence. Once again, I fear the Jews will have to move to a new land.

Isaac's words reminded Roland of what Hubert had said when his friend died of a snakebite: nothing was certain. He looked out the window and saw a beggar child wandering down the darkening street and picking up scraps of food. Roland had left Barcelona of his own choice; he could not imagine being forced to move, as the Jews had been so many times.

Considering all this, a plan that he had been considering became firmer in his mind. Although he knew that things would never return to the way they once had been between Christian and Jewish doctors, Isaac and he *were* exchanging remedies more or less. He would return to the university and become a doctor, thereby fulfilling Carlos's wishes. But he would spend most of his time not studying useless notes from lectures based mostly on Galen's work but poring over translations of medical texts from a variety of ancient texts in the library. He would share the remedies for the body that he found with Isaac and Hubert, and they would observe the effects of the remedies on their patients. He would also look for remedies for *maladies de l'esprit*, but he would share those only with Isaac because Hubert seemed to have no interest in healing such diseases. After Isaac had observed their effect on his patients, Roland would try them with Magali.

He paced back and forth, his excitement growing until he stopped suddenly, his heart sinking. If he returned to the university, he would no longer tend to patients under Hubert's tutelage, helping them to heal and in the process learning so much about the body. A memory suddenly came to him . . . his mother putting an aloe salve on a beggar's burned arm. Roland could follow her example, helping beggars in Montpellier when he wasn't attending lectures or reading ancient medical texts. It wouldn't be the same as working for Hubert, but Roland would be able to help patients. His resolve returned and he resumed pacing.

Still, I must be cautious, he reminded himself. How would Carlos advise him to proceed?

His brother would make certain that Roland understood both sides of the decision about whether or not to seek new remedies for Hubert. Carlos would counsel him to consider the consequences of saying no to Hubert. Roland would be free of the man's sway over him, but Hubert would be furious. Even worse, he could threaten to ruin Roland's reputation.

Carlos would devise a plan so that Roland could gain what he wanted from the bargain while preserving as much of his freedom as possible. And Carlos would advise setting the plan onto parchment and having both parties sign two copies of it.

The smell of fish simmering in wine wafted from Hubert's kitchen into his study as Roland sat down on the other side of the surgeon's desk. He handed his master the recipe for the salve, as well as the new recipe he had found for dropsy.

"I noticed that your face and arms have been swollen recently," he said. "This remedy for dropsy was in a treatise I was reading. I am not certain, but it may help you."

Hubert took the recipes eagerly. "I don't have dropsy—it's just the hot weather—but I will take the remedy for other patients."

"I have important tidings for you, Monsieur Hubert," Roland continued. "I have decided to return to the university. As of September, I will no longer be your apprentice."

Hubert was silent for a long moment, his jaws clenched. His eyes were like a cat's, yellow in the afternoon sun. "But you will still be in my employ," he finally said. "You will be my procurer. These recipes for the salve and dropsy are the first of many remedies that you will obtain for me. I will pay you so well that you may decide that you do not need to return to the university after all."

"I can easily accomplish both tasks, for the library in Montpellier contains many remedies."

Hubert grinned like a boy. "Ah, so you can complete your studies *and* work for me." He unrolled a piece of parchment. "Let us draw up a contract."

"I have already done so." Roland removed rolled-up parchments from his satchel and handed them to Hubert. "We will try this arrangement until Christmas; after that, we will both decide whether we want to continue our partnership."

Hubert nodded his approval. "I see that your brother has taught you about contracts."

"Yes."

The surgeon put on his spectacles and read the parchment. In the left column, Roland had written out his side of the agreement: to find remedies in ancient medical treatises, and to hire translators and scribes as needed to make copies of the remedies in French. On the right side, Roland had listed the things that Hubert would agree to do: "1) allow me to end my apprenticeship in September; 2) pay me to hire scribes and translators; 3) observe whether or not the recipes or treatments were effective and inform me of the outcome; 4) pay me at least one gold ecu for each remedy; and 5) refrain from trying to persuade me to do anything other than what was laid out in this document."

Hubert stopped reading and peered over the top of his spectacles. "There is something that you have omitted," he said. "I still expect you to ride to Arles every week for Mass and to have dinner with my family."

Roland had considered this demand, but it would be difficult to fulfill as the two cities were a day's journey apart. Yet he wanted to continue seeing Bertine. "Once a month, I could arrange to do so and bring you the recipes I have found."

Hubert's surprised look at Roland's firmness mirrored Roland's inner surprise at himself for speaking up for what he wanted.

"Let us compromise," Hubert proposed. "You will visit us every fortnight."

Roland hesitated, thinking of how much he enjoyed Bertine's company. "I suppose, but you will need to pay for my carriage."

Hubert nodded and, after adding those final stipulations to the contract, signed both copies and passed them back to Roland, who decided to imitate Carlos by making the *R* of his name much larger than the rest of the letters.

"A very confident script," Hubert said approvingly.

On the way home, Roland wanted to skip like a child. He was more like Carlos than he'd once thought.

Six

"If it were customary to send maidens to school and teach them the same subjects as are taught to boys, they would learn just as fully and would understand the subtleties of all arts and sciences."
—CHRISTINE DE PIZAN, A FIFTEENTH-CENTURY FRENCH WRITER

Lady Beatrice's Château

18 AOÛT, 1478
Lady Beatrice's Secret Book

All these years, I have protected Magali from offers of betrothal. No longer. King Louis summons me to his court in Toulouse, and I fear that he seeks to arrange a marriage between Magali and one of his relatives. Of course, I will do everything in my power to persuade the King of the merits of a better, more profitable prospect, as I have before. But I know that King Louis—or the Spider King, as he is called—is far more formidable than René, the "Good" King of Provence.

My child . . . my girl, with her strong will and her sharp wit. How I yearned to find a way for her to remain free, as I have. I fear that forcing her to marry a stranger will cause her maladie de l'esprit to return. I know full well that King Louis, or any nobleman for that matter, will care not a whit that she is ill—above all, he will only care that she is young and able to bear a child.

I have told only Père Etienne of this terrible summons—he and I have often discussed my course of action should the Spider King take an interest in betrothing Magali to one of his kinsmen. Père Etienne helped me to understand that many people of Arles are afraid that the town will soon lose its municipal power to the king of France and the nobles of Provence. He has advised me that I should impress upon the people of Arles that I will intercede on their behalf with the king. To prove my support, I should acquire more relics for the coffers of Saint Trophime. Furthermore, I should arrange for a wealthy townswoman to become a companion for Magali. He suggested a young woman named Bertine, the daughter of Roland's master surgeon, Hubert. Père Etienne assured me of her great wit and her good manners. Through Bertine's conversations with her mother and sisters and their conversations with other townswomen, the idea of congeniality between the townspeople and nobility will be spread. Thus, I will help to keep the peace between the two groups, as I have always tried to do between all of the Provençal nobles and our townspeople.

I do not want to be separated from Magali on my journey, but I must shield her from the king's plans for as long as I can. She must remain at the château.

I am not blind to the affection between Magali and Roland— he is such a serious young man—but I believe it has arisen simply because they have found a match in each other's wit. I should dismiss him—but I believe that his Sunday morning visits have helped Magali's humors remain in balance, and I cannot bear to take that comfort from her. Furthermore, Isaac continues to advise Roland on Magali's remedies and send him translations of ancient texts that might help her. Roland has not yet found a treatment for maladies de l'esprit, but I pray that, with the Virgin's help, he may discover one soon.

I will keep him in my employ for the time being, therefore, and when I go on my journey to Toulouse, I will make sure that Alienor keeps a close watch over Magali and him. No one, other than Père Etienne and me, is to know of the king's plans for Magali. Not until I have done all I can to change his mind.

When the turrets of the château appeared in the distance, the muscles of Roland's stomach knotted. It was not his usual time to come to the château. Lady Beatrice had sent him a message to come late one afternoon after work, in secret. She'd even instructed him to conceal himself under a blanket to avoid detection.

But there was no one else traveling at this late hour so he sat up, enjoying the cool breeze on this hot day.

It had been a month since his arrangement with the countess began—his trial was over. Given the rumors about the French king's plans for Provence, it was in Roland's best interest to stop visiting the château.

A carriage approached, coming from the direction of Lady Beatrice's lands. It was well made and looked familiar—it was Hubert's! Suddenly frightened, Roland quickly lowered his upper body to the seat and covered himself with a blanket, but not before catching a glimpse of the passengers: Bertine and Solange.

The road was fairly wide; still, he hardly breathed until the carriage passed. When he could no longer hear the rumbling of its wheels, he sat up and looked back at the road to Arles. The carriage was already a tiny black spot, which soon disappeared around a bend in the road.

He could think of no reason for Hubert to permit his daughter to take a carriage ride in the countryside . . . unless Bertine and her maid had been visiting the château. As he clutched the edge of the bench, he knew what he must do. He must tell Lady Beatrice that he could no longer attend Magali.

His resolve strengthened during the remainder of the ride.

After paying the driver, Roland walked up the winding road, passing olive groves on the way to the courtyard. Lady Catherine, the countess's lady-in-waiting, greeted him at the door to the tower and escorted him inside.

Lady Beatrice was seated at the table near the stained-glass pieces that formed part of a horse. Why was she meeting him here? It must be that she did not want Magali to know he had come.

"Catherine, you may wait in the courtyard," she bade her lady-in-waiting, who bowed and took her leave.

Even in the shadowy room, Roland saw full well the strain on Lady Beatrice's face, the shadows under her eyes. It kindled a feeling of dread in the pit of his stomach.

"Milady, did something untoward happen to Magali?" he asked.

She twisted her handkerchief in her hands, struggling to compose herself, before finally shaking her head. "I need to speak with you about an important matter," she said. "In a few days, I am going on a journey. Magali will remain here. I want to make sure that her good health continues in my absence."

Had the rumors come true? Would Magali be wed to one of the king's relatives?

The countess gave no clue as she continued, "You have served me well as a messenger to Isaac and have served Magali well as her companion. It is of utmost importance that you attend her at each week's end from now until I return, and inform Isaac of any change in her so that he can adjust his remedies. Do I have your word?"

He stared at the tile floor, too stunned to reply. Serving Magali was not his choice but her mother's command. What might she do if he refused her?

Carlos had told him about the powerful instruments at the disposal of noble courtiers. False claims of heresy, witchcraft, and adultery—each of which could lead to the execution or banishment of someone who had fallen out of favor—were common, but murders disguised as accidents also occurred.

"Yes, milady," he replied weakly as a sinking feeling came over him.

"Thus far, you have conducted yourself in a virtuous manner in my daughter's company," she continued. "I expect that to continue in my absence. Know that all the members of my household have been instructed to set a careful watch over Magali."

His fear of what the countess could do to him joined with the weight of the responsibility she was laying on his shoulders. "You have my word that I will act in an honorable way toward her," he said. "In exchange, I have a very important request—"

"I know what it is," Lady Beatrice interrupted. "Do not fear. No one in Arles, not even my confessor or your master, knows that you are in my employ. It will remain that way." Her eyes narrowed. "Did Bertine and her maid see you on the road?"

Roland shook his head vigorously. "No."

"Good," she said, and told him about the new arrangement. "Bertine and you will not be here on the same days, so you will never pass each other on the road again. Magali knows that you will no longer be able to visit if she tells Bertine about you. Besides, Lady Alienor or Nina will always be with her. I have impressed upon everyone in my household how important it is to keep your visits a secret and have threatened to punish them severely if they do not, just as I would if they were ever to reveal anything about Magali's disease of the mind."

This arrangement seems very ill-advised. Roland barely kept himself from speaking these words aloud.

"From the look on your face, I can guess what you are thinking," Lady Beatrice said grimly. "It is risky, I know, but I have no choice. I must try to keep peace between the people of Arles and the nobles." She nodded toward the door. "Now you must leave."

He rose to his feet. "One last question. If Magali's illness returns, will you end your journey early and return to her?"

There was a long silence, during which he dared not lift his gaze to observe the countess.

"I do not know," she finally replied in a voice drained of the power it held only a few moments ago.

21 AOÛT

Early Sunday morning, Roland arrived at the château as thick gray clouds were quickly blanketing the sky. Magali burst out of the front door and ran to greet him. He smiled at how the wind whipped loose strands of her hair around her face.

Magali's spirit was much like her hair, free and untamed. Bertine, on the other hand, always kept her hair pinned and coifed, a mirror of her restrained demeanor. They were very different young women, and yet their love of learning would make them good companions.

As Magali led him inside, he observed her as discreetly as possible, trying to decide if her mania had returned. No, he decided, she just seemed happy to see him.

She told him a new Greek tale today—that of the Gorgons, who were part animal and part human. He had come to love these stories she told him, and this one enthralled him because of the power of these monstrous women, who could kill a person simply by looking at them. Bertine's poetry enthralled him too because of its power to make him consider new ideas. It struck him that he enjoyed Magali's enthusiasm and companionship as much as he enjoyed Bertine's.

Inside the château, servants were carrying wooden chests and satchels to the front hall. These signs of Lady Beatrice's journey stirred Roland's worry. What was the purpose of her journey? What if Magali's spirits descended into blackness when her mother was gone? Of course, Isaac would advise him, but the weight of caring for Magali would fall most heavily upon his shoulders.

"Come join us," Lady Beatrice called to them from the great room, where she was conferring with Lady Alienor and the ladies-in-waiting. No doubt she was informing them about the final arrangements for her journey.

"When Mama is away, I will have a companion who will come to teach Nina and me Latin," Magali told him as they entered the great room. "Tell me, have you met the surgeon's daughter?"

"Yes," he said. "Bertine is quite learned."

"Have you told her that you attend me?"

"No, milady, I have not," he replied, glancing at the countess, who had paused in her instructions. As Magali turned toward the bookcase, the countess met Roland's gaze and put a finger to her lips, clearly warning him not to mention their conversation in the tower.

"That is good," Magali said. "I have never mentioned to her that you are also my companion, either." She turned to her mother and frowned. "Bertine does not suspect that I have need of a doctor for the spirit. Why would she? After all, I suffer no such sickness as you believe, Mama."

Lady Beatrice glanced at Roland with bewilderment while Lady Alienor and the two ladies-in-waiting bowed their heads. Everyone in the room had witnessed Magali's illness, but Magali herself refused to accept it. In one of his messages, Isaac had written that such blindness of a patient to his own *maladie de l'esprit* was common. He'd also instructed Roland not to debate the matter with Magali.

Lady Beatrice resumed her instructions for the three other women, who were working on embroidery while they listened. Noticing this, Roland realized he had never seen Magali or her mother doing needlework.

He returned his attention to Magali. "Do you enjoy Bertine's company?" he asked as they continued toward the bookcases.

"Yes, I enjoy talking and reading with her, as well as riding together," Magali replied. "But it is not the same as spending time with you."

His face reddened; what was her intent? But he dared not look at her, so instead he watched how the wind slashed sheets of rain against the windowpanes and hurled twigs and leaves into them.

"Like the three Furies," Magali murmured, and told him about the three goddesses who punished those who committed serious crimes such as murder or offenses against the Gods. Indeed, the story befitted the stormy day.

Later that morning, Magali asked Roland to tell her about his schooling—grammar school, college, and now his medical studies at the university. As he described the lectures and scholarly debates, Lady Beatrice met with Hugo, her seneschal and Alienor's husband, and instructed him on many important matters in preparation for her journey, including the collection of rent, the settlement of disputes among her tenants, and the repair of fences, olive presses, and gates.

From Carlos's letters about the royal court of Spain, Roland had begun to understand the workings of Lady Beatrice's estate. Actually, its management reminded him of how the pieces in a chess game worked together. The countess was the queen, her deceased husband would have been the king, and her confessor, Père Etienne, was the bishop. Lesser nobles, such as Lady Alienor and Hugo, played the part of the rooks as they toiled each day to oversee the upkeep of the countess's household and lands. As the housekeeper, Lady Alienor oversaw the work of some of the "pawns"—the chamber maids, scullery maids, keepers of the pantry and the buttery, and many others. To think that Lady Beatrice had overseen this vast estate for over a decade since the death of her husband. For the first time, Roland wondered how she had managed to remain a widow for all that time. And what was the purpose of her mysterious journey?

When he was finished telling Magali about how to engage in a debate, she jumped to her feet, her eyes sparkling with excitement. "Now I want to try debating you. Please, could you think of a subject?"

In his past few visits, Magali and he had read more of the book by Lucretius, as well as passages by other ancient philosophers, and Magali had grown just as intrigued with philosophy as she was with her stories. Discussing passages with her helped Roland to understand the texts more deeply, and he had come to appreciate the quickness of her mind.

"Let us debate the importance of writing," he said, remembering a favorite debate mentioned in one of Plato's books. "I will argue that writing is important and you will argue that it is not."

He gave her time to think about the topic and glanced at Lady Beatrice. She had finished talking to Hugo and was sitting very still, staring at Magali with a pensive expression. How he wished that he could know her thoughts.

When Magali was ready, Roland began the debate.

"Without writing, we would not be able to learn about knowledge from the past," he began. "For example, without her quill and the invention of writing, your mother would not be able to keep a record of how many barrels of olive oil and wine her estate produces and how much money she receives from selling them."

Magali rose to her feet. "I disagree. My mother could use tokens or entrust a loyal servant with a good memory to keep her accounts. We have come to trust writing too much. Just because an idea has been set in writing does not mean it is true . . ."

They continued their argument back and forth before presenting their conclusions.

Lady Beatrice was fighting tears as she rose to her feet and Lady Alienor took her place in front of the ledger. "Magali, you would make a fine scholar," she said in a trembling voice. "I pronounce your first argument a draw. Now I must go to my chamber and choose clothes for my journey. I will come to your chamber to bid you farewell tomorrow morning."

Magali was so proud of completing her first debate that she didn't seem to notice her mother's sadness. "Sometimes I wish I were a man," she whispered to Roland as her mother left the room and they sat in front of the hearth. "As a man, you are free in many ways that I am not."

I am not free from your mother, he thought, but what he said aloud was, "Your mother is right. You would be a fine scholar. You are more serious about your studies than some of the students I know at Montpellier."

She looked pleased. "One day I would like to attend lectures with you."

"You would not be allowed to do so," he said as gently as possible.

Her mouth drooped.

He wanted to lift her spirits by telling her about the Italian women who supposedly dressed in men's clothing in order to attend the university. *No*, he decided. *She might want to try that ruse, and she is too small-boned and delicately featured ever to disguise herself as a man.*

Instead Roland said, "I think you would scoff at the pompous professors. We students had to rise from our seats and bow to them when they entered the lecture hall, as if they were kings dressed in their sumptuous robes with ermine collars. They read their lectures from an elevated podium while we were expected to simply take notes without asking questions or even worse disagreeing with their ideas."

"I would guess that remaining quiet was difficult for you," Magali said thoughtfully.

"Yes and it would be difficult for you too." A strand of hair had straggled onto her face and he had to stop himself from tucking it behind her ear. "The university may be a privilege reserved for men, but for me, the only reason to attend lectures is to fulfill the requirements to become a doctor."

She looked up at him, puzzled. "So the lectures teach you nothing new about the body?"

Be careful of speaking heresy, he warned himself silently. "That is right. I am learning far more on my own than from them."

"How do you know?" she asked.

"I can observe whether or not what I read corresponds with what I see as a surgeon and what I observe about the effects of remedies. The doctor Isaac has taught me to seek the truth through observation."

"I think I understand," she said, leaning forward in her chair. "You have three sources of learning about medicine. They are like unto three rivers that flow into a sea of knowledge. You learn from Isaac, from your work as a surgeon's apprentice, and from your books. And you confirm what you have learned in one of these sources by comparing that knowledge with what you are learning in the other two."

"Yes," he replied, grateful that she understood. He told her about the salve that could seal bleeding wounds and the boy whose life it had saved.

"Like a miracle," she said, smiling wistfully at him. "I see full well that you have a calling to be a healer. I have no such path."

"Yes, you do," he said. "You are a student and a reader, probably also a writer."

"In my mind, yes," she said, "but something always stops me from setting my thoughts onto parchment."

"Devote an hour each day to take a quill in hand and write whatever comes to your mind," he advised. "In that way you will plant a seed that will grow with time."

"I will try this method," she said, nodding. "Tell me, how did you come to know that you wanted to work as a healer?"

"My mother," he replied fondly. "When I was a little boy, she brought me with her to heal beggars on the streets of Barcelona. Although she knew many remedies, she admitted that she knew very little about the parts within the body. Above all she wanted to know if each part worked on its own or if the parts worked together like the cogs of a water wheel."

Magali grinned at him. "And now you are trying to find answers to your mother's question." Her smile faded as she glanced at Lady Alienor, bent over the ledger. "I have no interest in following in Mama's or Lady Alienor's footsteps. How tedious it would be to spend most of my time recording sums of money in ledgers and conferring with servants."

As they walked back to the great room table, Roland considered what Magali's future would hold. She was of an age when many noble young women were married, but with her disease of the mind, Lady Beatrice might not force her to wed a stranger. She had some semblance of freedom to choose a spouse, whereas most women did not.

Taking no notice of his musings, Magali glanced at his leather satchel on the floor. "I have often wanted to look inside. May I?"

Actually, she had looked inside of it, the night they spent at Isaac's house. Roland wondered if she would remember. "Yes," he said.

She took out the book by Lucretius and held it to her heart. "My first book of philosophy," she said. "Thank you for introducing it to me."

Next she took out the book that Felise, the elderly woman at the tavern, had given him. Magali opened it to a picture of a young woman astride a horse and carrying a banner as she led an army into battle. "An Amazon!" she exclaimed, turning to the first page of text. It began with a miniature of two girls playing chess at a table set before a hearth. "I want to read this book," she said.

Roland knew nothing about the book except that it was about the old woman's girlhood and the long war between England and France. He glanced at Lady Alienor, silently asking her what to do. "Let me see it," she said.

She opened the book and looked at the first few pages. "Ah, this must be the story of Jeanne, the maid who saved France from English rule," she said.

Roland had heard tales of a girl who led the French into battle and restored the French king to his throne many years earlier. Shortly thereafter, she'd been captured by the English and burned at the stake as a heretic and witch.

"I believe that Lady Beatrice would approve of this book," Lady Alienor said. "I too would like to listen to it. Let us begin the next time that you visit the château. Tell me, where did you get it?"

"I met the writer in Arles," Roland said.

"I wish to meet him too," Magali said.

"The writer is a woman," he said, "although she did not sign her name."

Magali's mouth opened in wonderment. "What? I have never heard of such a thing."

He told her the little he knew about Felise.

"A woman who owns a bookshop with her husband—that I have never heard of either," she said as Alienor handed the book back to them. "It will be difficult to wait for your next visit to begin reading this book."

She continued looking in his satchel and found the leather case that contained his notes from medical treatises and his drawings of surgeries. Roland glanced at Lady Alienor, but she had risen to her feet and was talking to a servant.

"These drawings might disturb you, milady," he warned quietly as she began to untie the cloth ribbons.

"If they do, I will put them away," she said. "Please do not call me 'milady.' You are not my servant and you may call me Magali."

"As you wish," he said, but he could not bring himself to add her name.

The first sketch was of his dissection of a dog. "You cut into the body of a dead dog?" she asked, studying it.

"Yes," he said. "I wanted to see how the parts within were arranged."

She looked closely at the rest of the sketches. "You are a very detailed artist," she said.

"It is how I learn and remember how to perform various surgeries," he said.

She ran a finger along a vein in the palm of her hand. "I have never considered that we are all the same inside—the same blood, muscles, and bones."

"In some ways, yes, but people sometimes suffer from diseases that make their bodies different from others." *And minds*, he silently added.

She looked into his eyes so intently that he had to look away. "I wish to see things through your eyes. What is it like to be a surgeon as you are, seeing blood and the inside of the body day in and day out?"

It pleased him that it was so important for her to understand his work. "It is both a miracle and a mystery to witness how the blood flows and how all of the parts of the body fit together. I have many questions about what each part does."

"And do you ask Bertine's father those questions?"

"Sometimes," he said. "He is interested in muscles, the flow of the blood, and tumors. But I also learn about the inner workings of the body from Isaac, your new doctor. Your mother knows him because he came with his father, who was also a doctor, to attend your grandmother."

"Tell me how you came to meet him."

He hesitated but then decided that his answer might help her understand her disease of the mind. "It was you who caused us to meet."

Her brow furrowed. "I do not understand."

In a low voice, he told Magali the story of how Isaac and he met.

When he finished, they were silent for a long time. He glanced at her and saw that her mouth was quivering, as if she were fighting tears. How cruel he had been to tell her of her illness.

"How can this be?" she asked in a trembling voice. "I do not feel sick and I don't remember doing any of those things. And yet I trust you and know that you would have no reason to lie about what I did."

He wanted to take her hand, but instead he searched for words that might soothe her. "Isaac tells me that you are not alone. Often patients who suffer from a disease of the mind are also not aware of it as they would be aware of a bodily disease. Yet medicines can help to heal both kinds of diseases. Isaac's remedy has helped you to be well, for he believes that it restores your sleep. Without it, you suffer from mania and melancholia. You are lost to other people, locked in your own mind and unable to find a way back."

He kept Isaac's warning about the return of the illness to himself.

She nodded, wiping away her tears. "I think I am beginning to understand. My illness is like the labyrinth that Daedalus constructed," she said. "It was so complex that no one could find his way out. Except for Theseus."

She told him of this hero who entered a labyrinth and killed a monster, half bull and half human, who was imprisoned there and who devoured the young men and women who entered his lair.

"The only way Theseus escaped," she finished, "was through the help of a young woman named Ariadne. She fell in love with him and gave him a spool of thread when he entered the labyrinth. He then was able to retrace his steps and find his way back to the outside." Once again, she gazed intently at Roland; once again, he was uncomfortable. "You have given me more than a thread," she said. "You followed me inside."

Isaac's words echoed within Roland: *Follow her mind wherever it takes her.*

Yet he must always remember to keep the entrance to the labyrinth in sight.

8 Septembre

It was the feast of the Holy Virgin when Roland next came to the château. Lectures had now begun at the university, so he did not have to attend Mass every Sunday with Hubert and his family or dine with them—giving him more time to read Felise's book with Magali. He would miss seeing Bertine, but he would spend time with her again in a week's time.

Under Lady Alienor's watchful eye, Magali and Roland started reading at breakfast. The tale began when Felise was only fifteen. Magali read clearly but quickly in her eagerness to find out what would come to pass. Soon, she had reached a part in which Felise described her work as an apprentice scribe and her discovery of a woman writer named Christine de Pizan.

This book was very different from any book Roland had ever read. Unlike Lucretius, who made him feel small and insignificant in the realm of time and space, caught between the tiny particles within the body and the vast expanse of the stars, this book made him feel that a person's life could be examined closely, as if seen through a pair of spectacles. That in itself was strange—but what was even more unsettling was that Felise had chosen not simply to tell the story of the Maid of Orleans but also to try her best to convey what lay in her own heart. He could not imagine exposing his inner feelings in such a way. Suddenly uncomfortable, he longed to return to the tower room, where he could continue searching for remedies in the medical treatise Isaac had given him.

But his charge was to provide companionship to Magali—so, other than meals, he and she spent the whole day taking turns reading, with Lady Alienor sitting at her desk close by.

Not since he was a child had Roland read a book out loud, and it was strange to hear his own voice, now much deeper than it had been then. But even stranger was that Felise, Georges, and Jeanne came to life through the words—he did not understand how a writer could accomplish that. Their love story also made him feel as if he were a trespasser into their private world. It was like he'd felt the night he saw Thomas with the dark-haired woman named Lucienne.

As dusk fell, Magali read about Georges and Felise leaving a battlefield surgeon's camp (a description that especially interested Roland) and riding free through a moonlit meadow. "I feel free when I ride Belle," she said.

"As I do when I walk on the beach," Roland mused. He suddenly imagined walking on the beach with Magali, feeling the same freedom and love that Felise felt as she rode with Georges. *No, it is just a story, a beguiling one, but not real.*

He felt Magali's gaze upon him and glanced up at her. Her back was to Lady Alienor so he alone could see Magali's face. She was smiling, but in a way he had never seen her smile before. In a tender way . . . for him. "I want to ride across a moonlit meadow with you," she said softly.

He quickly looked away. *No . . . it cannot be. I am here to help you heal. No more.* What had he done, letting Magali read this love story?

Lady Alienor gave no indication that she had heard Magali. "Please continue reading," she bade them.

It was Magali's turn to read the ending, which told about Georges and Felise witnessing the Maid's death at the stake. She looked up from the passage she was reading. "Do you know from your studies if Jeanne suffered?" she asked Roland.

He had seen people with serious burns, but never someone being burned to death. "Only for a short while," he replied, guessing at the answer based on what he knew. "Once she was overcome by smoke, she would have felt no pain."

Tears welled in her eyes. "How could the English be so cruel? First they used writing to record lies about her being a heretic and a witch. Then they murdered her, when her only true sin was to dress as a man!" Too distraught to read any more, she handed the book to Roland.

"Should we stop?" he asked.

She shook her head vigorously, and so did Lady Alienor.

As Roland read on, he felt as if he were standing beside a young Felise and Georges, surrounded by a crowd of solemn people bearing witness to Jeanne's final moments.

Magali and Lady Alienor were both crying as he closed the book.

"I have never read such a good book," the housekeeper said through her tears.

"I want to write a book like this," Magali said in between sobs.

How he wanted to hold her in his arms and comfort her. *What have I done?* he asked himself again. *To both Magali and myself?*

One more day at the château . . . one more day of fighting within himself. The rain fell steadily as Roland and Magali read and debated just as they had done the previous day—but everything had changed between them. Hopefully, Lady Alienor had not noticed. Roland tried his best to avoid Magali's gaze, but when he met it, he saw full well her tender feelings.

No, he scolded himself. *I must not surrender to mine.*

"Let us play a game of chess," she said after they supped in the gray, rainy twilight.

"Yes," he agreed.

It was a good idea, he thought. They would be looking at the board and not at each other.

Magali's maid, Nina, followed them to the game table with its jade and ivory pieces. Magali picked up two pawns to hide in her hands. Roland chose the darker jade and would make the second move, which he always preferred.

Magali stared at the pieces before opening with a central pawn. They each moved several more times, establishing their position mostly in the center of the board, without capturing any of each other's pieces. She played as she had at the tavern with Giraud: boldly and quickly . . . and with great skill. But so much had changed since then; Roland found it difficult to settle his mind and think of which piece to advance.

"Why do you move so slowly?" she asked.

Because of you, he thought, but only said, "My mind does not work as quickly as yours."

"I have never thought about the pace of the mind," she said pensively. Her face was aglow in the firelight, her hands folded in her lap. He had never seen her so calm and happy. "You have helped me to think about many things I have never considered before."

"As you have helped me." He dared not look up from the board.

They returned to the game, exchanging pieces evenly. She moved her bishop to a square in the corner, positioning it so that it could capture any of his pieces in a diagonal line across the board. In Montpellier he had taken to playing chess against himself if sleep eluded him. One night the previous winter, he'd discovered the subtle power of this move, which his opponent usually did not take as a threat, and tried to use it whenever he could.

She touched the bishop's miter. "Here in the corner, he is often forgotten. But I think you will remain vigilant."

His blood froze in his veins. *How do you know what I am thinking? You have crawled inside my mind. Everything within me is exposed . . . I cannot hide from you.*

He pretended to study the board, calmly considering his next move, but inside it took every bit of his resolve not to jump to his feet and pace furiously. *How have I not seen what is happening between us? That I have found a friend and a woman in the same person . . . a womanly version of myself.*

Roland glanced at Magali's small hand—outspread on the chess table, burnished by the summer sun. How he wanted to grasp it tightly and bring it to his heart. *I don't want to hide from you; I want you to know everything within me. As I want to know everything in your heart.*

"Is something wrong?" she asked.

I cannot tell you. He shook his head and turned his attention to the board, but his heart pounded and he could not think of a good next move. He advanced an unimportant pawn while she moved a knight to join the bishop in her attack.

He stared helplessly at the board. He should defend his king, but instead he made another small move to bide his time.

Within a few moves, she put him in checkmate. She glanced at him, confused. "It is like a light extinguished in your mind and you could no longer see your best choice. What happened to you?"

I love you. He stood abruptly. "I am ill."

Her brow furrowed in concern and Lady Alienor looked up from her needlework.

"Do you want me to send for the village physic?" the housekeeper asked.

"That is not necessary," he said. "I will rest in my room."

He crossed to the door, grabbed his satchel, and fled into the rain.

Roland slept fitfully and rose before dawn. After lighting a candle, he paced back and forth. He returned to the moment of his discovery. Every sinew of his body resonated with joy . . . he'd never known such love was possible. He lay back down, letting himself be cradled in the warmth of this new feeling.

The village church bells rang. He strode to the basin and splashed cold water on his face. How could he have feelings for a woman suffering from a sickness of the mind? He was a messenger to her doctor, a conveyor of remedies, not her lover. She was a noblewoman, far above him in rank, to whose mother he had made a vow to behave chastely toward her.

Magali did not feel the same way about him. Though she might have tender feelings toward him, she simply wanted him as a companion, someone to help her pass the time of day. Hubert had been right to instruct him to avoid her. He should never have agreed to come here, and would leave this very day.

He dressed hastily, gathered his things, and walked downstairs.

As he reached the bottom step, someone knocked at the door. He put his satchel down and went to open it.

Dressed in hooded cloaks, Magali and Nina stood in the rain. The rust color of Magali's cloak brought out the same hue in her cheeks.

Roland's resolve faltered. He stepped aside to let them enter.

"Are you feeling better?" Magali asked.

"Yes, but I am still a little weak."

She drew back her hood. Her dark hair was neatly plaited and pinned at the nape of her neck. Her eyes shone with . . . not only tenderness, but love. No, he was imagining her sentiments.

She touched a satchel tied to her belt. "I brought you some food in case you want to rest in your room this morning."

He glanced at his own satchel, lying on the floor. "Yes, I will rest."

"First I want to break my fast with you," she said.

His mouth opened in protest but she was already spreading a cloth on her father's worktable. From the satchel she took out plums, a loaf of bread, a sprig of lavender, and a flask of water. "You may wait outside under the covered archway," she bade Nina.

Roland's jaw tightened and she frowned. "But milady, Lady Alienor bade me—"

"I will not be here long," Magali said, touching her maid's shoulder gently. "If Lady Alienor asks where I am, tell her that I am in the stable."

The girl nodded and took her leave, closing the door behind her.

Roland moved to the other side of the table from Magali. "I promised your mother that I would not harm you," he whispered. "I should leave at once."

Magali shook her head. "You could never harm me. Please, don't go." She broke the bread in two. "I did not sleep at all last night. I was thinking about you."

He clenched his hands behind his back and looked down. Isaac would not be pleased to hear of this. He sensed that Magali was looking at him, and he could not stop himself from lifting his eyes. What he saw was not his imagination. Her eyes brimmed with love for him.

"Will you help me act out a story?" she asked.

He widened his eyes, surprised by her request. "Why?"

"Trust me," she said.

"You wish to see me make a fool of myself as an actor again?" he asked wryly.

She smiled. "Of course not, although it was amusing to watch you play Zeus. We are going to act out the story of a hero named Odysseus who is on his way home after the Trojan War. He meets many obstacles and strange creatures on his journey. I could spend the whole morning telling you about them . . . but we have so little time." She sighed and looked down at the lavender in her hand. "His wife, Penelope, had her own adventures at home. She warded off unwanted suitors and never gave up hope for her husband's return. At the end, she recognized him even though he was disguised as a beggar. That is the part I wish us to enact."

The story of a husband and wife? His heartbeat quickened.

"Go to the corner," she bade him, "near my father's stained-glass window. Usually Nina plays the part of Odysseus, but today you will, and I will play the part of Penelope. Only through the expression in your eyes will I know who you are."

He went to the corner and stood facing the muted light of the Nativity window. Never before had he been in this part of the room, and for the first time he noticed the tender expressions on Mary's and Joseph's faces as they gazed at their infant son. Magali's father had captured the love they felt for him.

"Magali," he interrupted her as she recounted the story of Odysseus and Penelope, "could you come here?"

She quickly crossed the room and stood beside him, facing him in front of the stained glass. They were so close to one another, he could hear her soft breathing join with his. He felt a warmth encircling them, drawing their bodies even closer to one another. He took her hands in his. Small and trembling though they were, they steadied him.

"Magali, I do not want to act out the story of another man and woman," he said softly. "I wish for us to share our own."

She nodded as everything he felt for her coursed its way from his heart to his eyes and across an invisible bridge to her.

"I love you," she said softly.

A feeling of peace washed through him as he clasped her hands more tightly. "And I love you."

They held each other in a long embrace as the sun rose and illuminated the stained-glass window. Outside the tower door, Nina called Magali's name.

"I do not wish our story to end," Magali said as they drew apart.

"Nor do I," Roland whispered.

Seven

" ... But he who does not let his infirmity be known can scarcely expect to receive a cure. Love is an invisible wound within the body, and, since it has its source in nature, it is a long-lasting ill."
—FROM THE POETRY OF MARIE DE FRANCE, 1160-1215

Montpellier, France
17 SEPTEMBRE, 1478

I do not believe you made the wrong choice to allow Magali to read a book by a woman writer. You did not unknowingly open a channel for the mania to return. Mania or melancholia return when they will. Reading the book was good for Magali because it helped her to enjoy these days when she is balanced between melancholia and mania.

In the room he rented in Montpellier, Roland burned the message from Isaac, regretting that he had not asked the doctor about how his feelings for Magali would affect her illness. But he could not bring himself to write those words.

He took everything off of his desk except for a candle, a piece of parchment pinned down at the corners with four chess pieces, and quill and ink. He pulled his chair close to the desk and squeezed his eyes shut. Magali appeared behind his closed lids, standing in the courtyard of the château as she had when he last saw her. He stood an arm's length away from her, aching to take her hand in his. But only their minds had touched during this visit.

The day was sunny, the sky pure blue without a single cloud, and the air smelled of fragrant autumn leaves. Lady Beatrice was still away on her journey, and Lady Alienor and the ladies-in-waiting were walking toward the carriages that would take them to the village church. Roland's stomach rumbled, for he had fasted with Magali. She would take Holy Communion at Mass, while he would spend the morning in a carriage returning him to Montpellier. There he had resumed his studies, but more importantly his search for remedies—especially ones for diseases of the mind.

Magali's dark hair was pinned beneath a white coif, but as usual a few curls straggled down around her face. She wore a deep blue gown with an amethyst necklace at her throat and a sprig of lavender pinned near one shoulder. With servants close by, he dared not look into her eyes.

"I have been intending to ask you about something," he said. "I know you seek to understand the meanings of the Greek myths in your own way. I wonder if you also try to understand the meanings of the Bible stories and the other teachings of the Church."

"Yes. To me they are simply stories, no different from the stories that the Greeks told, and each story has a lesson," she replied eagerly. "Some of the lessons are very clear, such as when Jesus instructed his followers to 'love one another as I have loved you.' But other stories are not so easy to understand. They must be solved like puzzles."

"I have never thought of that. Have you solved the one about the story of the Last Supper?" he asked. "As a child, I found it hard to understand how ordinary bread truly changes into the Body of Christ. Please tell no one, but even today I find this miracle difficult to believe. Maybe the meaning that you have found will help me to understand."

"Of course, I will tell no one of your doubts!" she assured him.

"The Eucharist is one of my favorite stories. Abundance, that is what the host means. Even when we are starving in body or spirit, there is always abundance to share with one another."

Abundance.

In his candlelit room in Montpellier, Roland dipped his quill in the ink pot and began his drawing. He worked slowly, stooping over the parchment to see better, and drew every detail he could remember about her face: the roundness of her cheeks, the faint shadows beneath her eyes, and her smile. The church bells were ringing the hour before the new day when he set his quill down and studied what he had set on parchment. Never before had he drawn a person's face, yet somehow an invisible figure from one of Magali's Greek stories had hovered over his quill and guided him to form every line and curve of her face just as it truly was. Not only that but the muse had helped him to capture her love for him, a mirror of his own.

Hardly breathing, he willed the drawing to break through the barrier of the parchment, to become Magali in the flesh. Instead, a terrible image took shape in his mind: Magali in the throes of melancholia.

"I could cause it to return," he whispered, and rose abruptly to his feet. He must protect her—and the only way to do so was to never see her again. Chess pieces, quill, and ink pot fell to the floor as he snatched the parchment from the table. Rolling it up, he tied it with a ribbon and thrust it into his traveling chest.

Even if I go away and never see her again, I will always love her.

The candle had by now diminished to a stub. In its flickering light, he collapsed into the chair and laid his head on the empty desk, unable to hold the tears back any longer.

22 Septembre

Roland walked briskly across the main square of Montpellier, clutching his cloak as a shield against the cold rain. Decaying leaves from beech trees lay scattered beneath his feet.

"Roland!" someone shouted. The square was crowded with people on their way home for dinner and he could not see who it was, nor did he recognize the voice.

Then he saw Thomas, waving to him from across the square. Beside him was Hubert, who appeared much larger in his traveling cloak. Roland abruptly stopped walking; why were they here?

As the two men got closer, Roland saw that Hubert was scowling. His face was still distended. As they stopped an arm's length in front of Roland, Thomas's eyes flashed a warning.

"I need to speak with you, Roland," Hubert said curtly.

It was raining harder now, and Roland led them quickly to the Red Capon, where he often dined. Hubert chose a back table and ordered wine. The three of them were silent while all around them students talked and laughed. The serving girl brought the wine and filled their cups. Roland took a long swig to steady himself.

"You lied to me," Hubert began, his voice low but clear. "You are not going to the countryside to explore Roman ruins. Instead you are visiting the countess and her daughter at the end of nearly every week."

How had Hubert learned the truth? Roland kept his gaze down and gripped his cup. "What concern is it of yours how I spend my time when I am not finding remedies for you?" he choked out.

"Because you are too guileless to be concerned yourself." Hubert's tone was so ominous that Roland looked up. The surgeon's pursed lips trembled as he looked around to make certain no one was eavesdropping.

Roland glanced in bewilderment at Thomas, whose eyes continued to warn him silently of some impending danger.

"Tell me the truth—how did you really happen to meet the countess's daughter?" Hubert demanded.

"I have already told you," Roland replied tersely.

"I doubt that was the whole truth," the surgeon snapped. "After talking with the taverner, I have come to understand what really happened. That night, the countess's daughter drank far more than her measure of wine. It was the first time that the girl comported herself in such a wild manner within the walls of Arles, but who knows how many times she has done so at other places."

"Why, then, do you permit Bertine to spend time in her company?" Thomas challenged his father-in-law.

There was silence. Roland looked up to see Hubert reprimanding his son-in-law with a cold stare. Thomas's expression burned with anger held in check for too many years.

"My reasons are private," Hubert clipped. "And I am not concerned that the countess's daughter will sully my Bertine. She may be a woman, but she is neither weak-willed nor wild."

His gaze returned to Roland, who quickly looked down.

"I have come to know you well, Roland, as a man with a strong desire to help those in need. I believe that you helped the countess's daughter that night and continue to help her so that she does not fall prey to drink or wildness again."

Disturbing though it was that Hubert had discovered his secret, he had not yet mentioned Isaac. Roland held on to that one piece of good fortune.

"Have I guessed your purpose in visiting the countess's home, or is there something else that you are hiding from me?"

It was as if Hubert could see his mind! Roland drove away all thoughts of Isaac's safety and his own discovery of love as he traced his finger along the grain of the wooden table.

"Your silence speaks for itself," Hubert said slyly.

Roland flattened his hand and pressed it against the table. "My silence says nothing other than that my purpose in going to the countess's home is a private matter between her and me."

"And the king of France," Hubert countered.

"What does it matter to King Louis that I attend the countess?" Roland asked.

"For someone with your great wit, you can be quite stupid at times," Hubert scoffed. "And I must say, the countess herself is more foolish than I thought her to be, allowing you to come to her home."

"Stop baiting him and just tell him," Thomas snapped.

"Very well," Hubert said. "I will explain the matter so simply so that even a child would understand." He cleared his throat. "Roland, I want you to pretend to be the king. Would you want a Spaniard, your enemy, to visit the home of a young woman whom you sought to wed to your nephew?" The surgeon paused. "For all you know, this young man might try to steal the daughter's virginity."

Heat rushed to Roland's face but he did not protest, certain that Hubert would twist his words into an admission of guilt.

"Ever since I met you," Hubert said in a somber voice, "you have acted as if you were able to make your own choices. But you are wrong. You have no freedom, no power."

Yes, I do. Roland barely managed to suppress these words as he took another gulp of wine.

"You are a pawn—a pawn from an enemy land, at that," Hubert continued. "It was only through my patronage that you managed to remain in Arles. I may have been able to protect you from the magistrate and his son when you blackened Giraud's name, but I cannot protect you from the king of France."

Roland stared at the red wine in his cup, which suddenly reminded him of blood.

"Roland, you must stop attending the countess," Thomas broke in. "For your own good."

"Thomas is right," Hubert said gravely. "If rumors came to the king's ear that you had affection for or even contact with the countess's daughter, at the very least you would be banished from Provence and France. At worst, King Louis could easily hire assassins to kill you."

Roland's heartbeat quickened. Hubert put a hand on his shoulder. It was a gentle touch, like a father's, but it made Roland cringe.

"I know what I am saying frightens you," Hubert said softly, "but I can help you now, just as I have been helping you ever since you came to Arles. Your betrothal to Bertine would silence those rumors. You would protect yourself from the king's assassins. And you could remain in Montpellier and keep discovering remedies in ancient texts. I suspect that you take much joy in this work."

And joy in my love. Roland said nothing as a sense of urgency supplanted that love. Urgency to protect himself commingled with his urgency to protect Magali from her illness and find a cure for it.

Hubert rose to his feet. "There is much for you to consider. Come to Mass in Arles this Sabbath and let me know what you have decided."

27 Septembre

It has been so long since I received a letter from you. I hope all is well, but I fear that something untoward has happened to you. I beg of you, even if it is only a short note, send word of how you fare.

I am pleased to hear that you are no longer an apprentice to a surgeon and that you have returned to your studies. Might I have hope that come May, when you finish your studies and become a doctor, you will return to Spain?

It has been almost a year since I last saw you. Please come to Burgos at Christmastide. There is so much I want to tell you and I cannot wait to hear of your adventures in full.

Your impatient brother,
Carlos

Roland rolled up the letter and put it back in his satchel. In part, Carlos was right. Something untoward had happened to him. At the same time, something wondrous had happened to him, something that he had never imagined possible.

The carriage swayed from side to side in the wind, which began gusting shortly after he left Montpellier. Yet again, he checked to make certain that no one else was riding along the road to the château. He had begun his journey well before first light and had spent most of the way lying down on the seat so that spies would not notice him.

No one was on the road, but he imagined Carlos riding furiously toward his carriage all the way from Burgos. When he reached the carriage, he would rein in his horse and speak harshly to Roland: *"You love the daughter of a countess? A young woman who is not only mad but also soon to be betrothed to the king's nephew? My God, Roland, that is even more foolish than wanting to become a surgeon. You must return to Spain at once."*

Lady Alienor herself opened the door of the château. She rubbed her eyes, the flesh below them red and puffy. Even before she spoke, Roland dreaded what she would say.

"Magali has not slept more than a few hours each night in the week since you last saw her," she informed him.

He clenched his lips together. He should never have revealed his heart to Magali.

"Before Lady Beatrice left on her journey," Lady Alienor went on, "she gave me instructions about Lady Magali's care. If she did not sleep well, I was to ask you for a stronger remedy."

He opened his medicine pouch and handed Lady Alienor two small satchels containing the valerian and St. John's wort. "Double the amount of each herb and give it to her an hour earlier tonight," he bade her, remembering Isaac's instructions in his latest letter. "It will likely be a few days before it takes effect."

Or it may not work at all, Isaac had written.

"*Merci.*" She put the herbs into a leather pouch that always hung from her belt next to her many keys. "You may go to Magali in the orchard, where she insists on helping the servants gather apples.

God willing, her labor will tire her and she will find sleep tonight."

"Let us hope so." Roland strode around the château and through the garden. He wanted to tell Magali everything that Hubert had revealed . . . to share his heart and mind with her fully. But no, the surgeon's tidings would disturb her greatly and might even heighten her mania. Mania that he may have wrought by revealing his love.

I must not touch her or speak any words of affection, he warned himself silently as she called to him from the far side of the orchard. Wearing a hat with a wide brim like the peasants picking fruit from every tree, she ran to him with an apple in her hand. As she drew closer to him, he winced to see the dark shadows beneath her eyes.

Panting to catch her breath, Magali reached for his hands.

He ached to take them even as he shook his head. "The servants will see us," he whispered. "How have you been faring this week?"

"Never better," she replied. "I have been thinking of you day and night, waiting for you to return. I brought this for you." She handed him the apple, small and of a deep crimson color with white specks.

Their hands brushed as he took the apple, and at once warmth radiated from within him.

A movement caught his eye: Nina walking across the meadow toward them. His pleasure swiftly changed into anger—at the illness and at everything else that kept him apart from Magali.

"You may rest, Nina, while Roland and I walk in the plum orchard," Magali said when the maid joined them. She also had dark shadows under her eyes, likely from keeping vigil over Magali.

"Yes, milady." Nina yawned and went to sit on a bench nearby.

"We will just go a short way," he said as they began walking toward the plum trees. Their decaying leaves lay like a pale brown carpet, rustling beneath their feet. "You have not been sleeping and should retire to your chamber right after supper tonight."

She shook her head vigorously. "Bertine has taught me how to write poetry. It comes to me at night."

"Let us go to bed early tonight and rise early tomorrow," he coaxed. "You can write poetry and I can take notes on the text I am reading."

"I will try, but I cannot promise that I will find sleep."

He looked over at a branch of a plum tree that they were passing. "I know."

Magali stopped walking and ran her hand along the tree's smooth bark. "I knew something troubled you when I first saw you today. You are worried about me, I know, but is there also something else?"

He quickly lowered his gaze, hoping she had not seen his surprise. She was suffering from mania and yet still she noticed changes in him? "You are right," he replied with a sigh, thinking of some small morsel of all that had come to pass that he could tell her, something to help settle her mind. *And settle mine too.*

"You know that I have returned to the university, but did I tell you that I am still working for Bertine's father?"

He was fairly certain that he had, but she shook her head. "How can that be, when you are attending lectures in Montpellier?"

He told her about searching for remedies, like the salve that took the place of the cautery iron, in ancient texts—but he omitted his search for remedies for *maladies de l'esprit*. "Hubert is paying me to find remedies, which he then tests upon his patients to determine whether or not the remedy is effective. But another surgeon, Thomas, who is married to Bertine's sister, has warned me that Hubert wants to control me. Tell me, should I take his advice seriously?"

Magali resumed walking. "I am not sure. This is like another puzzle that we must solve together. First, tell me everything that you know about Hubert."

He did so, including the death of Hubert's father and that of his infant son. He was as brief as possible, because he was not sure how much of what he said Magali was absorbing.

"His story of his son's death made me feel pity for him," he concluded, "and yet ever since I came to Arles, Thomas's advice has been to sever my ties with him. I believed that I could outwit him and remain free; now I am not sure. I wish I knew whether I could trust him once and for all."

"Just like I wish I knew whether I could trust Mama or not," Magali said bitterly. She stooped down to pick up a dead leaf and quickly crushed it into little pieces that drifted back to the earth. "She wants to hold me captive forever."

Roland remembered Magali's mistrust of her mother when he first came to attend her. He was a fool to have awakened that mistrust again.

"Hubert is both truthful and deceitful just like Mama," Magali continued, her voice shrill. "He wants you to be the son he never had so that he can command your every move, as Mama commands mine."

Don't try to soothe her with more ill-chosen words, he chided himself as they continued to walk.

Nina must have heard Magali's raised voice, for she hurried toward them.

She and Lady Alienor know more about how to care for Magali than I do, Roland reminded himself. *I am nothing more than a messenger from Isaac and a provider of remedies. The only way that I can be useful is to discover a more effective one.*

As he followed Magali and the maid to the château, the sun sank in the west. In that direction lay the royal city of Toulouse, where the French king resided when he visited the southern part of his kingdom. It was likely where Lady Beatrice had been summoned . . . where Magali's fate was being sealed.

Roland could not protect her from the king, nor could he protect her from her illness . . . unless the ancient treatises revealed a long-lost remedy.

28 Septembre

Before first light the next morning, a servant knocked on the tower door and summoned Roland to the kitchen. Magali sat at a small table with a weary-looking Lady Alienor beside her. He guessed that Nina had been allowed a good night's rest to compensate for her sleepless nights earlier that week.

"Good morrow," Magali greeted him. "I slept well."

"Only a quarter of an hour more than you have slept for the past week," Lady Alienor corrected her.

"Still, I feel rested. I want to write."

"Milady, could you not consider writing after you sleep for a few more hours?" Lady Alienor pleaded.

"No."

"Very well." The housekeeper sent a servant to fetch Magali's writing supplies.

"Magali, at first light I must leave to attend Mass with Hubert and his family," Roland said as a servant brought three cups of water to the table. "Here is what I would ask of you until I return: You must remain in bed until daybreak and try your best to return to sleep. If you cannot do so, keep your writing supplies near your bed so that you can write poetry without rising. Maybe after writing, you will be able to sleep again."

"I will try," she said, smiling in spite of the deep circles under her eyes.

Lady Alienor accompanied him to the door while Magali set out her writing supplies.

"Will you return next Saturday?" Lady Alienor's voice lifted anxiously.

"Yes, unless I am needed before then."

"I will send word if that is the case. Tell me where you live in Montpellier."

"The only half-timbered house on the street of ink sellers."

Roland took one last look at Magali, bent over her writing, and made a quick prayer: *May she be as calm as she is now when I return.*

As he forced himself to turn away from her and walk outside, he remembered what she had given him. His hand gripped the apple in his pouch, as if that small gesture could protect her from her illness and her betrothal to a stranger.

At the north gate of Arles, Roland bent over the fountain and splashed water onto his face. The cold water refreshed him at least for the moment, making him feel as if he had not been robbed of sleep. Yet unless he stayed here all morning, his fatigue would surely return. If only he could remain here or fall asleep on the riverbank instead of doing what he had to do.

Shouts and screams coming from inside the gate startled him. Water dripped from his face. It was a Sunday, early in the morning, and yet he heard angry voices shouting in the distance and the sound of wood striking stone in the church square.

The commotion was loudest to the east, so he chose a western route to Saint Trophime. The roads were crowded with other townspeople on their way toward church. Roland spotted Hélène, the woman who had taught him to cook Provençal dishes. Their lessons had taken place only a few months earlier, and yet much more time seemed to have elapsed.

"Ah, Roland," she greeted him. "Thomas the Surgeon tells me that you have returned to the university. I miss teaching you how to make my recipes."

"I miss your lessons too," he said. "Madame Hélène, what is all the shouting about?"

"Fights between those loyal to the Provençal king and those loyal to the French king," she replied solemnly. "The magistrate's men ride through the town armed with clubs, putting an end to these fights, but already some men on each side have been killed."

Roland remembered the rumblings of unrest the day that Magali's horse was found. "Things have gotten worse," he said quietly. "Why is that?"

"There are rumors that the Countess Beatrice has arranged for her daughter to wed the French king's nephew. With that union, her lands would become part of the royal domain and the French royal family would control our city," Hélène replied, her eyes wild with fear. "I pray each day that we will not go to war."

"I will too," Roland promised.

The church square was heavily guarded by the magistrate's men, who patrolled on horseback brandishing clubs. No fights broke out, but insults were hurled back and forth.

Vincent and his family arrived, surrounded by an entourage of guards. He stepped forward with his son by his side. Giraud looked broader than Roland remembered him being, and his father older.

"People of Arles, it is the Lord's Day, a day of rest!" Vincent shouted. "Attend Mass and then go to your homes."

His words only provoked the crowd. Roland's height enabled him to see fights erupting and the guards hitting people with clubs. Bleeding men were everywhere, many of them howling in pain.

For once, Roland was glad to enter the cool darkness of the church.

Mass passed by quickly, and Roland's dread of dinner at Hubert's house grew. As they left the church, Thomas gave him a quizzical look and Roland responded with a nod, trying to appear confident.

The armed guards had succeeded in dispersing most of the crowd in the church square. Roland scanned the injured, who lay moaning on the ground, attended by their wives. From what he could see, most of the men still lying there suffered from minor injuries like bruises and black eyes.

"I know you want to help them, but they will have to wait until tomorrow." Hubert had come to walk beside Roland.

The surgeon's swollen face and the tight set of his jaw disturbed Roland greatly. He shifted his gaze toward the wall of the Roman arena that they were walking past, gathering strength from stones that had been laid in place thousands of years ago. "Monsieur Hubert," he began, "I must delay my decision to announce my betrothal to Bertine."

Hubert pointed in the direction of the fights still raging on the east side of the city. "You fool—I am offering you protection!"

"I know," Roland said hastily, "but if I do not seek my brother's approval first, he would withhold my share of our inheritance from my father."

"When will you speak with him?" Hubert demanded.

"At Christmas."

"Write to him before then," Hubert commanded. "Even though we don't know his reply, I will still announce your intentions today."

"Please, monsieur, wait until after Christmas," Roland pleaded.

Hubert turned to him with a fierce look. "Even the announcement of the betrothal is for your own good!" His voice was urgent, even more so than it had been in Montpellier.

"Have you received some new tidings about the French king?" Roland whispered.

"I cannot tell you."

Hubert's fear was not feigned and it kindled Roland's. "Very well," he said. "Announce my intentions."

At dinner, Roland sat in his accustomed seat beside Bertine.

"*Bonjour*," she said with a demure bow of her head.

"*Bonjour*," he managed to reply, but he could not bear to meet her gaze in their usual greeting. For months they had been Sunday companions—no, it was more than that. They were friends. He enjoyed her company, as she seemed to enjoy his. Maybe she even had tender feelings for him. She deserved honesty from him, not the lie that Hubert was about to reveal. Shame burned in his belly.

Hubert recited the prayer before the meal, and Roland joined the family for the "amen" and the sign of the cross. As usual, everyone talked in small groups, mostly ignoring Roland. Only Bertine engaged him in conversation.

"I have a new book that I would like to read with you after dinner," she said eagerly. "It is by the Italian poet Dante. He inspires me, and I am writing a poem in his style. One day I would like to read it to you."

"And I would be pleased to hear it," Roland made himself reply.

All too soon, it happened. Once the soup bowls were cleared, Hubert rose to his feet. He smiled as he looked around the table. "*Ma famille*," he said, his voice swelling with pride, "today I wish to announce the future husband of my youngest daughter."

He turned to Roland, as did everyone else. The blood drained from Roland's face. He barely stopped himself from jumping to his feet and declaring the truth. "I-I must first seek the approval of my brother, who holds my inheritance in trust," he stammered instead.

Hubert dismissed this concern with a wave of his hand. "Your brother will surely approve of your betrothal to a learned young woman who attends a countess's daughter. And I am certain that all the burghers of Arles will be pleased as well."

Hubert turned to François. "My son-in-law, I know that we have talked about Roland's mistakes when he first became my apprentice, yet he shows great promise as a surgeon and a doctor. He will also soon finish his courses at the university in Montpellier, making him both a doctor and a surgeon." Hubert's gaze shifted from person to person around the table as he spoke. "But most importantly, he procures wondrous remedies and techniques for my surgeons to use. It is a miracle that we no longer need to use the cautery iron as often as we once did. I do not consider Roland a foreigner or the enemy, as some of the elderly people of Arles do. This young man brings us great fame and wealth . . ." There was a catch in his voice; he cleared his throat. "This young man allows me to set right the pain and suffering that my father inflicted on many of his patients."

Even the children stopped fidgeting as silence descended. Roland was not accustomed to Hubert revealing something deep within his heart.

The moment passed swiftly; donning his usual mask once again, Hubert raised his cup and smiled at Roland, who forced himself to return the smile. "To Roland of Barcelona," Hubert said jubilantly, "who has declared his intentions to wed my Bertine."

Everyone drank and offered formal words of congratulations. Only Thomas and Perronelle, both of whom frowned at the news, said nothing. But Clare was the only family member who rose from her seat and came over to her younger sister, who smiled joyously at Roland.

He pasted a smile on his face but inwardly he was groaning. How much easier this day would have been if Bertine wanted no part of this betrothal!

"*Ma chère soeur*," Clare said tenderly as she embraced Bertine, "I know that you will be a dutiful and kind wife to Roland and that your wit will match his own. I will help you prepare for your wedding."

Bertine returned her sister's embrace. "You must play the lute at our wedding feast," she said, blushing, as she held Roland's gaze. "And when I bear his children, I want you by my side to help me, just as I helped you with Nicholas and Arnaud."

Stop! Roland wanted to shout, and then flee from this pretense. But no, he had to protect himself from the Spider King. He felt disoriented and ashamed of his deceit but relieved that no one, not even Thomas, seemed to detect it.

Somehow, Roland endured the rest of the afternoon reading with Bertine. Just as last time, she sat closer to him than usual—not touching him, but clearly claiming him as her future husband.

The book they read was about wandering off the path of righteousness and descending into the levels of hell. Roland wondered if he, too, had strayed from his true course as Bertine and he read about the horrors of Satan's lowest, most agonizing lair, where unrepentant sinners suffered forever.

At long last, it was time to take his leave. He bowed to Bertine. "I have enjoyed your company, milady," he said.

She curtsied in return, her eyes shining with excitement. "And I yours."

"I must warn you," he whispered. "Despite your father's confidence that my brother will approve of my betrothal to you, I am not so sure. I hope you will understand if he forces me to break it."

Her eyes misted with tears. "I will pray every day that he grants you his blessing."

Clare came over and put her arm around Bertine, who leaned her body into her sister's like a child nestling against her mother.

I am so sorry to have lied to you! Roland said to her silently. *You are my friend, and were it not for my love for Magali, I might truly want our betrothal to take place. At least, when my deceit becomes apparent, you can take solace in your sister's love.*

Hubert came from his study to walk with Roland to the front door.

"I will return to Montpellier on the morrow," Roland announced. "I will send you more remedies by courier as soon as I find them."

"*Bon*," said Hubert, patting him on the back. "I would advise that you write your brother of your betrothal plans this week so that he is prepared to discuss them with you."

"Yes," said Roland, bowing to hide his face. "Monsieur, your face is still distended. For your own good, you need to take the remedy for dropsy that I gave you."

Hubert waved his hand dismissively. "My illness will pass, but I thank you for your concern. Fare well until we meet again."

A cold wind assailed Roland as he walked toward the inn where he had secured his belongings and where he would stay the night. It was late afternoon, and soon it would be time for Magali to take the remedy. How he hoped that she would sleep better tonight.

He had not gone far when he heard footsteps behind him. He wheeled around and saw Thomas hurrying to catch up with him. The sounds of fights in the distance continued, but no one other than the surgeon was out on this street. Still, Thomas motioned to an alley where they could speak without townspeople seeing them from the windows of their great rooms.

"It has been a while since we have spoken privately," Thomas began. "First of all, I have sad tidings. Do you remember the carpenter's apprentice who had splinters in his hand?"

Roland nodded.

"The wound festered, and a fortnight ago I had to cut off his hand. The stump festered. I could not save him. He died yesterday."

The carpenter's boy . . . his pale face shining with hope that he would keep his hand. And Roland had been so confident that he had removed all of the splinters. He bowed his head. "I am sorry to hear of this."

"I am too," Thomas said. "He was not much older than my sons."

They fell silent, and the only sound was the wind knocking against shutters.

"I have more tidings for you," Thomas continued. "Hubert is not in good health. He feels weak at times, even when he is at work. He must give his knife to me or one of the other surgeons."

"I have tried to tell him to take a remedy I found for dropsy," Roland said.

"As have many of the surgeons and me. He doesn't listen to us. Instead he spends much time trying your remedies on his patients. Then he works late at night, making and storing the effective ones. He has even rented a warehouse for his work."

"You must warn him that he needs rest to stave off his illness," Roland said.

"Must I?" Thomas asked.

Roland's eyes widened. "What are you saying?"

Thomas crossed his arms against his chest. "You know full well. I wager that neither of us would feel sad if Hubert took to his bed . . . or died."

Roland stared at the mud below, suddenly feeling weak himself.

"I'm sorry to disturb you with such talk," Thomas said. "Let us speak of other matters. Do you really intend to marry Bertine?"

Roland jerked his head upright and stared at Thomas, whose question was as direct as he always was. In the year that Roland had known him, the surgeon had been a skilled teacher and had consistently given him practical advice. It would ease Roland's burden to tell someone about his lie. "Can I trust you to tell no one of my answer?"

"Of course," Thomas said. "It is not my way to reveal secrets that are entrusted to me."

"I do not intend to marry Bertine," Roland admitted. "I only said that I would do so to protect myself from the French spies and assassins that Hubert warned me about. Should I believe him, Thomas?"

The surgeon's brow wrinkled. "I do not know. I do believe that Hubert has heard tidings from Vincent or Père Etienne that few of the rest of us are privy to. But hear this: regardless of whether Hubert is telling the truth, he will try to find a way to force you to marry Bertine."

A chill swept through Roland. "Hubert is like King Louis, trapping me in his web. Again and again, he unearths my secrets without my understanding how. How did he discover that I was advising the countess on remedies to help her daughter?"

"I do not know, but I wish I had never invited you to come to Arles with me this summer," Thomas said. "You see, I falsely believed that Hubert would find fault with you due to your Spanish blood and dismiss you after just a few weeks. I surmised that even that short time working in the shop would allow you to understand the daily work of a surgeon and help you decide if that was the path you wanted to follow. I never suspected that your love of book learning would lead you to knowledge of secret remedies that truly work. Nor did I know that Hubert would embark upon a partnership with you." He leaned closer to Roland, his expression somber. "As I have advised you before, return to Barcelona or go to the university in Salamanca, which has an excellent school of medicine. Put as much distance as you can between Hubert and you. I fear that the longer you gather remedies for him, the more he will attempt to trap you. One day he may well succeed. Remember, it is not merely fame and wealth that he wants. He wants to control you, body and soul." He kicked a rock against a wall. "As he controls me."

"But you escape him when you travel to Montpellier," Roland pointed out. "Tell me, was it your idea to assist the professors there, or Hubert's?"

Thomas smiled faintly. "Mine, but Hubert saw at once the prestige that such a position would bring to his shop. And now he is making use of you in the same way, increasing his reputation through the remedies that you are finding for him."

"As I am making use of Bertine to shield me from danger," Roland said bitterly.

"But you seem to truly have affection for her," Thomas countered, "and she for you."

"Yes, but I am not ready to wed. And I am wary about Hubert's power over me if I do so."

"As you should be."

Thomas and he had so much in common—both their interest in surgery and their ties to Hubert and his family. Roland wanted to find out about another possible similarity. "I have a question for you," he said, "but it may be too private to ask."

Thomas looked at him with surprise. "Go on."

"I was wondering . . . do you have affection for Clare as I do for Bertine?"

Thomas sighed. "I am not given to trust most people, but for some reason I trust you. Promise not to tell anyone what I am about to tell you."

"Of course."

"I have affection for Clare but not love. From the moment I met her, I have admired her wit. I also feel pity for her, because her father either ignores her or finds fault with her. She is a loving mother to our sons. I believe that she once had feelings for me, but the love she offered me was like a mother's love for a son." He drew in a deep breath and exhaled slowly. "In Montpellier, I found love with Lucienne—I remember introducing you to her. But about a month ago, I became ashamed of deceiving Clare. I have told Lucienne, and we have agreed to remain apart until I can obtain an annulment from my marriage."

Roland's face grew hot with shame. His lie to Bertine made him worse than Thomas.

"Tell me, is there another reason that you do not intend to marry Bertine?" Thomas asked softly. "Do you have tender feelings for the countess's daughter?"

The muscles around Roland's mouth stiffened. Thomas suddenly reminded him of Hubert.

Protect Magali . . . protect myself. Roland shook his head, willing himself to remain impassive. "Not at all," he said. "Hubert guessed rightly that my sole purpose in attending the countess is to help her daughter. You see, she suffers from a *maladie de l'esprit.*" Roland's explanation of her illness tumbled forth, hopefully hiding his true feelings from Thomas.

"Ah, your answer to my questions fits with what I have seen of you with your patients," Thomas said.

Good, he did not seem to notice Roland's deception.

"You have too much concern for them and blame yourself when your treatment is not effective," the surgeon said gently. "As I am sure that you are blaming yourself for the death of the carpenter's son."

Roland bowed his head. "You are right."

"As for diseases of the mind, some surgeons resort to trepanning," Thomas went on, "but I would never agree to perform such a surgery, for many patients die of it. One day, I hope there will be a more effective surgery to cut such an illness from the head. Look for that remedy in your books."

Roland shuddered as he imagined one of King Louis's surgeons shaving a circle of Magali's dark hair and preparing to drill a hole into her skull. Never! He had to find a safer treatment.

Eight

"The time was now at hand when the King had ordered [the Jews] to leave France altogether, and it could not be in any way prolonged. Then did the Jews sell all their movable possessions in great haste, while their landed property reverted to the crown."

—FROM A CONTEMPORARY HISTORY OF THE REIGN OF KING PHILIP AUGUSTUS OF FRANCE IN THE LATE TWELFTH CENTURY

Lady Beatrice's Château
4 OCTOBRE, 1478

Monsieur Roland,

Last night, M. refused to take the remedy, saying that it no longer helps her to sleep. She was awake all night and we barely managed to keep her inside. You must come as soon as possible. You are to help keep watch over her tonight and seek advice from the doctor at once.

—Lady Alienor of Provence

As the sun began to tint the orchard with rose-colored light, Magali met Roland at the front door of the château, with Nina right behind her. The shadows once again rimmed Magali's eyes and her pupils were larger than usual. Roland was overcome with a desire to take her in his arms and soothe her into a good night's sleep.

She did not even look at him, much less try to take his hands in hers. She scowled at the pouch of remedies hanging from his belt. "I will not take the medicine you have brought," she said. "It makes me sleepy and I cannot write my poems."

"Let us talk about that after supper," he said.

Neither Magali nor he ate very much—he out of worry for her and she because of the wildness that had taken hold of her in the four days since he'd last seen her. Instead of eating, she drank far more wine than her usual measure, just like the first night he'd met her.

As servants cleared the dishes, she slammed her cup down and began to sway from side to side. "I want to dance," she said. "Fetch a lute player, Nina."

Nina glanced at Lady Alienor, who said firmly, "No, Lady Magali, you must take your medicine soon and go to your chamber."

Magali crossed her arms against her chest and narrowed her eyes at Lady Alienor. "You are my servant and must do my bidding."

Never had Magali shown such disrespect for the housekeeper, but Lady Alienor did not flinch. "No, milady, I serve your mother, and she gave me instructions on how to care for you during her absence."

Magali's expression darkened. "My mother does not need to care for me. I take care of myself. Go, fetch a lute player."

Roland rose to his feet as the memory of the first day he met her flashed in his mind. "We will hire a lute player soon, but for now let us play a game of chess," he said. "I often do so to calm my mind before I go to sleep."

"*Bon*," she said, standing up and pouring more wine into her cup.

He chose his words carefully. "You are a very skilled player and I must have a clear mind to play well against you. Therefore, I will drink no more tonight."

She shrugged. "Then I am different from you, for the wine steadies me and helps me to think clearly."

That made little sense, but he did not argue with her as they walked to the table.

Nina followed them and settled with her embroidery in a barrel-shaped chair. Lady Alienor sat at a small table in the arched doorway between the dining room and the great room, less than a stone's throw away from their gaming table. Her drawn face etched with worry and fatigue, she directed a host of servants who were bringing in firewood, lighting sconces, and drawing the curtains for the night.

By the time Magali and he had set up the board and played several opening moves, Nina was already dozing, exhausted from keeping watch over Magali. Tonight, that duty would be his. Unlike the last time it had fallen upon him, however, he accepted it fully, for it was the only way he could give his love to her. He would enter the labyrinth of her illness—but he had no thread to lead them back out again. A wave of anger coursed through him at the mania that took the true Magali away from him.

He allowed her to win the game—not in an obvious way but subtly, by choosing the second or third best move at important impasses. She did not notice, having drunk the entire large cup of wine. It seemed that something had shifted inside of her; she was far away in her thoughts as she fingered the crown on the queen's head. He searched for some way to bring her back.

The Compline bells of the village church rang the hour of reciting prayers before bed. Lady Alienor rose from her chair and came to the table. "Lady Magali," she said, "it is time to take your remedy and prepare for bed."

"I do not have to obey you!" Magali shouted.

Rubbing sleep from her eyes, Nina joined them. "Milady, please, let us go to your chamber."

Magali shook her head. "I am thinking . . . of a poem," she slurred. "Go to bed . . . by yourself . . . if you are tired."

Nina looked helplessly at Lady Alienor, who turned to Roland with pleading eyes. He had to act on Magali's behalf. Doing so would surely reveal his feelings for her, but there was no choice.

He laid a hand on her shoulder and she turned toward him. "You have lost sleep," he said quietly. "The medicine will help you find it again."

She shook her head and rose unsteadily to her feet. "I want to write."

"You may, as soon as you have a good night's sleep."

He tried as best he could to sound firm like Isaac, but instead he sounded tentative.

"No." She grabbed her empty cup and thrust it toward Nina. "Fetch me more wine."

Nina started to take the cup, but Roland stepped forward. "Magali," he said, more firmly this time. "Listen to me."

She turned to him, her eyes glittering in the candlelight. She was so unsteady on her feet that she had to clutch the table for support.

"The wine is the wrong remedy and it does you no good," he said. "Hand me the cup."

"No."

"Lady Alienor will prepare the right remedy for you. Agree to take it, or I must leave at once."

"No," she moaned, "stay."

"I will, but only if you take the medicine."

She stared into his eyes for a long moment.

I love you, he silently told her. *Please, do what is best for you.*

At last she handed him the cup, which a servant quickly took from him, and then, before he could stop her, wrapped her arms tightly around him. He could not stop himself from embracing her too.

After Magali took the remedy, she collapsed against Roland, falling into the same deep slumber as she had that night long ago on the streets of Arles. He checked her breathing and found it to be very faint. Although this time he was not as concerned that she would die, he longed for her to return to her full health in a way he had not known possible that July night. To return to the vibrant Magali he had captured in his sketch.

He carried her to her chamber, laid her in her bed, and covered her with a blanket. Nina settled into a smaller bed next to Magali's, and Lady Alienor and he left the room. As she locked the door from the outside, Roland noticed a pallet in the hallway and realized it was hers. She was on duty night and day, and yet she was unwavering in her service.

"As I said in my message to you," Lady Alienor said, "Lady Beatrice instructed me that if Magali became very unsettled, you must go to the doctor who advises you, whom she never refers to by name, and beg him to come here to attend Magali."

It was just after Compline on a Thursday night. Tomorrow was the beginning of the Sabbath, which would continue through Saturday. If he didn't go to him before it began, Isaac would not be free to speak to him for two days. He had to go now.

As he turned to leave, Lady Alienor caught his arm. "I see that you have tender feelings for Magali and she for you," she said, one eyebrow arched, "yet I trust you. Return as quickly as you can."

The groom dared not drive the countess's carriage all the way to the town wall. When it was just visible, bathed in the light of the waning moon, he steered the horses into a clearing on the side of the road.

Even from this distance, Roland could hear shouts and screams from the city.

"Return as quickly as possible," the driver told Roland, and he and his son drew their knives to protect themselves from those who opposed the countess's alliance with the French king.

Roland descended from the carriage and walked in the shadows along the side of the road until he reached the wall. Instead of entering through the north gate, he followed the wall until he reached the Rhône.

This part of the wall was mostly in ruins, for the town magistrates saw no reason to protect the Jews, so Roland easily climbed over it and ducked into the shadows of the houses. Since he did not know how to reach Isaac's shop from here, he would have to find the temple first.

As he made his way toward the faint outline of the temple's domed roof, he heard shouts in the distance. Though it was past curfew, people were still on the streets, riled up by fear and drink to brawl with fellow townsmen about a matter over which they had no control. He quickened his pace.

Upon reaching Isaac's house, he thrust a note under the door and knocked, all the while regretting his disruption.

Footsteps, and then the door opened. Isaac, wearing night clothes and holding a candle, motioned for him to enter. He spoke in Hebrew to his wife, who was peering around a corner. Her face softened and she returned to her room.

"Are you certain that no one saw you?" Isaac asked as he led Roland to his shop.

"Yes."

"You must leave very soon." They sat at the shop's small table and Isaac set the candle between them. "I assume you are here because of Magali."

Roland nodded. He felt tears rising but held them back, knowing that he had to remain strong through the long night ahead. "As I wrote in my last message to you, she is suffering again from mania. It is at its highest point, just as it was the first night I met her." He drew in a deep breath and exhaled. "But I could not write to you about another matter. I have changed; I am no longer a stranger who simply wants to learn about diseases of the mind by helping her. I love her and want her to return to her true self. At first I tried to deny my feelings, but I could not. I even convinced myself that my love would protect her from her illness."

"In my years as a doctor, I have seen no evidence of that," Isaac said gently. "I believe that her disease will always be within her. It is more difficult for you to bear now that you have learned to follow the turnings of her mind and walk with her along the pathways of her thoughts. When her illness returns, a door is locked so that you cannot join her."

Roland nodded grimly. "Did revealing my love to her cause her to become ill?"

"I do not believe so. As I have said before, a *maladie de l'esprit* comes and goes as it will." Isaac stared at the flickering candle between them. "Does Magali return your love?"

"Yes, although her mania now comes between us."

"I did consider that the two of you might come to love one another," Isaac said. "It has happened many times before between doctors and their patients. Sometimes, a doctor misuses a patient's love to his advantage. I do not believe that you would do such a thing, but still I must warn you to consider several important matters." He held Roland's gaze in his. "First, you are learning to be a doctor and have promised Lady Beatrice to care for Magali to the best of your knowledge, with my guidance. Your love for her might overshadow your judgment as a doctor, and then you could not provide the best care for her. Secondly, as a noblewoman, Magali is not free to love whomever she chooses. If she is forced to marry against her will, she might become overwrought and make dangerous choices. You must protect yourself against all manner of things here—mainly, the countess's anger if she discovers your secret. I strongly advise that you no longer serve Lady Beatrice and her daughter."

Groaning, Roland pressed his hands to his face. "I promised the countess that I would attend to Magali once a week until she returns from her journey. And now that Magali is ill, I cannot leave her . . . at least until her mother returns."

"You may need to break that promise to protect yourself," Isaac said gently. "If you choose to keep it, make sure that Magali keeps taking the increased dose that I advised last week. I must warn you again that there are no guarantees it will continue to work." He placed his palms on the table and pushed himself up to his feet. "Now, you must go."

"Could you come to the château with me?" Roland asked as they walked to Isaac's door, although he already knew the answer.

Isaac shook his head. "I must ask you not to return to my shop again. It is dangerous for my family, but also for you."

"I understand."

Roland was just about to step out onto the street when he heard loud chanting coming from beyond the Jewish quarter. The voices grew louder and the sounds of drums mingled with the chant. Isaac quickly closed the door. Roland and he glanced at one another, their bodies very still.

As the crowd advanced toward the Jewish quarter, a familiar Provençal drinking song rose into the air, but the words had been changed. "Burn the Jews—roast their flesh," men sang loudly.

They were going to set fire to the quarter! Fleeing to the tower would offer the Jews no protection. Fear rooted Roland to the spot. He hardly breathed until the song faded in the distance. Sniffing the air, he smelled no smoke. His momentary relief was quickly replaced by an overwhelming sense of helplessness that he could do nothing to stop such hatred. He turned toward Isaac. Never before had he seen such terror and rage on the doctor's face.

"I am sorry for the cruelty of my fellow Christians," Roland whispered.

"You are not part of it . . . it is not your fault." Isaac opened the door. "Go now. I must prepare for my family's journey to Aix-en-Provence. My wife and I have been planning to live with my cousins there should this day come to pass."

No more messages from Isaac. No more visits to this refuge. As Isaac clasped Roland's arm, compassion softened the doctor's fear and anger. At once, Roland felt steadier, and he also clasped Isaac's arm. "You have taught me so much. May you and your family be safe on your journey."

5 OCTOBRE

In the courtyard, Roland descended from the carriage. Though it was past midnight, sconces illuminated the front windows of the château.

Lady Alienor met him at the door looking very distraught. "Lady Magali slept for but an hour," she said. "We tried to keep her in her chamber, but she flew into a rage. Come and see..."

He strode into the great room and stopped suddenly, taking in what lay before him. The barrel-shaped chairs were overturned and most of the books had been swept down from the shelves and lay scattered on the carpet. Late-blooming wildflowers and lavender sprigs were strewn across the hearth, with chess pieces scattered amongst them. Fanning out from the hearth in the shape of a semicircle were torn scraps of paper and parchment. Each one contained a jumble of tiny words that filled every bit of the cream-colored space. Roland picked one up and held it close to his eyes. Words were strung together—*Saint Michael the Archangel flying high in the sky searching for a walnut, lost toad, come to me*—and then there were words written so close together that he could not discern what they were.

"Where is she?" he demanded.

"She wanted to ride to the sea again," Lady Alienor replied. "I am sorry, but we had to tie her to her bed."

Roland hurried to her chamber with Lady Alienor close behind him.

"Taking care of her is like taking care of a helpless babe," Lady Alienor said, defending her decision. "Tying her to the bed is no different from swaddling a child."

"I understand why you had to do so." Roland stopped and handed her a pouch containing more of the remedy. "I will untie her and take care of her the rest of the night. Have a servant prepare these herbs in a cup of boiling water, then you and Nina must sleep. On the morrow, send a message to Hubert the Surgeon that his daughter is not to visit for at least a fortnight."

"Thank the Virgin you are here." The housekeeper turned to fetch a servant.

Magali's screams were audible from all the way down the hall. Roland ran to her door and entered her chamber.

She had been writhing so violently that her wrists were raw and chafed. He sat on the edge of the bed and brushed the hair from her face. Her eyes darted wildly around the room before they settled on him. When she recognized him, they filled with tears and she began to sob.

Nina, seated in a chair on the other side of the bed, bowed her head in prayer as Roland untied Magali and held her tightly.

18 OCTOBRE

"A little broth?" Roland asked when Magali stirred.

"No." Her eyelids fluttered and closed again.

A ray of late-afternoon sunshine was slicing across her bed, creeping closer to her face. Nina rose to close the curtain.

"No," he bade her, and she returned to her chair and to her endless prayers for Magali. In the past two weeks they had done no good, but neither had Isaac's remedies, other than to burn away the mania. Was it melancholia or a mixture of the remedy and exhaustion that imprisoned Magali in sleep day and night? It was yet another question that he could no longer ask Isaac.

Even as the sun's rays spilled onto Magali's face, she slept. It was time to gradually decrease her herbal remedies.

Closing the text set on the table beside him, Roland stood and paced in the sunlight. Everything was suspended in waiting . . . for Magali to return to the middle part of her wheel, if that was even possible; for the countess to return from her journey; for the rumors of Magali's betrothal to be revealed as true or false.

For Roland to decide what he should do.

The jangling of keys announced Lady Alienor's arrival, and he turned toward the door. The circles beneath her eyes had vanished; she looked more rested than she had for weeks. He nodded a greeting, once again grateful for her presence and for her acceptance of what had come to pass between Magali and him. *But she is not the countess,* he reminded himself yet again.

"Lady Beatrice sends word that she will return around the feast of Saint Raphael the Archangel," the housekeeper said.

Six days hence. This time of waiting would soon end.

"I also have a message for you," she said, handing him a parchment scroll.

As soon as she left the room, he broke the seal and read Thomas's message:

> *If you are at the château, as I suspect, I urge you to go to Spain at once. The fights on the streets of Arles worsen, and some young men (like Giraud and his friends) falsely blame the Jews for the unrest. Many of them have fled Arles. Like the Jews, you are a foreigner. If your service to the countess is discovered, you too might be blamed or attacked . . .*

Roland shook his head slightly, trying to dispel the fog that had settled in his mind. Over the past two weeks, as he cared for Magali, he had not once thought of his contract with Hubert, his betrothal to Bertine, or the unrest in Arles.

Hubert was enraged at your sudden disappearance, both in person and in your letters. He suspected that you were still attending Magali and treating her hysteria, especially after he received word that Bertine's lessons with her were suspended for the time being.

I told a lie on your behalf—that you traveled to Spain earlier than you intended, in order to seek your brother's approval of your betrothal to Bertine.

Again, I urge you to leave at once . . .

22 OCTOBRE

They dined in silence, Magali and Nina on one side of the table and Lady Alienor and Roland on the other. Magali ate—not heartily, but more than she had eaten in many a week. Roland had no appetite, but he made a pretense of savoring the meal to encourage Magali's enjoyment of it.

Magali pushed her plate away and gazed out the window. The air had warmed in the past few days, and the sky was bright and clear. "I want to ride," she said.

Lady Alienor, Nina, and Roland exchanged a quick glance of relief. At last, her melancholia seemed to be lifting.

"As you wish, Lady Magali," Lady Alienor replied. She called for a servant.

As they walked to the stable, Roland saw fifty or more groomsmen and villagers who pledged fealty to the countess. All of these men were on horseback and armed with swords and longbows. Denis, the keeper of the husbandry, was directing them to set a watch around the countess's lands. Roland recalled the day that Denis and a groom had led him from stable to stable, searching for Magali's horse, which they believed he had stolen. That day, Roland had witnessed the first sign of the conflict between the townsmen and the nobility. And now that conflict had intensified as everyone awaited the countess's return and the fate of the governance of Provence.

Denis turned to Lady Alienor. "Lady Marguerite is not to ride near the boundaries of her mother's lands," he warned. "No one on the road, be they Jews or people of Arles, must lay eyes on her, for they might try to harm her."

Roland's apprehension grew as grooms led four horses to the courtyard and helped the three women to mount. They set out in a slow walk, with Lady Alienor in the lead and Roland and Nina flanking Magali. When they reached the kitchen garden, Magali reined in her horse and turned to Nina. "Ride by Lady Alienor's side," Magali bade her.

Nina gave an obedient nod and joined Lady Alienor, who solemnly faced Magali and Roland. "Roland, see that you stay close behind Nina and me or else all four of us must ride alongside one another," she said firmly. "We must do so to remain safe."

"We shall," he replied.

As soon as Lady Alienor and Nina set their horses to a faster walk, Magali turned to Roland. Her face was gaunt and pale and her smile faint. The muscles of his shoulders, stiff with worry for so long, slackened a bit.

"How long have I been ill?" she asked as they resumed their ride.

"Close to a month."

"I have been thinking," she said, her voice wavering. "My illness is too much for you to bear."

Such pain he had never before seen on her tear-streaked face. "No," he said softly. "You have no choice but to bear your illness. I do have a choice, and I choose to help you bear it."

"I am sorry it is such a difficult choice."

"I would have it no other way."

They rode in silence to the orchard, a stone's throw behind Lady

Alienor and Nina. Only a month ago, they had been alone together there. Now the trees were bare, their leaves brown and shriveled. She met his gaze again, her sadness transformed into resolve. "We are already wed in spirit. Let us journey far away so that we can be wed in the flesh."

Flee to Spain with her! At once, doubt silenced that urgent voice. "We would have to leave secretly and hide from the men that your mother would surely send to find us," he said. "Even if we did succeed in eluding them, you would long to see your mother again. And she, of course, would long to see you."

"I do miss her," Magali admitted, "but if I were forced to choose between you and her, I would choose you."

"Maybe at first," he said gently, "but as the months passed, you might well come to resent me for taking you away from her."

"Never," she insisted.

Lady Alienor turned around to see where they were; seemingly satisfied that they were close enough, she faced forward again.

"There is something that we must prepare for," Roland said, even more quietly than before. "Lady Alienor will surely reveal to your mother that we have grown close. Your mother might forbid me to see you ever again."

Dread suffused her face. "Then we must flee . . . before Mama returns!"

"I have another idea," he said quickly, for already Lady Alienor was steering her horse back to the château. "I will tell your mother the truth about us. Then I will bargain with her. I will search for a remedy that helps with mania and melancholia on the condition that she allow me to continue to attend you."

"I will pray that Mama agrees to your bargain," Magali said eagerly. "Surely the Virgin will hear my prayer."

With great difficulty, he feigned to share her hopefulness. For once she did not comment on his skill as an actor, for she seemed not to be aware of his deceit.

24 Octobre

Roland was sitting at his desk in the tower, reading a medical text he had brought from Montpellier, when Lady Beatrice and her entourage returned. He rose from his chair and watched the countess and her men enter the courtyard. They were surrounded by an outer ring of armed guards, several dozen in all, wearing the royal colors of red and blue. Along the road from Toulouse, these guards would have sent a clear message to the people of Provence, as they now sent a clear message to Roland. He suddenly felt very small and insignificant . . . trapped.

He paced back and forth in his chamber for an hour before someone finally knocked at the tower door. He bolted downstairs and opened it. Lady Beatrice and her lady-in-waiting, Catherine, stood there, and he greeted them with a bow. The countess's jaws were clenched tightly, her expression strained.

"Wait in the courtyard, Catherine," she said, and entered the tower.

Now that he had drawn the sketch of Magali, Roland was even more aware of the strong resemblance between mother and daughter. A fire blazed in the fireplace, but Lady Beatrice did not remove her traveling cloak of deep blue wool. She sat down at the worktable, tracing her finger across the surface of the stained glass that formed the horse's head. Roland stood awkwardly across from her in almost the same spot where, months ago, Magali and he had been alone together for the first time, sharing a breakfast of bread and plums.

"I give thanks to the Virgin," she said, her eyes on the table, "for sending you to rescue Magali from the streets of Arles. I also give thanks for the care Isaac and you have given her since then."

Roland told her about Isaac's flight to Aix-en-Provence with his family.

Still fingering the stained glass, she frowned. "I was afraid that such trouble for the Jews would come to pass. May Isaac and his family be safe."

She lifted her head and looked directly at him. He quickly averted his gaze.

"Please, look at me," she said firmly.

He forced himself to obey. There was a softness in her eyes that belied the strain etched on her face.

"I wish for the two of us to speak the truth to one another," she said. "I promise not to tell anyone what we discuss in this chamber. You must promise too."

Not even Magali? But he kept that question to himself as he nodded his assent.

"I know that Magali has grown close to you," she began. "Lady Alienor has just informed me that you have also grown close to my daughter, even in the midst of her illness."

He searched her face and saw not anger but regret, even sorrow.

"Milady, I promise you that I have done nothing to harm Magali."

She smiled wistfully. "I know. I doubt you have ever harmed anyone." She paused. "I should have dismissed you before I went on my journey. But I allowed you to keep attending her because I believed that you were as much a medicine for her as the valerian and St. John's wort."

"I wanted to believe that too," Roland admitted, "but Isaac tells me he has never seen any evidence that love is a remedy for a disease of the spirit."

"And yet you love her still, even though you cannot cure her?"

Overcome by everything he felt for Magali, he could only nod.

"She loves you too—Alienor says that she calls for you in her sleep," Lady Beatrice said, her eyes filling with tears. "And yet I must give her to another man."

A horrible image seized hold of his mind: Magali crushed beneath the weight of a stranger's naked body. "Must you?" he cried.

She nodded through her tears. "I am bound to obey the king; I had no choice but to agree to Magali's betrothal to his nephew."

The air was suddenly stifling, and Roland struggled to draw breath. "But, milady, surely her disease of the mind—"

"That does not matter to him. What does matter is that she is young and capable of bearing a son, the embodiment of the union of France and Provence."

Roland stared at Lady Beatrice, trying to absorb her words. "Milady, these tidings will upset Magali greatly—maybe even cause her melancholia to return. I beg you to think of what is best for her."

"I have," she said, "but I am at the mercy of the Crown."

As she covered her face with her hands and wept, her commanding presence vanished and she became a small and fragile figure. He, too, felt weak and was glad to be sitting down, gripping the edge of the table for support.

She uncovered her face and wiped the tears from her eyes. "My only hope is to try to negotiate a betrothal for the king's nephew with a young woman from another house of Provence."

At her words, Roland felt a glimmer of hope.

"To that end, I have asked the king to give me some time to make my decision," Lady Beatrice continued. "However, the prospects of finding another suitable young woman are very small indeed. I have resigned myself—"

"I have not," Roland said fiercely, jumping to his feet. "I wish to marry Magali."

She shook her head. "That is impossible. You are a fool to think that you could step in front of the king and claim her."

"But you may yet find a suitable young woman for the king's nephew," he said. "Would you then allow Magali and me to wed?"

"I do not know." Tears sprang to her eyes again. "I love my daughter and could not bear to part with her. You must accept that she will most likely wed the king's nephew, and I will move with her to the royal court."

Her words echoed in the silence. It was not Lady Beatrice who held the key to Magali's and his future. It was the king of France. Roland's only means of bargaining with him, the possibility of finding a remedy, would be useless. The glimmer of hope he had felt a few moments ago vanished.

She rose to her feet, her face blotched from her tears. "I should bid you to leave at once, but I need your help to tell Magali of these tidings. After today, you cannot write to her or see her again until the matter of her betrothal is settled once and for all. I will have many visitors from the king's court in the next few months, including his nephew. I cannot risk having him or another guest notice her affection for you. That would be dangerous for Magali and you."

"Milady, Magali has seen me every day for the last moon. My absence will be very difficult for her." *As not seeing her will be difficult for me.*

"I know. I will give her a token of hope; I will tell her that if I am able to arrange another match for the nephew, you might attend her again."

"But you doubt that will come to pass," Roland said. "Why give her false hope?"

"So that she will remain calm."

Roland clenched his jaw. He could not bear to be a part of this deceit, and yet he had to see Magali one last time.

Montpellier
7 NOVEMBRE

In his room, Roland unrolled his sketch of Magali and secured the four corners with books. The memory of the last moment he saw her filled his mind—Lady Alienor, Lady Catherine, and Nina holding her back from following him out of the tower. He'd barely stopped himself from returning to Magali and pulling her to him. Fleeing with her to Spain.

"We will find a way, Roland," she'd wailed as he left.

Her words kept echoing in his mind, but in his heart he knew the truth.

8 NOVEMBRE

Roland pushed his chair away from the table at the library and rose to his feet. Passing tables where students and professors read and took notes, he walked to the north window and gazed at the Pyrenees, their peaks covered in snow. The ancient mountains stretched before him, so vast and powerful that no king could command them.

He turned from the window and strode back to his seat. A stack of dusty tomes lay to the side of the table and one book was open beside his parchment, quill, and ink. He rubbed his eyes. He had found so many remedies today for diseases of the body—no longer for Hubert, now only for himself and Isaac—that the fingers of his right hand were sore from copying them onto parchment. But still he had not found a single remedy for Magali. He would keep searching until it became too dark to read.

An hour later, a shadow fell over the page he was reading. Thomas, his hair wind-swept and a dusting of snow on his cloak, stood next to him. "You look terrible," he exclaimed. "Have you been ill? Is that why you have not returned to Spain?"

Roland glanced around the library. Everyone else was gone. *I can speak freely and tell Thomas everything. But no, I must keep it to myself!* he argued to himself.

"Why are you here?" he asked.

"To assist with a dissection," Thomas replied, "but I also wondered if you truly had gone to Spain." He glanced down at the text that Roland was reading, his brow furrowed. "You are still looking for remedies? But Hubert says that you are no longer sending them to him. Come, Roland, explain yourself."

Thomas is my friend. I can trust him. After revealing what was in his heart to Thomas, Roland slumped over until his head was resting on the table.

Thomas clasped Roland's shoulder. It was the first time in many weeks that someone had touched him.

"I promise to tell no one your secret," Thomas said, "just as you promised me you would tell no one about the woman I love." His expression grew somber. "I miss being with her, but I cannot bear the shame of deceiving Clare any longer."

"I love Magali and am ashamed of deceiving Bertine," Roland whispered.

They fell silent as the candle burned low.

Thomas sighed. "I know full well that you cannot stop your feelings for the countess's daughter, but you must protect yourself, not just from Hubert but also from the French king and Lady Beatrice."

Roland lifted his head and stared at a shelf of books. "I want to stay here and keep searching for a remedy for Magali. If I were to flee far away from Provence, I would want to take Magali with me, but that is nigh on impossible."

"Not nigh on impossible, but simply impossible," Thomas said bluntly, gripping Roland's arm so tightly that it hurt. "You must accept the fact that you cannot have the countess's daughter."

"No," Roland moaned. "I am bound to her forever."

9 Novembre

"You were too distraught last night for me to speak of some other important matters," Thomas said. He and Roland sat in a dark corner of the inn where they always supped together in Montpellier.

"First of all, Hubert is still sick but refuses to take a remedy," he said. "He is now suspicious about whether you actually traveled to Spain to speak with your brother. It has been over a month since you supposedly went away, and he has not had a single letter from you."

Roland swilled wine, trying to dismiss the memory of lying to Bertine in front of her entire family. "I do not wish to contact him ever again. I want to be free of him—and free from King Louis—forever."

"Good," Thomas said. "Secondly, I wanted to inform you about the conflict in Arles. There is much uncertainty about Magali's betrothal. Luckily, though, with the coming of cold weather, the fighting between the two sides has lessened."

"What of Bertine?" Roland truly missed her company. *I will never have it again—it is my just punishment for lying to her.*

Thomas paused as the serving girl brought their fish stew. "Clare tells me that her sister misses you very much. She trusts that you did indeed go to Spain and remains hopeful that you will return to wed her."

Roland groaned.

"For most of the month of October, Bertine remained at her father's house," Thomas continued. "No one knew for certain why she had been dismissed from attending the countess's daughter, but Giraud and others who were in the tavern the night you rescued Magali spread rumors that God punished her by causing her hysteria to return. Now that Bertine has returned to being Magali's companion, Hubert has pressed his daughter to tell him how Magali comports herself. He also dismisses her disease as imaginary and calls it a woman's wildness."

Roland set his fork down. If Bertine had such symptoms, Hubert would better understand what it was like to suffer from a disease of the spirit and would certainly believe the disease was real. "Does Bertine tell him how Magali fares?" he asked.

"Some days she seems to enjoy her studies with Bertine, but on others, she hardly talks and casts angry looks at her mother."

Magali was not bed-ridden! Roland felt the muscles of his shoulders slacken.

"Hubert presses Bertine to discover if the rumors about Magali's betrothal are true, but so far nothing has been revealed," Thomas went on. "However, Bertine has observed that courtiers bearing the livery of the king of France have been visiting the château. Their meetings with the countess are always conducted behind closed doors."

Roland thought of Lady Alienor's and the other servants' loyalty to the countess—an allegiance that had thus far thwarted Hubert's wishes. And it also seemed that Magali had confided nothing in Bertine. How could she, with her mother or Lady Alienor or a maid always hovering close by?

Roland suddenly thought of something that had not occurred to him before. "Has Bertine told Magali about her betrothal to me?"

"I do not know." The surgeon scowled. "How I want to tell Bertine not to trust her father. You see, I believe he is already plotting to wed her to another man."

"Without telling her?"

"Of course. He even encourages her to keep believing that you will return."

Roland tightened his grip on his cup. "Bertine does not deserve this duplicity, from me or from her father. One day I hope to ask her forgiveness."

"I doubt that you will ever see her again," Thomas said in his usual direct manner. "Now, I have one last piece of news. My oldest son will begin his studies here at the university in January, which saddens Clare very much."

"Ah, I will need to move elsewhere so that your son does not see me here and tell his grandfather," Roland said.

Thomas nodded.

Roland considered his choices. He wanted to go to Fontvieille, the nearest town to Magali, but it was too close to Arles and it had no university. "Avignon," he decided aloud. Other than Arles it was the closest city to the château, and it had a university where he could finish his lectures and keep searching for remedies.

Thomas and Roland paid for the meal and walked out of the inn together.

"It is the most difficult choice I have ever made, not to lodge with Lucienne when I am in Montpellier," Thomas said. "She is a widow who did not love her husband, but she was faithful to him while he was alive. She longs to see me too, but she understands my shame. She has promised to remain unwed until I am free from Clare. I have decided to find a priest who will annul our marriage." Thomas's eyes narrowed in anger. "I will have to pay him a large sum of money, of course."

With that, Thomas took his leave and Roland lifted his face to sleet that stung his face and chilled him to the bone.

Nine

"Guard their bodies and do not show a joyful face to them."
—Advice from Vincent of Beauvais to Margaret of Provence, Queen of France, about caring for daughters

Lady Beatrice's Château
14 Novembre, 1478
Lady Beatrice's Secret Book

What am I to do? I have tried to arrange a marriage between the king's nephew and every possible noblewoman in Provence, but none of these prospects have born fruit. Magali descends further into her illness each day. At first I thought to dismiss Bertine because I did not want her to witness Magali's sickness and tell her family about it. But Père Etienne assured me that Bertine's father would not spread rumors about Magali in Arles. Furthermore, my confessor believes the continuance of Bertine's service will reassure the people of Provence that they will still have a beneficial relationship with me even after Magali weds, and that Bertine is a good influence on Magali. On the last matter, I have to agree with him. The surgeon's daughter has no maladie de l'esprit, and her even temper often helps to lift Magali's spirits. And yet there is a sadness to

Bertine now that I had not noticed before I went away on my journey.

I have made sure that a servant is always watching the two young women. Even when they are riding, there is always someone between them so that I can put a stop to any confidences about Roland that Magali might share with her friend. (That is an extra precaution, since I believe I have already deterred her from such a disclosure by telling her she can never see Roland again if she reveals her love for him.) Alas, this means I have also prevented Bertine from sharing the cause of her sadness with Magali.

In the evenings after Bertine returns to her father's house, the dark looks Magali directs at me all day transform into angry words. She assails me about my plot to wed her to the king's nephew and calls me a traitor. Yet she is even angrier with me for banishing Roland. Again and again, I try to explain why I had to make that choice, but she will not listen. She begs me to allow her to write to Roland, but I cannot. He does write to me often, to make sure that Magali is still taking her remedies, which I now purchase from an apothecary. Thank the Virgin, Magali continues to take them; at their final meeting, Roland made her promise him that she would.

In his latest letter, Roland informed me that he now attends lectures in Avignon and continues to search for a better remedy for Magali buried in ancient texts. Dear Virgin, guide him to find something that will heal her!

King Louis has given me until the Feast of the Epiphany, twelve days after Christmas, to inform him of my decision about Magali's betrothal. Yet it is really not my decision to make but rather a command on his part. I would be a fool to refuse his betrothal offer. He has much of the choleric humor and would punish me, as well as the people of Provence, if I were to oppose his will.

Each night, after Magali takes her remedy, she becomes quieter as sleep begins to take her. She offers only one prayer and begs me for only one gift for Noel: to see Roland again.

I would be a fool to allow this visit to come to pass. It would only make her yearn more for his permanent return.

Rocamadour, France
12 DECEMBRE

Roland entered the great room of the inn, clad in a traveling cloak made of coarse wool. Beatrice, alone by the fire, rose to her feet from her chair. As he drew back the hood, Beatrice barely managed to stifle a gasp. His face was drawn, his cheeks gaunt, and his beard was straggly and uncombed. Magali and he both suffered because of her, because of her foolish decision to hire him to help care for her daughter.

You had to make that choice, she reminded herself. *You had to do everything in your power to try to heal Magali. Forgive me, Roland, for what I must do.*

She went to him at once. Before he could speak, she whispered, "Quickly walk down the hall. The third door on the left is open. Enter the room and wait for me there. Remember what I wrote in my letter. We must pretend to be strangers to one another."

Roland abruptly obeyed.

She'd barely had time to sit back down and pretend to do needlework when a group of the king's men entered the inn, laughing as they passed around flasks of wine. *Her guards.* She knew full well why the Spider King had sent them to Provence soon after she journeyed to his court. It was not just to protect Magali and her but also to imprison them. After all, they were now his property.

Beatrice barely contained her anger as she walked toward the men's leader, a burly man who liked to brag about his prowess in war. He was clearly bored with his present duty: guarding a group of Provençal noblewomen on a pilgrimage to the Shrine of the Black Virgin.

He did, however, bow to Beatrice with due courtesy.

"Captain Pierre, many thanks for your protection on our journey today," she addressed him. "My ladies, my daughter, and I will presently retire for the night. We have our doors locked and will be quite safe." She spoke in the certain, imperious tone that she always used when dealing with powerful men. She loosened a money bag from her belt and handed it to him. "You and your men deserve a fine supper after the arduous journey. The tavern across the street is known for its victuals, as well as its music and other entertainment. On the morrow you will accompany us to Mass, and on the day following to the shrine."

"At your service, milady," he said, bowing again. "You are most generous. I will set guards at the door to your inn as a precaution. They will come to fetch us if they suspect any danger to you and your ladies. *Adieu* until the morrow."

As she walked quickly down the hallway, Beatrice could hear the men leaving amidst raucous laughter and bets about who would secure the whores first. She had far more important matters at hand.

She opened the third door on the left and found Roland pacing in front of the fire.

He did not bow with his usual courtesy. "How is Magali?" he asked, his expression distraught.

Every bit of composure she'd had with the captain and his men drained from Beatrice's body, and she collapsed into a chair. "I have tried my best to find another Provençal woman to marry the king's nephew, but to no avail. When I told Magali that she must marry him, her melancholia became so great that she has mostly stopped eating."

She looked up toward heaven and offered yet another silent prayer to the Virgin Mary. Many times a day she prayed, desperate for a miracle that would save her from making this terrible choice.

Her prayer done, she turned back to Roland. "I have tried every possible way to set her free. I decided to take this journey so that you and Magali could say farewell to each other."

"You, her own mother, would imprison her in an unwanted marriage and make her surrender her joy?"

The anger in his voice brought tears to her eyes. "Please, you must forgive me for what I must do."

Roland fell to his knees in front of her. "I beg of you again, milady, let me flee to Spain with her!"

"For someone with such intelligence, how could you be so naïve?" she asked in a trembling voice. "Do you wish to start another war between France and Spain?"

He shook his head.

The countess's voice was filled with an urgency Roland had never heard in it before.

"The fate of Provence also depends on Magali's union to the crown," she explained. "If I refuse to agree to the proposal or send her secretly to Spain, the king will see my choice as a sign of rebellion on my part, but also on the part of the king of Provence, as well as other counts of our land. Louis might well take arms against our kingdom, causing great bloodshed."

The countess was being forced to sacrifice her own daughter to save the lives of the Provençal people! Roland had read of such marriage/treaties, but never had it occurred to him how their cruel finality made the woman suffer. *And me, the man she loves.*

As he paced back and forth, his mind whirred, searching for any means to extricate Magali. "Lady Beatrice, please forgive my ignorance about the workings of the nobility," he said, "but do you have any allies who could help you plead your case with King Louis? Perhaps the king of Provence?"

Beatrice glanced at him as if seeing him in a new light. "I never knew you to be aware of matters politic, Roland, but in answer to your question, no. It was actually King René who suggested to Louis that my daughter would be a good match for his nephew. The king of Provence himself has only sons, each of whom are already wed to French noblewomen. You see, King René believes that if the people of Provence accept French rule, King Louis will not interfere as much with our governance. After all, Provence has been its own kingdom for close to six hundred years."

Roland continued to pace. "Does King Louis know about your daughter's illness of the mind?"

"Yes, and as I said, to him it matters not. Her illness is not a reason for a king or nobleman to reject a bride. She only needs to be capable of bearing him a son." A look of resolve came over her tired face. "At least if I go to live with her at court I can continue to protect her and make certain that she takes her remedies."

"Please, let me take care of her in your place," he pleaded, all the while knowing that King Louis would never allow a Spanish doctor to attend a member of his court.

She shook her head, her mouth trembling. "I will take you to her now," she managed to say. "You and I will stand strong together and tell her she must marry the king's nephew." She paused, breathing deeply to steady herself. "But the most important reason that I have allowed you to attend her is that you must urge her to eat. Do I have your word that you will do so?"

Roland was already striding to the door. "I can make no guarantees."

Lady Beatrice led him to another door farther down the hallway. Inside, Lady Alienor, Catherine, Nina, and Magali were kneeling in prayer before a small statue of the Virgin Mary.

Magali sprang to her feet. "Roland!"

He struggled to conceal his shock at the sight of her—her face so gaunt that for the first time, her cheekbones protruded sharply from beneath her flesh. Her rust-colored bodice and skirt, which her body had filled only a few months earlier, hung loosely on her thin frame.

Her eyes were the only part of her that had not changed. They shone with love for him as he encircled her with his arms. He lost himself to their embrace, the warmth of her frail body, the smell of lavender in her hair. Closing his eyes, he willed this moment to continue forever.

"Day in and day out, I have prayed for God's guidance in helping me to accept what I must do," Lady Beatrice said in a tremulous voice. "His silence and Père Etienne's counsel have caused me to understand that I must submit to His will. Magali and Roland, you too must submit to His will."

Magali clung to Roland. "How could God do this to me? Roland, take me to Spain this very day!"

"The guards would follow us," he said softly, stroking her hair. "And even if we managed to escape them, you would never see your mother again."

"If Mama gives me only two choices, to wed a stranger or to never see her again, I will take the latter," Magali wept.

Glancing at Lady Beatrice, Roland saw the depth of her anguish.

"It is the king of France who is making the choice for all of us, Magali," the countess said. "At least there is hope that I will be allowed to live at court with you and help care for you."

Magali lifted her head abruptly. "I will refuse to take the remedies and I will not eat. I have no reason to live if I cannot be wed to Roland!"

Her words hung in the air. She did love him, he had no doubt. But to take her own life for the sake of that love? Surely the source of her words was not that but instead her *maladie de l'esprit*.

Roland tightened his embrace. "Magali, please listen. Do not take your own life; even though we will be separated, I will still know that you are alive. After you are wed, I will journey to Toulouse and stand outside the king's castle and rejoice that you are there. And your mother will try her best to come to the court with you. I beg of you!"

"No, I cannot live without you," Magali moaned and buried her face against his chest.

Lady Beatrice reached out to grip her daughter's shoulder. "You must understand that there is nothing I can do to prevent your betrothal."

Rash words rushed into Roland's mind and he barely stopped himself from saying them aloud. Instead he pleaded, "I beg of you to listen to me, Lady Beatrice. Please consider your choice carefully, for it will determine if your daughter lives or dies."

Lady Beatrice shook her head. "Magali must accept her new life, just as I did when I was betrothed—just as many noblewomen must do," she said in a resigned voice. "All I can do is pray that she will do so quickly."

Still holding Magali, Roland stared, open-mouthed, at Lady Beatrice. Where was the powerful woman who'd forged treaties throughout Provence and ruled her lands on her own for over a decade? He could hold his tongue no longer. "Milady, did you not hear your daughter? She just told you that she will take her own life if she is forced to marry the king's nephew. You will lose her . . . *forever*. As will I."

Lady Beatrice's eyes widened and her body tensed. "Magali, you would really commit that grave sin?"

"Yes, Mama," Magali wept as Roland embraced her more tightly.

Invisible walls closed in on Beatrice, squeezing air from her lungs. She left the room and, stumbling down the hallway, opened the front door. A fierce wind nearly knocked her to the ground and fought her efforts to close the door. When at last she succeeded, she pressed her back against its hard surface and looked up into the night sky.

Above her, stars pierced the blackness like sword points flashing in firelight. The sentries, warming themselves by a fire, turned to her with concern.

"I just needed a breath of cold air," she assured them. "I do not need your help."

They resumed their talk, passing a flask between them.

Magali and Roland were united against her, against the finality of what she must do, against the king's power to force his will to be done. Even if she urged them again to listen to her, they wouldn't hear and they wouldn't understand. Never had Beatrice felt so alone.

I would sacrifice my own child? I would cause her to take her own life? Dear Virgin, surely this is not your Son's will, as Père Etienne believes it to be . . . as I believed it to be until Magali and Roland shook me awake. The icy wind stung her face as she stared at the stars. *It is no use pondering this matter further. I have no other choice but to seal Magali's fate. Yet I will not abandon her to die . . . I will die with her. Forgive me, Dear Virgin, for what I must do.*

The warmth was quickly vanishing from her body; her face and hands were growing numb. Yet she stood rooted in the doorway as the embrace of the frigid air tightened its arms around her.

Her legs weakened and she felt herself slipping to the ground—but suddenly, a force within seized her and held her upright. *I must live! Magali must live!*

Clasping the iron handle, she pushed the door open and closed it behind her. She crept down the dark hallway to the room where Roland and she had spoken privately.

The fire had burned low, so she pulled a small blanket from the bed and wrapped it around her shoulders. She remembered pulling such a blanket over Magali's body when she was a child, and then covering her with a blanket the previous summer on their boat as they sailed away from the dangers in Arles to the safety of the château.

Tears filled her eyes. Her love and care for her daughter were not enough. First her illness had descended and Beatrice could not protect her from its blackness. Then she had not been able to keep her free from this unwanted betrothal. And now, worst of all, she could not protect her from wanting to die. But her illness, not the prospect of living without Roland, was surely the cause. Her illness was stronger than her will to live.

"I must find a way to save you," Beatrice whispered.

She fell to her knees before the hearth and silently began praying the Ave Maria. But she could not attend fully to her prayer the way she could in the quiet chapel of the château.

She was further distracted when her womb began to coil in pain. She abandoned her prayer to lie on the cold floor and massage her belly. The cramping caused by her monthly courses always lasted for days, making it very difficult for her to work and make decisions. She groaned. The courses, her punishment from God for Eve's sin, could not have come at a worse time. She kneaded the muscles of her womb, as she did each month. As the midwife had done during the racking pain that had led to Magali's birth.

Suddenly, Beatrice grew very still. *I gave birth to one living child and many others who died. I am still able to bear children . . . I am still able to bear children! I could be the woman who gives birth to a child who will seal the union of the French crown with the crown of Provence. Why did I not think of this earlier?*

The door opened and Beatrice quickly sat up.

"Mama?" Magali called to her.

Her pain forgotten, Beatrice leapt to her feet and smiled at her daughter. "I may have found a way to save you from your betrothal," she whispered excitedly.

"How?" Magali asked.

Beatrice closed the door firmly, then took Magali's hand in hers. "I will offer myself in marriage to the king's nephew in your place," she said.

"Oh, Mama." Magali's face crumpled. "You would lose your freedom so that I could gain mine?"

Beatrice squeezed her daughter's hand. "My sacrifice is a small thing compared to your happiness . . . your life."

Magali threw her arms around her mother and the two women held each other tightly. As they rocked back and forth, a weight began to lift from Beatrice's shoulders—until a sudden thought unsettled her.

"I must warn you, *ma chère*, that even though I will try my best to persuade the king, I do not know for certain that he will agree to my proposal."

Magali's body stiffened.

"I do believe that his nephew would," Beatrice said quickly. "Remember the day that I tried to persuade you to sit for your portrait to be taken?"

Her daughter nodded slowly. "Yes."

"When you refused, I posed for the portrait in your place. We do resemble each other greatly, after all. The king told me that his nephew was quite enamored of the painting."

"Let us hope he holds some sway over his uncle," Magali said in a small voice.

"Yes." Beatrice drew in a deep breath. "I have decided something else, too. If the king accepts my proposal, I will allow you and Roland to wed one another."

With a cry of delight, Magali hugged Beatrice even more tightly. Another pain shot through her belly, this one stronger than the ones before.

When she recovered, she took her daughter's hand. "Come, let us make haste to tell Roland—but then he must leave before the guards return."

Holding hands, they walked to the room where Roland and the other women were gathered.

When Magali announced what would come to pass, Roland smiled more broadly than Beatrice had ever seen him do, lifted Magali from her feet, and spun her around, sending her skirts flying.

The countess stood alone until Lady Alienor came over to her. "You are brave, milady," she said softly. "I believe that you have made the only choice that could possibly change your daughter's fate."

Beatrice had been to the Shrine of the Black Virgin at Rocamadour many times, but this time it was as if she was seeing it anew. Even with her monthly pains, she felt lighter than she had ever since the messenger from King Louis had come to the château with his terrible summons. She only wished that Roland could be with Magali and her, rather than hovering in a crowd of pilgrims separated from the nobles.

But the guards, having slept off their revelry of two nights ago, were keeping a close watch over Beatrice, Magali, and their attendants today. The king's men hovered over the four women as they entered the basilica to pray over the bones of the hermit-saint Amadour.

Outside, they saw the place where Roland, the famous warrior of Charlemagne's army, prayed that his sword would be magically preserved in stone. How fitting for the flesh-and-blood Roland to be here . . . had he been to this shrine before? There were so many things that Beatrice did not know about him. Yet she knew the most important thing: he and Magali loved one another.

Ten

> "I know that many have been, are, and henceforth will be touched by this sin of sadness that proceeds from disordered will, currently called in most cases an illness of the melancholic humor which physicians say comes in many forms."
>
> —A PERSONAL ACCOUNT OF MENTAL ILLNESS BY THE FIFTEENTH-CENTURY KING DUARTE OF PORTUGAL

Avignon, France
29 JANVIER, 1479

"Hear ye, hear ye," the royal herald shouted.

Despite the rain, people gathered around him as he stood on the steps of the cathedral.

Roland shouldered his way to the front of the crowd.

"Hear ye, hear ye," the herald repeated. "I come from Toulouse bearing news from King Louis of France."

"Down with the Spider King," a man shouted, and others took up the cry.

"Silence," the herald roared. Royal guards on horseback drew their swords and circled the crowd. People quieted at once.

"The King's nephew Philippe will wed Lady Beatrice of Arles," the herald announced. "The wedding will take place on March the twelfth, the last Saturday before Lent."

All around Roland, jeering rose; he, meanwhile, barely stopped himself from cheering. His month of waiting was over at last. He lifted his face to the sky, letting the cold rain wash over him and trickle into his parched mouth.

Those around him backed away.

"You are mad, Spaniard!" a man shouted. "Begone, lest you make us mad too."

Roland gladly obeyed. He ran through the rain, splashing in puddles, as Carlos and he once had on the streets of Barcelona. This time, however, his childish exuberance transformed into pure joy.

2 Février

Thomas was waiting for Roland at the inn where he usually supped. The surgeon had come to see him several times since Roland's move to Avignon. For once, he did not dread hearing his friend's tidings about Hubert.

Just yesterday, Roland had received a message from Lady Alienor. (Lady Beatrice had arranged to communicate with Roland through her housekeeper in order to protect him from the king's spies.) In veiled words, the message had reassured him that Magali and he would be free to marry! The only problem was the long wait, for the countess had made it clear that they should not see each other or even write to one another until after her own wedding.

Thomas and he sat down at a corner table and ordered wine.

"This time you cannot take away my hope," Roland said, and in a low voice he told his friend about his upcoming wedding.

Thomas neither smiled nor congratulated him. "I pray that Hubert will not find a way to stop it," he said somberly. "After all, he did announce your betrothal to Bertine to his family. The courts might well force you to wed Bertine . . . if Hubert could find you. He is still angry at you for disappearing and breaking your agreement with him to find new remedies. But more importantly, he told me that he knows about your love for Magali."

Roland slammed his hand on the table. "How? Magali and her mother have assured me that they do not speak of me in front of the servants. And I have not visited them at the château since late autumn."

"I don't know," Thomas said glumly. "As usual, Hubert just has his ways of learning the secrets of others."

The serving girl brought wine to their table, but Roland asked for water instead to cool the anger that enflamed his cheeks. "Did Hubert not receive my letter stating that my brother had already betrothed me to a Spanish noblewoman who serves at the queen's court?"

That letter was a lie, of course. Roland had not even mentioned his proposed betrothal to his brother when he saw him at Christmas. Nor had he mentioned Magali.

"Hubert does not believe a word of what you wrote," Thomas said. "He does not speak of your love for Magali publicly, wanting to protect Bertine, but he told me of it in confidence and seemed convinced it was true."

Roland stared at his cup of water, trying to absorb Thomas's news.

"It is possible that Hubert was merely making a conjecture without any evidence," Thomas continued. "At any rate, he told me he would find a way to force you to wed Bertine—or, failing that, punish you for breaking the betrothal."

Roland's shoulder tensed. "Did he truly say that?"

"He spoke in anger, but yes." Thomas drew in a deep breath. "Over the years, I have come to understand that Hubert is not a purely evil man as I once thought. True, he seeks power over others, but he also helps to improve their lot in life. He truly believed that his partnership with you and his offer of Bertine's hand were of mutual benefit to both you and him."

If Roland had not fallen in love with Magali, that might have been true. No longer. Roland's thoughts turned to Hubert's threats. "I am trying to understand how he could truly prevent me from marrying Magali."

Thomas cupped his wine and swirled it around. "I don't know," he replied. "To my knowledge he has never caused bodily harm, but he knows well how to poison the mind and turn one person against another. As he turned my father against me . . . as I am afraid that one day, he might try to turn my sons away from me."

"Why?"

"Jealousy, I think. He saw full well the love my father and I shared, in contrast to the scorn Hubert had for his father, a drunkard who harmed his own patients. Having only daughters, Hubert wanted a son-in-law who would revere him. Marie's husband, François, was never that man, but Hubert had hopes for me. So he lied to my father, saying that I'd told him he was more of a father to me than my flesh-and-blood father."

"What a terrible lie!" Roland gulped more water, but it did nothing to cool his anger.

Thomas bowed his head. "Despite all my efforts, my father went to his deathbed believing that it was the truth."

"If Hubert could secure an audience with Magali, he might try a similar ruse, saying that I love Bertine and not her," Roland said, horrified at the idea. "If Magali were in the depth of her illness, she might even believe him. I should take her to Spain as soon as possible."

Thomas sighed. "If my marriage can be annulled, I would have similar thoughts of fleeing to Montpellier with my boys. But I fear that escape from Hubert will only be possible when he dies."

"I am beginning to feel the same way," Roland said. He had never wanted to murder a person before, but looking down at his hands now he imagined clenching Hubert's neck—choking him until he could no longer draw breath. He covered his face with his hands, but the terrible image persisted.

"What is wrong?" Thomas asked.

Roland told him of his dark fantasy.

"I too have thought of killing him," Thomas admitted.

Roland dropped his hands from his face and they stared at one another, the fire crackling in the hearth behind them.

"But I could never bring myself to do the deed," Thomas added, "unless he hurt my sons or turned them away from me."

"Nor could I, unless he did the same to Magali."

Roland's murderous thoughts subsided as something else occurred to him. "Maybe Hubert suspects that you are in contact with me; maybe he even suspects that we are friends," he said. "He wanted you to bring me this news so that he could arrange for someone to follow you."

"You are thinking as Hubert would, but no, I am certain that no one followed me." Thomas shook his head. "As for Hubert suspecting we are friends, he asked me that question directly and I lied. I have made sure of convincing him of that by insulting you at every turn. He claims that my disdain for you is born of my jealousy." Thomas smiled. "In truth, I am jealous of you, for you may be more successful in escaping from him than I am."

"In several months' time, we will know," Roland said grimly.

In several months, and he and Magali would be wed in Spain!

Despite that hopeful thought, Roland's fear returned. "Hubert might suspect that the countess bade me to remain hidden from the king and his nephew. He might even be setting a trap by trying to force me to disobey her."

Thomas stroked his chin. "Though your idea sounds far-fetched, you might have discovered his plan," he said. "Maybe I should ask Clare discreet questions about what Hubert knows."

Roland frowned. "No. That might make the family suspect that you are helping me. Again, you are absolutely certain that Hubert does not know my whereabouts?"

"Yes, and your disappearance infuriates him to no end. After all, he was your patron and helped you establish your reputation as a surgeon in Arles, even though you have Spanish blood. He fully believes that in return, you owe him complete loyalty and obedience . . . as if you were his own son."

Roland shuddered at the memory of Hubert's fatherly touch on his shoulder. But his disgust was quickly supplanted by overwhelming shame and regret. He could never take back the lie he had told Bertine. It would haunt him forever.

Avignon
27 Mars

His hood thrown over his head, Roland ran through the rain with the treatise clutched inside his shirt, hoping that his thick cloak would protect it from getting wet.

He reached the half-timbered house where he rented a room. A gangly boy of around ten opened the door, and Roland entered the great room. The aroma of the fish stew simmering in a big pot over the hearth filled the air inside.

Madame Anes looked up from her sewing, as did her three younger children, who were playing with their dolls on the floor beside her. She nodded a greeting. "Will you join us for supper tonight?"

"Not tonight, thank you," Roland said. "I have work to do. I will take food in my room."

As he climbed the stairs, he thought again of Magali and what she was doing at this very moment. Several weeks had passed since her mother's wedding day—was she in Toulouse with her, or at the château with Alienor and Nina?

Lady Beatrice had been absent from the château for nearly three moons, and the last time her mother was gone on a long journey, Magali's illness had raged within her. Had it returned? Four months . . . that had been the lapse of time between her illness when he first met her and the return of it last October.

No, her illness had not returned. Surely, the quick-witted Lady Alienor would have sent word to him. But what if Magali was with her mother in Toulouse and had succumbed to her illness? How would the royal physicians care for her? He imagined Magali, free of mania and melancholia, sitting in the château's great room and staring at the chess board, set up for a new game, and his disquiet lifted. He entered his room, already warm from the fire that Anes had lit for him.

The room was hardly more than a closet—a bed and a small table near the hearth—but it was all that he needed. He set up his chess pieces on his board and made his first move. In his mind's eye, he saw Magali seated across from him and moved a pawn for her. He continued the game with her as an imaginary opponent, writing their moves on a piece of parchment. As the two of them had discussed when they met at Rocamadour, she was also playing imaginary games with him at the château. When they saw each other again, they had agreed to play some of their recorded games again, making novel moves as needed.

After finishing the game, he opened the treatise, which a scribe near the university of Avignon had copied for him from a manuscript that he'd found at the library. Good, the rain had not smeared the ink. From his satchel of books, he took out his drawing of Magali. He felt as if she were sitting at the table beside him, her chair pulled so close to his that strands of her loose hair brushed against his face. In his mind, he heard her soft breathing and saw her fingers ruffling the feather of a quill pen, as she always did when she read.

"May I find a remedy for you," he whispered, as he did every night, and he began to read.

The second candle had burned low by the time Roland had read nearly a third of the translation. He came to a new section entitled "Ancient Remedies." The Jewish doctor who'd compiled the treatise had discovered the writing of a Greek doctor named Soranus of Ephesus. Roland leaned closer to the page and read quickly. To treat patients suffering from mania and melancholia, Soranus advised bathing in the warm mineral waters of a spring near his city.

Roland jumped to his feet. Where could he find such a spring nearby? It was far too late to ask Anes—he would have to wait until morning. He clutched the drawing of Magali and paced back and forth in front of the fire. Isaac would advise him to try the remedy on many patients before making conclusions about its efficacy. Still, Roland could not contain his excitement; what if this was the remedy he'd been searching for?

He had trouble falling sleep until sometime after the bells rang the midnight hour—and soon enough he found himself awake again, gasping for breath.

He bolted upright in the bed, his heart pounding. He tried to grasp hold of the vivid dream which had just ensnared him, but it was already vanishing from his mind. All that remained was an urgent desire to go to Magali.

28 Mars

Drawing his hood over his head, Roland emerged from the carriage into the pelting rain.

"Remain here until I return!" he shouted to the driver.

He made his way out of the thickest part of the olive grove, where the carriage was hidden from view, in utter darkness. He finally reached the path to the château. Olive branches hung over it and raked against his mantle as the cold rain soaked his hood and dripped down his face.

He was shivering by the time he reached the courtyard. After making certain that no one was there, he crept forward, remaining in the shadows of the stable. A light shone from within the tower; from a fire or from a candle, he could not be certain, but by that light he saw smoke curling from the château's chimney and the drawn curtains of the great room.

Maybe Magali was in the tower. On their last day together, she'd told him that she would use his room in the tower as her own chamber. Sit at his desk to read and write and sleep in his bed.

He darted to the tower's back side, where no one in the château could see him and where its eaves protected him from most of the rain. He heard not a sound coming from inside. Huddled in his mantle, he waited there.

He knew not how many hours had passed and still smoke rose from the chimney of the great room. Maybe Magali was inside the château after all.

A noise coming from the main road to the château startled him, and he retreated farther into the shadows. It was the unmistakable sound of horses' hooves and the creaking of carriage wheels . . . the beating of his heart quickened.

The light from a lantern illuminated the courtyard, but he dared not look to see who it was. The latch of the tower door slid noisily as it opened, and footsteps struck against the cobblestone. Roland took a quick look. Bertine, Nina, and Solange had their backs to him as they ran toward Hubert, who was descending from his carriage. Lady Alienor and several servants emerged from the main door of the château and hurried toward Hubert's carriage.

Quickly retreating to his hiding place, Roland listened intently.

"Papa, did you find her?" Bertine cried out.

"No, *ma fille*," Hubert replied, "though we searched along every street in the village and in Arles. In the morning, we will search the forest."

"This is my fault," Bertine wailed. "Solange, Nina, and I were taking turns to keep watch over her. It was my turn. Lady Magali fell asleep, and I tried to keep myself awake—but I must have fallen asleep. When I awoke, she was gone. Dear Virgin, keep her safe!"

"Let us go inside," Hubert said.

The sound of Bertine's crying diminished, but Roland waited until he heard the grooms leading the horses to the stable before thrusting his head out again to survey the courtyard.

Once he was sure that no one was there, he darted through the doorway of the tower, which had been blown open by the wind. Maybe he would find something that would help him figure out where she had gone.

Broken panes of colored glass were scattered on the floor and sparkled in the light of the dying fire. He strode to the Nativity window. On the floor beneath it, shards of blue and green glass were placed together in a large square about the same size as the window itself. The glass pieces depicted no figure; still the arrangement was harmonious, suggesting that Magali's mind, if she indeed had done it, was steady.

Ducking low so as not to be seen through the windows, he went to the fireplace. There were only a few flames left along the charred and smoldering remnants of logs. He found the stub of a candle on the mantel and lit it, holding his cloak around it to dim its light. Then, hunching down, he made his way to the stairs and quickly ascended to the top floor.

Clothes lay rumpled in an open chest at the foot of the bed, whose blankets were in a disarray. Avoiding the window, he crept to the desk where he'd once studied—such a long time ago, it seemed. Two books lay open upon it: the one about Jeanne the Maid doing battle to save France from English conquest and the treatise by Lucretius he had given Magali in Rocamadour. He grabbed both books, then stooped to examine the scraps and sheets of parchment strewn on the floor.

The script was Magali's; sometimes it was neat and contained notes from books. On other pieces of parchment, her handwriting deteriorated into a scrawl. Latin and French words were cobbled together in lines of poetry that made no sense. These were the words of a person suffering from mania, its pathway manifest in her changing script. But there were no dates on the parchment, so he knew not the order of the path.

He bolted back down the stairs. He had to find Magali before Hubert dispatched a search party at first light. She could be anywhere in the olive groves or in the forest that surrounded the countess's estate.

Last fall, Magali and he had looked at a book of maps in the château's library. On a map of France and Provence, he had pointed to the spot where the château would have been. Fontvieille, with its Roman ruins, was only a few leagues north of it and on the way to Avignon where he now lived. Would she have remembered the map? And on a rainy night without stars to guide her, how would she have known which way was north? There was her illness to consider as well, which would have robbed her of a clear mind.

He returned to his carriage and fetched a lantern. "Remain here," he bade the driver, who looked miserable huddled in his cloak. He had already paid the man generously for his troubles, but he gave him another handful of coins to ensure his obedience.

Roland spent most of the night searching the countess's lands, making an ever-growing spiral with his carriage as its center point. He found no sign of her. Finally, he returned to the carriage and bade the driver to set out along the road to Fontvieille.

At regular intervals, Roland descended from the carriage to shine his lantern into the forest on either side of the road. By first light, he was exhausted and drenched to the bone. He took off his wet cloak, wrapped himself in two thick wool blankets from the coach, and continued his search.

By the time the carriage reached the wall of Fontvieille, the rain had stopped but the air was cold and windy, more like autumn than spring, and though it was full morning, it remained dark as twilight. He came to a forest and found a familiar path—one he'd followed the previous summer that led to the ruins of Roman millworks. Magali might have stumbled upon the ruins and sought shelter there. He quickened his pace.

The trees blocked much of the wind and light. Just as last time, the forest disquieted him, but he pressed deeper into its darkness.

It was raining again by the time he reached the clearing where the ruins stood. The stone was darker than he remembered, streaked with rain but providing some shelter from it. He ran toward it but found no one under the first set of arches. In the shadows of the second, he found Magali asleep and shivering in a rain-drenched shift. He wrapped a blanket around her and lifted her into his arms. She was as light as a child.

She awoke with a start, her eyes wide and then filling with tears. "You found me," she whispered.

He pressed his cheek against hers. "I had a dream and knew that I had to come to you . . . later, we will talk. We must leave at once."

Before Hubert finds us.

Avignon
29 MARS

"The illness is different this time," Magali said, her voice weak. "The deepest melancholia I have ever felt. All I want to do is to sleep."

"From the scraps of parchment I found in the tower, I thought you might be suffering from mania," Roland said.

Magali lay on a bed in dry clothes and covered with blankets. He sat on the edge of the bed and threaded his fingers through her matted hair. Later, he would ask Anes for a brush for his "sister" who was ill. As he secured another room for Magali, his landlady had given him a look of curiosity but had said nothing.

"Those scraps were from October, when I was suffering from mania. I was reading them to try to remember how it felt, in the hopes that I could dispel some of my listlessness. I could not."

"May the remedy you just took begin to lift your spirits," he whispered.

That morning, while she slept, he'd bought it for her, making certain that the apothecary doubled the amount of St. John's wort in the recipe. At Magali's bidding, he'd also sent a message to Lady

Alienor, who would convey it to Lady Beatrice at the French court. Using indirect wording, Roland had informed her that Magali was very ill but safe with him in Avignon. He'd added something to the message that he had not yet told Magali: they would journey to Aix-en-Provence, where there were mineral springs.

"Tell me all that has come to pass since we last saw each other," he said to Magali.

She drew in a deep breath, as if gathering strength to tell her tale. "In January, I was joyful, awaiting spring when we would be wed," she began. "Mama assured me that she was at peace with her choice to marry the king's nephew. She was overjoyed that I was happy again. She rode with me often and read books with Bertine and me, including the book about Jeanne the Maid. Bertine and Mama cherish it as much as I do. Soon it was time for Mama to journey to Toulouse to prepare for the wedding. As you know, the king sent guards to protect our lands. Somehow, they did not find me last night."

"Nor me," Roland said. And Magali and he had also eluded Hubert . . . for the time being. Despite Roland's dry clothes and the crackling fire, a chill passed through him.

"After Mama left, my happiness began to fade," Magali went on, her voice faltering, "a little bit more each day, and I had no appetite. My stomach began to hurt whenever I ate. I longed to write to you and ask you to come to see me, but Mama told me to wait until after her wedding. I considered dismissing Bertine for a few days—without consulting Alienor—so that neither she nor her father would find out about your visit. But in the end, I decided it best not to do anything that might ruin our plan."

"Tell me about Hubert's visits to the château," Roland said, deciding not to mention Thomas's latest tidings.

"Right before Mama's journey to Toulouse," Magali began, "on the advice of Père Etienne, she arranged for Hubert to supply the remedy for me while she was gone."

Roland's shoulders tensed as Magali went on with her telling. "He came to our home with it and offered to help me if I became ill. He feigned great concern for me, and Mama believed him. I would have, too, if you had not told me of his deceitfulness."

"Did you try to warn your mother about him?" Roland asked.

Magali shook her head. "I did not want her to worry about me while she was away. I also had confidence that I could protect myself from him."

The same confidence Roland had once mistakenly had. "Is that the only time Hubert came to visit?" he asked, suspecting what her reply would be.

"No. Bertine was concerned about my illness, so, with Alienor's permission, she was attending me day and night, taking turns with Nina and Solange. The melancholia was causing me to vomit almost every day, and Alienor was giving me more of the remedy to replace what I lost. When it was almost gone, Bertine sent Solange to her father, and he arrived promptly with the remedy. Bertine told him about my nausea, so he bled me. I was too weak to stop him. He told me about a surgery that might heal my melancholia."

Roland turned to her, the horror of his dream returning. "Trepanning?"

"Yes, that was its name."

This must have been the source of the dream. He leaned down to embrace her.

After taking a little water, she continued her account. "Hubert decided to remain at the château to take care of me, but I also think he stayed there to be with Bertine. By yesterday morning, I was feeling so ill, both in mind and body, that I decided I would go to you."

"On that very day, I knew you needed me," he said in a voice made faint by awe. He told her about the dream.

She lay back down and took his hand in hers. "An invisible thread binds your heart and mine."

"That will never be broken," he murmured. He lay down beside her and held her to him. They lay in silence for a long time as birds sang outside the window.

"Tell me about how you found your way to the ruins," he said, marveling once again that she had not been caught.

"I waited until Bertine was asleep before leaving the tower and fleeing into the forest. The clouds obscured the North Star, so I hid behind a big tree, not knowing what direction to take. Then I heard Bertine shouting for her father, and soon the neighing of horses and Hubert bidding the groom to head south on the main road to Arles. After the carriage set out, I fled in what seemed to be the opposite direction, hopefully north toward Avignon. When I finally reached the ruins and knew that I was in Fontvieille, I was so tired that I decided to take shelter there and rest for a short while. I must have fallen asleep."

"Such relief I felt when I found you," he said as he stroked her cheek, as cool and damp as when it was drenched in rain that early morning. Yet her flesh had once been warm and dry. It seemed that her illness of the mind was now manifesting in her body. Isaac had once told him that he had observed such a condition in other patients.

"Tomorrow, when we are rested," he said, "we will go to Aix-en-Provence, where there are warm mineral springs. A Greek doctor of long ago believed that bathing in the waters could heal diseases of the mind. Isaac and his family also live in Aix-en-Provence. If you are not feeling better soon, I will seek his advice."

"At last, you may have found a cure for me," Magali said softly. She embraced him with her frail arms, and soon she fell asleep.

Aix-en-Provence

14 AVRIL

"I do not want to go to the baths today," Magali announced as she set down her quill. "They have done me no good."

Roland closed the book of remedies that he had not been able to attend to for the past hour and turned to look out the window. She was right. Several weeks had passed with no discernible change: her appetite was still poor and she continued to vomit several times a day.

He reached across the table to take her hand. "I think it best that you continue with the baths," he said. "It may take longer than several weeks for the melancholia to lift. And you may need to bathe three times a day rather than two."

She shook her head, her eyes cast down toward the blank parchment on which she had been attempting to write her thoughts all morning.

"Please . . ." His words failed him as a ray of morning sunlight fell across her face. Her flesh, like that of many people of Provence, had never been of a pale hue, yet for the first time he could see that it had darkened significantly over the past two weeks. There was no doubt.

"I have changed my mind," he said. "No more baths if you allow me to take you to Isaac as soon as possible."

She shrugged. "Very well, but I doubt that will do any good either."

He quickly wrote Isaac a note. "Come with me to find a messenger," he said to Magali as he sealed the parchment.

"I am too tired—"

"We can take a carriage."

She agreed and he supported her on the short walk to the stable, where they secured a carriage to take them to the cathedral square.

Mass had just ended and people swarmed out of the cathedral, in a hurry to dine after their long fast. Two women walked close to Roland and Magali's carriage, talking about the meals they had prepared. One of them boasted that she had made a stew with mussels and octopus fresh from the sea.

Once Roland might also have bragged about a dish he had prepared. But he had not cooked in many a month, and his worry about Magali took away his pleasure in eating.

"I want to go inside," Magali said, her voice weak.

Bidding the driver to wait for them, Roland helped her to descend and supported her as they entered the cool darkness of the nave, where only a few people remained inside, praying.

At a side altar, Magali and Roland halted.

"I have never seen a painting like this," he said, in awe of what he saw before him.

"Nor I," said Magali.

It was a triptych with a portrait of King René on one side of the main painting and one of Queen Jeanne of Provence on the other. But it was the central image that was the most startling. It depicted Moses and the burning bush, but instead of God appearing in the midst of the flames, it was the Virgin and Child.

"Moses looks surprised to see her—even disappointed," Magali said. "If I were him, I would have preferred a vision of the Virgin and Child to a vision of God the Father."

Roland squeezed her hand, grateful that her illness had not taken away her insights into the meanings of stories.

She bowed her head. "Blessed Virgin, help me to heal," she said, and then softly prayed the Ave Maria.

Though he no longer believed in prayers, something inside urged Roland to join her. He closed his eyes and spoke silently, not to God or a saint but to whatever it was that looked down on them from the stars: *Bring her back.*

When darkness fell, after making certain that no Christians were watching, Roland carried a sleeping Magali into the Jewish quarters, as he had done on the first night he'd met her. He was grateful Isaac had agreed to see Magali.

The doctor and his family were now living with his cousin, who treated patients with eye diseases and was letting Isaac use part of his shop until he could set up one of his own.

"Look for a sign with a painting of spectacles," Isaac had written.

Isaac's wife answered Roland's knock, holding a squirming baby in one arm and a candle in the other. She gazed at Magali with concern. "I remember this young woman." she said softly. "Come, my husband is waiting for you."

She led him down a hallway to the shop, which was lit with candles whose light glinted off spectacles arranged neatly on a shelf.

Isaac looked up from a table where he was preparing a remedy and greeted Roland warmly before turning to Magali. "She has lost flesh from her bones," he observed, and motioned for Roland to lay her on a bed against the wall. "Tell me what has come to pass."

As Roland did so, Isaac held two fingers to her wrist for a few moments. "Her heart is not beating steadily and her skin has a dark gray cast to it," the doctor observed. "How is her appetite?"

"She barely takes food or water because her stomach hurts," Roland replied. "She vomits several times a day and each day she becomes more listless, even though I have increased the amount of medicine I give her."

Isaac motioned for Roland to follow him to the hallway and closed the door behind them. His look of concern made Roland grow alert.

"Some of her symptoms could indeed indicate a disease of the mind," Isaac said, "but I believe that her illness is not of the mind but of the body. Her skin color, stomachaches, and vomiting make me think she has been poisoned."

It was as if a stone sank in Roland's belly. "No," he moaned, grabbing the doorknob to hold himself upright. "I believed that her melancholia was causing her lack of appetite and her vomiting. I should have come to you two weeks ago. Is it too late to save her?"

"I do not know," Isaac replied. "Do not berate yourself . . . you took the best care of her that you possibly could." He grew quiet for a moment. "If we knew what the poison was, we could give her a remedy to work against it."

A tiny flame of hope sparked inside Roland. "Do you have any ideas of what it could be?"

Isaac shook his head. "I do not know much about poisons. I have only treated a few patients who by accident took an excess of herbal remedies containing belladona or monk's hood. I do not believe that the poison in Magali's body is either one of those. It seems to me that it must have been given in small doses over a span of time, maybe mixed in with her remedies. Tell me, when did Lady Beatrice leave the château?"

"I do not know for certain." Roland massaged his temples. "Maybe January?"

"The poisoner may have begun to give Magali the substance then. That would mean she was being poisoned for a month or more. So it is likely a substance that works slowly."

Roland began to pace back and forth, his mind racing. "And to find what the poison is, we would probably have to find the person responsible."

Isaac nodded. "Until then, all we can do is to try and purify Magali's blood. Do not give her anything but chicken broth with parsley and water with mint for the next few days. We will see if she begins to heal."

Roland's chest tightened. There was only one person who could have done this to Magali. He beat his fist against the door so hard that his knuckles throbbed in pain. "It was Hubert's doing," he cried. "I will kill him!"

Isaac grabbed him by the shoulders and pulled him away from the door before he could slam his other fist into it. "Stop! You must turn your attention fully to Magali."

The urgency of the doctor's words wrenched Roland out of his rage. He had to find out what the poison was before it was too late. That would mean returning to Arles—but would Magali be able to endure the journey?

When he asked Isaac this question, the doctor shook his head. "Let her remain here in a hospital, where the nuns can care for her."

Roland's heart sank at the thought of leaving Magali, but he knew he must. It was the only way to try to save her life. And he must also send a message to Lady Beatrice this very day . . . His mind whirred as he considered everything he must attend to.

Isaac reached to open the shop door but Roland gripped his arm, stopping him.

"I will not tell Magali of your suspicion," he said.

Isaac shook his head. "It is more than a suspicion, and you owe her the truth. You told me that you try to share everything with her; you must share this too. She can fight for her life with you or surrender it with you by her side. You must accept whatever happens."

"You think it likely she will die?" Roland whispered.

Isaac bowed his head in sorrow. "Yes."

At the hospital, a large chamber with twelve beds for the patients, Roland slept fitfully in a small chamber reserved for the sick person's family. Throughout the night, he crept across the hall to check on Magali. The light of the nearly full moon bathed her as she lay facing him, her knees drawn toward her chest like a newborn babe. She was so peaceful and childlike in her sleep. Yet the moonlight also illuminated her hollow cheeks and the slenderness of the arms stretched out on top of her blanket.

He considered asking the nuns to add meat to the broth that he offered her every hour or so—but no, Isaac had insisted that fasting was of utmost importance to her healing.

In the hour before dawn, she became more wakeful. After she took a small amount of the broth, Roland told her about the poisoning.

Her eyes widened. "Is Isaac certain?"

"Yes." He held her hand against his heart.

"I have never harmed anyone," she said, her voice breaking. "Who would wish me dead?"

He did not answer, only took her tightly in his arms as she wept and felt his own tears rising.

"You must tell me." The strength of her voice belied her body's frailty. "I know that you want to protect me, but I want to face what has come to pass with you."

He slackened his embrace but her thin arms only encircled him more tightly. She was right—he could not protect her from the truth any longer.

"Hubert," he seethed.

She drew apart from him and met his gaze, her eyes very wide. "How could that be? Hubert loves Bertine and knows that I am her dear friend. He would not want her to grieve for my passing. Besides, his concern for me seemed so truthful."

Roland's fury returned—heat rising through his middle—and he had to contain it before he could reply. "He deceived you as he did me," he said at last, his tone level. But as he told Magali about Thomas's most recent warning, he could fight his anger no longer. He sat up and turned his head away from her, hoping she had not seen the blood rising to his face. "I will strangle Hubert with my own hands!" he snarled.

The bedclothes rustled as Magali sat up, and he felt her cold hands stroking his cheeks and gently turning his face back toward hers. Her eyes locked with his, pleading with him as she had never done before. "Stop," she said.

Hearing this one word, he felt his anger receding a bit; his shoulders slumped as he let her hold him in her gaze.

"Do you remember the day we looked at your sketch of the murderer and the inside of his body?" she asked.

"How could I forget that day?" he murmured. It was then that an inkling of what was happening between them had struck him for the first time. She had asked to see what was in his satchel—something that no one else had ever asked. In his leather case of sketches, she'd found the one of the murderer, his neck and face purple and swollen from the noose. "We talked about how we could not understand how a person could be driven to kill another," he said. His voice was cold, coming from a dark place that he had not known until recently was within him. "Now I understand."

She cupped her hands around his face, her gaze intent. "You are not a murderer, nor am I. If you killed anyone, even the person who was poisoning me, I fear you would become mad. Not like me, with waxing and waning spirits, but imprisoned in the darkness of despair forever."

Her words echoed in the quiet room as he squeezed his eyes shut. An image came to him: He was standing over Hubert's lifeless body, his hands trembling in the wake of committing the terrible deed. His hands, which no longer felt like they belonged to him.

Magali was right. If he committed this act, the hands that were now holding hers would no longer be able to heal. He would be alive on the outside but dead within.

She grew quiet but remained in a seated position. He thought perhaps she was drifting to sleep, but when he opened his eyes, she was still wide awake.

"Promise me!" In the dim light, there was a fierceness in her eyes, despite the frailty of her body.

"What you ask of me is the most difficult vow I have ever made," he said, his voice hoarse. "But I promise you."

Eleven

> "It is not far-fetched or difficult to place poison in a simple or complex food and succeed with this intention with any food or beverage taken. Even if it doesn't kill, it will cause harm and deliverance rests only in the hands of God."
> —From a treatise on poison by Maimonides, a twelfth-century physician

Aix-en-Provence, France
15 Avril, 1479

It would be the most difficult farewell Roland had ever said, knowing he must leave Magali with the nuns while he went to find the person who had poisoned her. How long would it take to do so . . . and how long would it be before Lady Beatrice received his message? He sent a message to Lady Alienor; surely, she had already sent word to the countess about Magali's disappearance.

Fearing that spies might read his message, he wrote very little—only that it was urgent for the countess to meet with him as soon as possible, and that she could send him secret messages through Thomas. How he wanted to meet the countess in Aix-en-Provence so that he could see Magali at the same time—but that would take nearly two full days away from his quest to find her poisoner.

At dawn, he woke Magali to bid her farewell. Taking her hand in his, he told her the only secret he'd kept from her.

"There is something I must tell you," he began. "First you must understand that I *am* Bertine's friend, but I do not love her as I love you."

She nodded. "Whenever you spoke of her, I could tell that you bore her much affection. She spoke with the same affection for you."

Roland went on to tell Magali how he had deceived Bertine and how, for many months, he had blamed Hubert for making him afraid of what would happen if he did not agree to the betrothal. "Now I know that only I am to blame," he said somberly.

Magali closed her eyes, and for a long time did not speak a word. He feared she would never forgive him for his deceit.

"Not a murderer . . . and not a liar," she said at last, her voice weak and halting. "Go to Bertine . . . ask her to forgive you . . . as I forgive you."

The muscles of his shoulders relaxed. A nun called to him that his carriage had arrived. He combed his fingers through her hair where it lay loose on her pillow, wishing nothing more than to remain by her side. But the quicker he found out what the poison was, the quicker he could find a remedy to counteract it.

Her deep brown eyes met his with intensity. "Know that I am with you on your journey," she said. "I have one final piece of advice to give you. Remember how we solve puzzles and riddles? We do it as Isaac taught you—never assuming that we know the answer until we collect all of the evidence. Now you must use the same method to find out who gave me the poison. Do not assume it was Hubert but consider everything you discover. Now go," she bade him, smiling weakly.

"I will try my best," he managed to say, thinking, *How can I go, knowing there is no guarantee that I will ever see you again?*

Despite the nun hovering over them, Roland could not stop himself from leaning down to embrace her. He then fled the room before either woman could see his tears.

Arles

17 AVRIL

Roland rented a room in a decrepit house. It was a hovel really, south of Arles on the river, a place where poor fishermen cast their nets, later to sell their catch in the city marketplace. A thick coat of dust covered the few pieces of furniture in the small room, and the straw pallet looked lumpy and was probably flea-ridden. The room faced east, and without the afternoon sunlight, it was chilly. Lacking a fireplace, it would only grow colder as darkness fell.

These discomforts mattered not a whit. This village afforded him secrecy. No one from Arles—especially Hubert or anyone from his family—would ever venture here and find him, except Thomas, to whom Roland had already sent a message.

Roland walked to a cove on the river where he and Thomas had once taken Thomas's sons fishing. He sat down on the shore and took out a notebook, quill, and ink from his satchel. He listed every person who might want Magali dead and who could have had the chance to poison her.

He was so engrossed in his writing that he did not hear Thomas approaching until he was almost upon him. He glanced up to see a look of surprise on his friend's face; Roland assumed it was because of the ragged garments he was wearing. He pointed toward a grove of trees where the fishermen could not see them, rose, and led Thomas to it.

"My God, Roland," Thomas whispered once they were alone, "I must tell you what has happened to the countess's daughter."

Roland bowed his head, fighting tears. "I already know."

Thomas grasped his shoulder, and they stood without speaking for some time.

Finally, Roland wiped his eyes and lifted his head, reminding himself that he could not waste a single moment. "Tell me exactly what you know and who else shares your knowledge," he bade Thomas, his voice clipped and urgent.

"She has disappeared," Thomas quickly replied. "Only Hubert, Bertine, Clare, Solange, and I know. Hubert has sworn us to secrecy and vows to punish us severely if we tell anyone else."

If only that were all that had happened to Magali.

"There is more," Roland said, looking around to make sure no one was nearby. "I trust you, Thomas, and know that you will tell no one else what I am about to tell you." As succinctly as he could, he laid out all that had happened since he was reunited with Magali.

When Roland was finished, Thomas kicked a rock from beneath his feet. "My God, I should never have invited you to Arles. Then Magali would have been spared this treachery."

Roland shook his head. "It is not your fault. I am the one who made the choice to come here. No matter what happens to Magali, I will never regret our love for one another. No one can ever take that away from me. Now, will you help me find out who did this? There is no time to waste."

"Of course. Will you dare show yourself to Hubert?"

"Not yet."

Thomas's eyes flashed with anger. "He must have had a hand in this foul deed! Surely it is his way of getting revenge on you."

"We do not know that for certain." Roland told Thomas about his promise to Magali that he would not assume any one person was guilty until he had gathered sufficient evidence. "Remember that above all else, we must find out what poison was used so we can find an antidote."

Thomas's face was grim. "It will be very difficult for me to work in Hubert's shop every day knowing what I now do, but I will hide my feelings as best I can. And when I am not working, I will do everything I can to help you."

"Thank you. Now, tell me what you know about Hubert and Bertine's visits to the château."

According to Thomas, Bertine had begun to stay at the château before the countess went to Toulouse for her wedding. The people of

Arles had been unsettled by that event, fearful that the Spider King would demand great sums of tax money. As for Hubert's visits to the château, Thomas revealed that around a week after Bertine went there, a messenger had come to Hubert's house with a note from her. She'd needed someone to buy more of Magali's remedy.

Roland grew alert. Maybe this was how the poison came to the château. "Who read the message?"

"Hubert."

"Did he read it aloud word for word?"

Thomas shook his head. "He read it silently and simply told us what it said before burning it."

Roland stared down at the grassy knoll where they stood. "I wonder if there was something else in the message that he kept to himself. Do you know who went to buy the remedy?"

"No, but I will try to find out from the apothecaries in Arles."

"Do not inquire yourself but send a beggar instead," Roland instructed his friend, remembering how Isaac and he exchanged messages . . . how he had just sent a message to the château. "A child would be best, for he will do just as you tell him and not reveal who sent him, especially if you threaten punishment." He paced back and forth. "Another question, Thomas. Do you know who delivered the remedy to the château?"

"Hubert," Thomas replied. "I know that because he left from the shop on a Saturday afternoon, right after the day's work was done, and did not return until Mass the next day."

The same day that Roland always visited the château . . . He frowned at the thought of Hubert taking his place, spending the night as he did, but he forced himself to return his attention to the important task at hand. "When did he return to the château?"

"Several weeks later," Thomas replied. Maybe the very night Roland had hidden behind the tower. "Bertine sent a message to Clare saying that she was very concerned about Magali's deep melancholia. Bertine wanted her sister and father to come to the château at once.

Clare begged Hubert to take her with him—she missed Bertine very much and wanted to comfort her—but he refused."

Roland continued pacing as he absorbed Thomas's observations and considered what to do next. He stopped suddenly and turned to Thomas. "You must be my eyes and ears. Observe Hubert and his family closely. But I just realized that there might be those other than Hubert who might wish harm upon Magali."

Thomas's brow wrinkled with confusion. "I don't understand."

"Perhaps someone in Arles wanted to punish Lady Beatrice for her alliance to the crown of France by poisoning her daughter."

"That is possible," Thomas said, "but how would that person have arranged for the poison to get to the château?"

"Maybe by bribing an apothecary?" Roland shrugged. "It is just an idea, but I am trying to remain open to all possibilities. Tomorrow I will go the cathedral square and secretly watch the preparations for the Easter feast. Lady Beatrice and her new husband may be there, as well as their servants and of course royal guards. I want to see how the townspeople receive them. Furthermore, one of Lady Beatrice's servants might reveal something important about what happened to Magali. I have often thought that servants know much more about the events that transpire in their households than they ever reveal."

"Maybe one of her servants was being bribed by the poisoner," Thomas said, nodding. "This method of solving puzzles as you and Magali have done gives one many possibilities of what the answer could be. We surgeons could use the same method to find out what is causing our patients' illnesses, could we not?"

Roland nodded but kept to himself the fact that a Jewish doctor had taught him the method. He trusted Thomas, but he could not risk endangering the doctor and his family, especially in this time of unrest.

As Thomas said farewell, he took in Roland's height. "When you are at the square tomorrow, remember to stoop so that no one notices how tall you are. It might cause them to recognize you."

Sweat trickled down Roland's face from beneath his wide-brimmed peasant hat. He yearned to take it off on this hot day, but the shadow it cast over his features seemed a necessary disguise.

Following Thomas's advice, he disguised his height as he stood in an alley amidst beggars seeking shade. From here, he could see the stable, the entrance to the inn, and the cathedral square. Servants clad in the royal colors of red and blue were tending to the horses and setting up trestle tables and benches for the Easter feast. One table was set on a raised platform—obviously for the countess and her husband and their retainers, a not very subtle way of reminding the people of Arles that the king of France was now their sovereign.

The noon bells rang and townspeople walked briskly across the square, going home for their midday meals. Roland closed his eyes and listened closely.

"By God's ear, I detest hearing them speak the French of the North," a man declared as he walked past Roland. "The king of France and his kinsmen cannot buy my loyalty by plying me with food and wine."

"Nor can they buy mine," his companion agreed. "But I will come to the feast to drink my fill nevertheless."

"I cannot stoop so low," the first man retorted.

"Do as you please. You will leave more wine for me."

Roland imagined the man shrugging as he spoke.

Their voices were drowned out by the rumbling of carriage wheels and horses' hooves clomping against the earth. Denis and another of the countess's servants whose name Roland could not remember were seated on the first cart. Many other carts followed, carrying barrels of wine, great wheels of cheeses, and loaves of bread. Royal servants came over to help unload these provisions for the Easter feast.

The smell of wood smoke filled the air, and Roland guessed that the meat would be roasted on spits throughout the day. His mouth watered at the thought of food—it had been many hours since he'd broken his fast, and he had eaten nothing more than coarse bread— but he forced himself to focus on the task at hand.

From his current position, he could not discern Denis's voice over the other men's. With his back pressed against the wall of a building, he made his way slowly toward the stable, where he would have a better view of Denis directing the servants. As he did so, careful to remain in the shadows of the eaves as he went, he reviewed in his mind the few things he knew about Denis.

The first day he'd laid eyes on the keeper of the husbandry was the morning that he and Isaac had returned Magali to her mother. Denis had appeared truly relieved that they had found her that day. He had also been relieved later that day when Magali's horse had been located and returned to the countess. And on the night that Magali had run away from the château, Denis had sounded truly concerned about her safety. According to Lady Beatrice, Denis had taught Magali how to ride and care for her horse. Other than those small bits of information, all Roland could recall about the man was that he was quiet and respectful, as was expected of servants. He supposed that all servants had to learn to be skilled actors who could never truly speak their minds to those they served. That would make it very difficult see beyond the façades of Lady Beatrice's servants and find out if any of them were involved in Magali's poisoning.

There came the sound of light footsteps as someone on the other side of the street passed by him. Drawing the hat farther down over his face, Roland risked a glance. It was a thin woman with light brown hair tucked into a coif—Solange, Hubert's servant. Roland grew very still. Other than Bertine and Hubert, she was the only other person from Arles who had been to the château. And she knew about Magali's disappearance . . . as did Denis, as surely did all of the servants at the château.

Solange strode purposefully toward the stable and called Denis's name.

Laughter rose up amongst the servants. "Girl, do you not see that he is busy?" a man with a thick northern accent joked. "He has no time for you to pleasure him."

Another burst of laughter and a volley of crude jokes ensued. Straining his ears, Roland heard footsteps. Denis and Solange stood across the street, a stone's throw away from Roland. He hunched over more, hoping that Denis would not recognize him in the afternoon light.

Denis and Solange—was it possible? Roland remembered Magali once telling him that Solange often went to the stables when Bertine and she were studying with their tutors. But Denis was much older than Solange; a widower, according to the housekeeper Alienor; and not a handsome man, though he had even features.

"Solange," Denis whispered.

"I knew you would be here," Solange murmured. "I miss you so much now that I do not go with Bertine to the château."

"As I miss you," Denis breathed. "One day, I pray you will be my wife."

They fell silent again, clothes rustling as they embraced. How Roland wanted to flee from this cruel reminder of what he might lose forever.

"How could Lady Marguerite simply disappear without a trace?" Denis asked forlornly.

Roland inched closer and strained to hear every word of their conversation. "My master commanded me not to breathe a word of her disappearance to anyone," Solange said in a low voice. "I wager that Lady Beatrice commanded her household to do the same."

"Yes, and most urgently," Denis said. "She and her husband have returned to the château and will preside at the feast here tomorrow."

Roland felt a wave of relief. He was certain Lady Beatrice would send him a message, and he could tell her about Magali at last. He would then have yet another person helping to find the poisoner— could it be someone in her household? That seemed unlikely, but they still needed to search in every possible direction for the person who had attempted to murder Magali.

"My dear one, you are close to Lady Marguerite in age," murmured Denis, who was now holding Solange's hands to his heart. "Her disappearance makes me worry that something untoward will happen to you too. I want to be with you day and night and protect you from anyone who would want to harm you."

"I, too, long for the day when we can be wed," Solange said softly. "But now I must return to Hubert's house."

She sighed. "It is very hard to serve Bertine. She weeps day and night. It makes me sad too. But then I put my thoughts on you . . ."

"I think of you all the time," Denis said.

They were quiet for a while, holding each other, before they finally parted.

Roland squeezed his eyes shut and imagined Magali enfolded in his arms. It did no good. She was a day's journey away.

Clenching his teeth, he barely contained himself from crying out in his sorrow.

All afternoon, the smell of roasting meat tortured Roland, especially when it mingled with the scent of bread baking in the public oven. He stood sweating in the shadows, mulling over the meager clues that he gleaned from Denis and Solange's whispered words. They proved nothing—the sadness that both servants felt at the troubles of their respective houses could well be feigned. The one thing he felt certain was true was the affection between the two servants.

It was well after dark when Thomas appeared and bade Roland in a whisper to follow him at a distance. They went to an alley nearby, where they were hidden from the lantern lights that illuminated the cathedral square. Thomas produced a cloth bundle containing a chicken leg, half a loaf of bread, and a crock of goat cheese. Roland devoured it all, then washed it down with a flask of wine Thomas offered him.

"A beggar boy helped me to find where the last batch of Magali's remedy was purchased," Thomas said in a low voice. "It was from the shop of a woman named Genevieve. According to the boy, the purchase was of a large crock, about the length of a woman's forearm and as wide as three of them."

"Are you certain it was the last batch purchased?"

"Yes. I went to the shop later in the day, pretending to need a remedy for a stomachache. When Genevieve's back was turned to mix the herbs, I looked at her account book and found an entry for March 11: St. John's wort and valerian in equal measure, with a half-measure of spearmint. Sold to Clare, the surgeon's wife. Twenty silver livres tournois. Am I right . . . is that the remedy you use for Magali's mania and melancholia?"

"Yes. Why did your wife purchase the herbs?"

"She often procures remedies for the family, especially ones for her mother's headaches. You see, of Hubert's three daughters, she is the one who most wanted to follow in his footsteps as a healer. But he would not allow her to do so."

Roland remembered the incident at the dinner table nearly a year ago—Clare pretending to be a battlefield healer in her son's game, her father reprimanding her. Roland had thought little of the exchange at the time, but after months with Magali, he now understood keenly how many women were prevented from doing work of their choice.

"The ledger contained no mention of a poison," Thomas said. "If it was put into the remedy, it must have been purchased separately and then added later. There are several apothecaries in Arles known to deal in poisons. The boy I hired could not discover which shop it might have been, for the owner of each one ordered him to leave as soon as he asked about a recent purchase of poison."

Roland's back straightened as an idea came to him. "Hubert is meticulous about his ledgers. Maybe we could discover if *he* made a purchase at an apothecary shop around March 11. If it was for a poison, I am certain he would have been clever enough to call it something harmless, but the date will give him away."

"It is a good idea," Thomas said, "but he keeps his ledger in his study. It is always locked when he is not working on his accounts or counting money, and only he has the keys."

"We must think of a way to enter, then," Roland said.

Thomas stroked his chin. "In the meantime, I have another idea. The watchmen are all posted around the cathedral square tonight to ensure that those who oppose the crown do not disrupt the preparations for the Easter feast. Let us try to see the apothecaries' account books with our own eyes."

All Roland wanted to do was to shed his heavy cloak and tumble into bed, where he could turn his thoughts to Magali. But no—with each task they completed, they got closer to knowing who was trying to take her life. "A good idea, Thomas," he said.

Roland and Thomas crept along in the shadows of the buildings they passed. When they came to the street that divided the Jewish quarters from the Christians, Roland paused. Candles were lit in only a few of the homes. According to Isaac, many of the Jews had fled to Aix-en-Provence and farther east, to Italy or the Turkish Empire. Roland's fear of losing Magali and the city of Arles' loss of skilled doctors, jewelers, and bankers . . . these two things would forever be linked in his mind.

He shook off his sadness and caught up with Thomas.

They came to the first apothecary shop known to sell poisons. The door was latched but one of the shutters was loose. As quietly as possible, they pried it open and crawled in through the window—one that, fortunately for them, was not covered in glass. As they had arranged in whispered voices on the walk here, Roland kept watch on the door that led to the apothecary's house while Thomas lit a candle and perused the account book.

After what seemed a very long while, he closed the book, shaking his head. They climbed back outside and secured the loose shutter as best they could before departing.

"Nothing on March 11 but other poisons were sold in that shop in March and April," Thomas whispered as they walked toward the next shop. "In fact, someone purchased belladona this very day."

"Surely the countess is prepared for someone trying to poison her or her husband," Roland said quietly, hoping that an unlucky servant would not die at the feast tomorrow when he or she sampled the food.

"Do you have *any* idea what kind of poison was given to Magali?" Thomas asked.

Say nothing about Isaac. Roland shook his head. "Only that it was given in small doses over a period of time to slowly weaken the body, thereby making the illness seem natural."

Deceit, as surely as the poison, had been the murder weapon . . . a tool used by a person working in the shadows. With each step toward the second apothecary shop, Roland imagined confronting Magali's poisoner and forcing the person to tell the truth.

This shop was sturdier than the first one, and its glass windows glinted in the light cast by an oil streetlamp. The door, of course, was locked.

Thomas pointed to the closest window to the door. "If we broke a small corner of it, do you think you could reach the latch?"

Roland held his arm up to the space. "I think so."

Using the hilt of his knife, Thomas shattered a corner of the window. Shards of glass crashed to the floor. Roland looked up and down the street, hoping the noises coming from the cathedral square were loud enough to mask the sound of breaking glass. No one on the street lit a candle or opened shutters. Thomas wrapped the cloth that had held Roland's supper around Roland's arm, and Roland reached carefully through the hole in the glass. Moving slowly, he found the latch and slid it open.

Slowly, they entered. There were enough embers glowing in the fire to light their way to the desk where the apothecary recorded the accounts. Gripping Thomas's knife, Roland kept his eyes on the inner door that led to the shopkeeper's living quarters. Behind him, he heard Thomas ruffling through the pages of the ledger.

The door to the back part of the house burst open. A man with a chiseled face gripped a knife, his eyes wide in the light of the glowing embers. "Begone, thieves," he growled, taking in Roland's ragged clothes. Roland shrank into the shadows. He had never met the man before, and the man did not seem to recognize him either.

Turning his attention to Thomas, the apothecary squinted. "Thomas, son-in-law of Hubert, what brings you to my shop like a thief in the night?"

Thomas did not answer and returned his gaze to the ledger: "The eleventh day of March. Angelica root, ground to powder," he read. "Sold to Hubert the Surgeon. Fifty silver livres tournois." He glared at the shopkeeper. "That is a very dear price to pay for angelica root, Jean. I believe there must be another substance you are disguising as that harmless herb."

Jean's eyes flickered from the ledger back to Thomas's face. "What concern is my ledger to you?"

"A private matter. Was the remedy a poison?"

"A private matter," Jean echoed, folding his arms against his chest. "Now pay me for the broken window or else I will have you thrown in jail for trespassing."

Keeping his eyes on Jean, Thomas slowly opened his purse. "Do you swear to me that you sold this remedy to my father-in-law?" he asked.

"Of course," the apothecary said. "Why would I lie?"

"You know very well. Someone could have paid you to lie. The person could even have promised you more money for not telling him about my interest in the sale."

"That person would be a fool to trust me," Jean retorted. "I could have made up any lie just to get the money."

"So, it is your custom to lie?" Thomas asked, scooping many coins from a small satchel. "Here's enough money to pay for the window—and to hold your tongue about me."

Jean snatched the money from Thomas. "Leave at once," he commanded, "and do not return unless you have come to purchase herbs."

"Or poison?" Thomas said softly as he and Roland took their leave.

20 AVRIL

Roland slammed his notebook shut. Hidden in his decrepit room, he had just recorded all of the new bits of knowledge he and Thomas had gathered, and they confirmed that the poisoner had to be Hubert. Roland fought an urge to go to his house and strangle the man with his own pillow as his meek wife watched. She might well applaud.

The sound of leaves rustling outside of his open window startled him, and then in his peripheral vision he saw something fly through his window and land with a thud on the straw-covered floor.

It was a sealed scroll tied to a stone. The seal was Thomas's.

Beatrice's heart pounded against her chest as she knelt before the Virgin's altar. She did not even pretend to pray as she waited for Roland to emerge from the alcove where she had instructed him to await her. Two royal guards and Catherine, her lady-in-waiting, stood just outside the door to Saint Trophime. She had only a few moments to speak with Roland and find out how Magali fared.

Every step she had taken to get here had been fraught with danger— the danger of revealing who Roland was to her husband, the danger of involving Isaac in any way, and the danger of unintentionally causing the unrest in the streets of Arles to worsen. She'd lost count of how many lies she'd told her husband about Magali's mysterious disappearance, including that tonight she was going to Saint Trophime to pray for Magali's safe return. Yet she had also answered many of Philippe's questions truthfully, with a tearful "I don't know."

At last, the bells marking the bedtime hour of Complines rang. Roland peered out from the alcove but remained mostly in the shadows. He understood as well as she did that no one could know he was here.

"Tell me quickly what has come to pass," Beatrice whispered.

When he was done, she rose to her feet. *Magali is alive . . . she is alive! Dear Virgin, may she heal! In this very moment, may the poison be draining from her body.*

She would start her journey this very night. No, she could not. She groaned softly. She had to attend the Easter feast tomorrow to placate the people of Arles.

She lit a candle and tried to settle her mind. But there were so many matters to consider, so many details to be arranged. Above all, what new lie would she tell Philippe about Magali in order to leave the feast early and go to her bedside?

"How I want to journey to Aix-en-Provence too," Roland said from his hiding place.

She could hear full well the longing in his voice and wanted to clasp his arm to bolster his spirits, but all she could do was murmur, "I will embrace her in your stead and tell her that I saw you." She glanced toward the door. "I must go now. Unfortunately I won't be able to go to Magali until after the first part of the Easter feast. At least while I am detained there I may notice details that will help us find the poisoner."

His face was in the shadows, but even so she could see the intensity of his gaze upon her.

"Before you leave, there is something very important that Magali wanted me to tell you," he said urgently. "She fears that we might kill the person who poisoned her with our own hands. She believes that we would suffer for the rest of our lives if we made the choice to avenge her death; she said she knows in her heart that we are not murderers. She wants our promises that we will not pursue revenge. I have already made that vow to her."

Lady Beatrice felt her blood turn cold. "Magali is guided by stories and is innocent to the ways of the world. I am not. This childish wish of hers comes from one of her beloved Greek myths. It is about Themis, the goddess of justice and the enemy of Nemesis, the goddess of retribution." She paused, struggling to control her trembling voice. "The only way I can make this promise to her is if I promise not to avenge this attempt on her life with my own hands. Instead, I will see to it that whoever did this foul deed will be put to a cruel death! Now, you must tell me whom you suspect."

Roland's face flushed, but he kept his mouth shut.

"Your silence informs me that you have someone in mind," she whispered harshly. "Tell me who it is, and I will choose Nemesis. I will summon assassins."

Roland clenched his jaw and shook his head. "Lady Beatrice, know that I too fight against my desire for vengeance. But as Isaac reminded me, the most important task at hand is to find the poison and give Magali its antidote!" His urgent voice shot like an arrow through the dark space between them. "I cannot tell you whom I suspect, but I can tell you that summoning assassins is no different from killing with one's own hands. Magali was right—even that choice would cause you great suffering."

His words echoed in the silence.

Her anger suddenly gone, Beatrice began to weep.

21 Avril

On Easter morning, as Beatrice dressed for Mass and the feast, her new husband, Philippe, came to her chamber, placed his hands on her shoulders, and kissed her on the neck. She forced herself to smile at his image in the looking glass, hoping she had succeeded in burying her fear about what would happen to Magali.

Thankfully, Philippe bore little resemblance to his vile uncle King Louis. His dark hair and beard were always trimmed and neat; his bearing was stately. At court, when he was drilling his men to prepare for inevitable war, he seemed entirely different to Beatrice: alert, like a falcon at the ready to swoop down on its prey, and formidable—a man rightfully entrusted to lead men into battle and win. But this Philippe remained hidden when they were alone together. She knew not whether to fear the fierce war captain within him. Yet hadn't she been concealing parts of herself from him too? Would he fear those hidden sides of her?

Philippe had never met Magali, had never had a child himself, and yet he had tried his best to soothe Beatrice ever since joining her at the château two days earlier. He offered her a clean handkerchief to dry her tears; when she merely pushed her food around her plate, he pleaded with her to eat. "God willing, you will find your daughter," he had reassured her just yesterday. "And if not, you will soon have a son to take her place; I pray that he will have no disease of the mind."

Her body had stiffened at these words, and although she'd said nothing, inside she'd screamed. *No child of mine, even one who is sound in mind and body, could ever, ever take Magali's place!*

Now, as they stood together at her mirror, she turned to him, cloaking all of the turbulent spirits coursing through her body—above all, shame that she must lie to him again. "I have tidings about Magali."

Magali's illness of the mind, she told Philippe, had driven her to run away from the château. A stranger had taken her to a hospital in Aix-en-Provence. In addition to her melancholia, she was suffering from a painful ulcer . . . She was in the care of Franciscan nuns who had informed Beatrice that her daughter might die.

Her story told, she let Philippe enfold her in his arms. "You must go to her—in disguise of course," he said, "but first you must appear briefly at the feast."

She could hold back her tears no longer. "The hours will be long until I can begin my journey, but yes, I know how important it is to appease the people of Arles."

As Philippe released her from his embrace, she could tell that his mind was far away. "If royal guards accompanied you, they would draw attention to you and your daughter and might cause unrest in Provence. I will arrange for some of your grooms to accompany you."

Philippe was right, of course. Still, she feared that soon he would take charge not just of such minor arrangements as sending grooms rather than royal guards but also of everything that she had once ruled.

In the church of Saint Trophime, as Père Etienne recited the Easter Mass, Beatrice thought only of Magali. Memories unfolded one after the other until Beatrice settled on one to fill her mind, even as her belly rumbled for food.

Magali was four years old, and Beatrice and she were dressing for Count Raymond's funeral in matching black satin robes and veils. "I don't like black," Magali whined. "I want to wear my blue dress."

Bright blue had been her father's favorite color and the predominant one he'd used in his stained-glass windows.

"After Mass, *mon chérie*," Beatrice soothed Magali.

The little girl stomped her foot. "No, now!"

It took the promise of a ride on her horse to convince her daughter to wait a few hours to wear the blue dress. Beatrice thought the matter was settled, but later, while she attended to matters concerning her late husband's estate and the servants were occupied in preparing for the funeral feast, she discovered that Magali had slipped away. No one could find her.

Silently bidding her confessor, Père Etienne, to continue the proceedings in her place, Beatrice abruptly left the table where her husband's relatives were arguing about the will that she and the priest had carefully drawn up for Raymond to sign. He'd never cared about his vast wealth and had been content to simply make stained-glass windows, play chess, ride with one of his favorites, and play imaginary games with his little daughter.

Beatrice and her servants frantically searched for Magali in all of her favorite places—the stable, gardens, and the upstairs room of the tower. At last they found her, next to a stream hidden in the olive groves. Beatrice had not considered this spot, for she did not know that Raymond had taken Magali there many times to look for frogs.

Magali had fashioned a necklace and wreath from flowers in the garden and was singing as she tossed the remaining flowers in the stream.

Beatrice held her tightly, too relieved to scold her. "You frightened us," she said. "Why did you leave?"

"To get flowers," the little girl replied, "for Papa and the angels to see me wearing. I gave the rest of the flowers to the frogs."

Beatrice returned her mind to the present and fixed her gaze on the Easter flowers: lilies and violets. *Please, Dear Virgin, may she live.*

She succumbed to fresh tears.

The Easter feast was unbearable but Beatrice forced herself to remain seated at her place on the dais, which was set higher than the other trestle tables. Philippe played the part of royal ambassador perfectly, conversing easily with the magistrate, Vincent, who was seated at their table, and the wealthy townsmen and men of the lesser guilds alike. As soon as a barrel of wine was emptied and a platter of roasted meat was devoured, others took their place. Philippe had employed a food taster at the main table, and nothing untoward was discovered; it seemed that no one had tried to poison them. Beatrice should have felt relieved, but her fear for Magali overshadowed everything else and took away her appetite.

Père Etienne was making his way through the crowd toward her, accompanied by Hubert, Bertine, and several women, probably his wife and daughters. Beatrice grew very still as she stared at the man's handsome face and light blue eyes, so like Bertine's. Could the surgeon be Magali's poisoner? She had allowed him to attend her daughter while she was in Toulouse, even after Roland warned her not to trust him. But Père Etienne's advice had prevailed in the end. Her confessor had persuaded her that his childhood friend was a skilled surgeon who could help care for Magali while Beatrice was away. Now, too late, she realized that the two men were from the oldest and wealthiest families in Arles. They could well be working together to punish her for aligning herself with the French crown. Why had she not considered this potential plot until now?

As they approached her, she dabbed at her nose with her handkerchief, struggling to conceal her rage. Rage not only at Hubert but also at her confessor. How could he, a man of God, be blind to the truth about his friend? Or, worse—could Etienne have conspired with Hubert? But the arrow of her rage pointed mostly at herself, for her blind obedience to Etienne since she was wed at thirteen.

Hubert bowed deeply to her. What a good actor he was as he played the part of a doctor who had not succeeded in healing a patient. "Milady, I have offered four Masses for your daughter's safe return," he said solemnly.

Liar! Beatrice's cheeks blazed but she managed to nod. "*Merci*, Monsieur Hubert."

She endured the introduction of his wife, Perronelle, a round, fair-skinned woman who said that she was praying to the Virgin every day for Magali's safety. Beatrice found herself believing this woman.

Bertine's two older sisters, Marie and Clare, were not pretty like Bertine. Marie, the older of the two, announced proudly that she and her husband were also praying for Magali's return.

The middle daughter, Clare, had her arm around Bertine, who was weeping profusely.

"I, too, pray for your daughter," Clare said, but her attention was fully on her younger sister.

Bertine released herself from Clare's embrace and fell to her knees before Beatrice. "Oh, milady," she cried. "I blame myself for Lady Marguerite's disappearance. I fell asleep the night she disappeared. I will never forgive myself, but I beg of you to forgive me!"

Thankfully, no one other than Philippe and Bertine's family were close by and they all knew of Magali's disappearance. Hubert came to his youngest daughter and gently lifted her to her feet. "*Ma chère* Bertine," he soothed. "I have assured you again and again that you are not to blame. You must forgive yourself."

He turned to Beatrice, his face softened with his love for his daughter. His daughter who did not suffer from a disease of the mind. How could a man with his own daughters try to take *her* daughter's life? Beatrice bowed her head, struggling to compose herself.

"Please, milady, accept my apologies for Bertine's outburst," Hubert said humbly. "I trust that you do not blame her."

It is you I blame! Beatrice barely kept those words to herself as she shook her head and turned from him to his youngest daughter. "Bertine, you were the best companion possible for my daughter. I cannot thank you enough for serving her as loyally as you did."

"We were more than companions," Bertine wept. "She was like unto my beloved sister . . . as surely as Clare is."

Marie frowned at being ignored by her youngest sister while Clare wrapped her arm around Bertine again.

"Let us go to church, dear sister, to pray again for Lady Marguerite's swift return," Clare said softly.

Twelve

"No priest can soften the heart of man like his wife can."
—FROM THIRTEENTH-CENTURY WRITER THOMAS CHOBHAM

Arles, France
21 AVRIL, 1479

Roland wriggled out of the grotto, and crept quietly to the front of the church, staying in the shadows along the side wall. He climbed the stairs to the choir loft and peered through the stained-glass window before him to the church square below, the rose petals tingeing his vision red. He frowned at the townspeople eating and dancing, without any thought that a poisoner—*Magali's* poisoner—might well be in their midst.

It came to him that Lady Beatrice's new husband had a purpose in providing a great quantity of victuals and music for the feast. He was lulling the people of Arles into accepting his governance.

Beneath this peaceful façade, buried in the heart of Magali's poisoner, was there the possibility of more violence?

He shifted his gaze to the food taster, dressed in the red and blue of France, who stood behind the royal couple and dutifully tasted each dish. Surely an opponent of the crown would not dare poison the king's nephew or his new wife at such a public occasion—but still Roland was relieved that the young man appeared to suffer no ill effects.

The mere presence of a food taster sent a warning but also a promise to the people of Arles. *The crown of France is strong and will provide for you. People of Arles, for your own good, you should submit to it. Even if you rebel against the crown, you cannot harm the royal family.* The choice to seat the magistrate and his family at the high table with Lady Beatrice, her husband, Philippe, and her confessor, Etienne, sent another subtle message: *The French king wants to show amity and good will toward the people of Arles.*

How different these messages would be if the French king ever found out that Magali had been poisoned. Lady Beatrice was right to withhold that fact from her husband. Roland turned his gaze on her. From this distance, it seemed that she was concealing her fear for Magali's life well behind her erect posture and brocade gown with shimmering gold filigree against a dark blue background.

Père Etienne and Vincent the Magistrate were conversing with Philippe. While publicly feigning approval of the French king's acquisition of Provence, had the two men secretly worked together to plan an attempt on Magali's life? And Giraud, who was also there but seemed hardly to be saying a word . . . was he part of the plot? Roland's thoughts intertwined into a tangle of speculations until in his mind, he heard Isaac's voice: *Observe carefully before making hasty conclusions.*

Roland scrutinized the table closest to the high table, where burghers of the city were seated—Hubert and his family first among them. Roland imagined bolting out of the church, running into the square, and shouting out his suspicion for all to hear.

Tonight, he vowed silently. Tonight, he would confront him.

He wrenched his eyes away from Hubert and sat down on the floor. Taking out his notebook, he read his notes but stopped at the word "angelica." From what he knew, it was a harmless herb used to treat headaches and toothaches, but it could well be that in the apothecary's ledger, "angelica" was a cypher for a poisonous substance. Had the poisoner used all of it or was there some left? If so, where was it hidden? Thomas and he would have to search for it in Hubert's shop, as well as look at his ledger to see if there was a record of the amount paid for the "angelica."

A sound from below startled him: the main door of the church opening. He crept back to the shadows and looked down to see Bertine and Clare walking toward the Virgin's altar. They knelt in front of it, Bertine weeping as her sister prayed the Ave Maria.

"I tried to help her," Bertine said through her tears. "I sent for Papa, and he tried too. And then she ran away when I was sleeping. If only I had stayed awake."

If only Roland had known about the poison. He felt a sudden kinship to Bertine—they had both tried to save Magali, but to no avail. Bertine seemed truly sad, but was her sentiment merely a ruse to conceal her guilt? He had never known her to be deceitful. Besides, what reason would she have to kill Magali . . . unless her father poisoned her mind?

Roland was reminded of what Thomas had told him about his father—how he had turned against him after Hubert convinced him that Thomas loved Hubert more than he loved him, his own flesh and blood.

Clare embraced Bertine, whispering words that Roland could not hear, and then the two women stood and turned to leave. He wished he could see their faces—perhaps their expressions would reveal some truth their whispering had not—but he could not risk craning his neck to catch a glimpse.

As Lady Beatrice, Philippe, and their entourage set out to the château, Roland saw Hubert talking to his oldest son-in-law. Even in the fading afternoon sun, he could discern the self-importance on Hubert's face as he and François spoke—probably discussing the success of his wine-selling, something the two men talked about every Sunday. As if Magali had not been poisoned.

Fury burning in his chest, Roland crept out of the church and made his way to the alley where Thomas and he had arranged to meet at sunset.

Thomas was not there.

Roland waited for what seemed like a long time before his friend finally joined him. When he did, Thomas was breathing heavily and Roland could see the angry set of his jaw in the fading light.

Thomas took something out of his satchel: a small pottery crock. Roland's shoulders tensed as his friend uncorked it. It contained a white powder. He took the crock and smelled the contents. There was no odor.

"What is it and where did you find it?" Roland asked, but even as he asked, he knew the answers.

"I do not know for certain, but I think it is a poison known as arsenic," Thomas said grimly. "I searched Hubert's shop while he was still at the feast and I found this on his shelf."

Roland let out a cry of anguish and Thomas clapped a hand over his mouth, silencing him.

"Wait here," the surgeon whispered. "When Hubert returns to his house, I will go there and show it to him. I will make him tell me what this substance is and whether there is an antidote."

Roland wrenched Thomas's hand off of his mouth. "I must go with you."

"No. I fear what you might do."

"You cannot stop me."

Roland strode toward the surgeon's house, Thomas close behind him.

Darkness was falling as they hid on the side of the house farthest from the oil lamp. Roland's body was taut, his heart beating fast. *You poisoned her . . . you poisoned her. You want to take her away from me forever.*

He heard footsteps coming from the direction of the square. Roland and Thomas shrank farther into the shadows.

"Papa, may I please go to Clare's house tonight?" Bertine asked, in a trembling voice.

"*Mais oui, ma chère*," her father replied. "Your sister always has a way of comforting you."

How dare he use such a tender voice! Roland took a step toward him, but Thomas grabbed his arm and held him back.

After Bertine, Clare, and her sons continued down the street, Roland and Thomas crept closer to the front of the house. They waited for what seemed a very long time standing near a partially opened shutter, just outside of the glow cast by sconces lit within.

"You can ignore this no longer!" Perronelle's voice burst out suddenly.

"You are distraught," Hubert said coldly. "Go to your chamber."

"I am not a child to be sent to bed," Perronelle retorted, "and you will hear what I have to say. When I bore you a third daughter, you promised me that she could devote her life to prayer in the order of Saint Francis. You broke your promise when you arranged for Bertine to marry your despicable Catalan journeyman—"

"Foolish woman!" Hubert interrupted. "You are too simple-minded to understand my reasons."

"Oh, I understand them all too well," Perronelle said bitterly. "You care only about your reputation and wealth, and now the strength of Arles against the crown of France—not about your promise to God."

"You are wrong," Hubert snapped. "I have given a great sum of money to the church of Saint Trophime."

"That is not the same as giving spiritual gifts."

"How is it different? My money was used to buy relics for the church."

Perronelle shook her head.

"You will never understand the difference between the earthly and spiritual realms, *mon mari*. But no matter, I will no longer try to instruct you. Even so, I have found a way to make you keep your promise about Bertine."

Hubert gave a derisive snort. "You are too late. I have listened to Père Etienne's counsel about how the burghers can continue to wield power even as the Spider King has caught us in his web. I have sealed an agreement with Vincent. Bertine will wed Giraud. Fear not, he is no longer as wild as he once was."

A sick feeling erupted in the pit of Roland's belly. Bertine's fate was his doing.

Perronelle let out a scornful laugh. "You think I am a fool, but I knew of this horrible plan of yours. Mark you, it will not come to pass after the letters I wrote to Vincent and Père Etienne. Solange just delivered them for me."

"What have you done?" Hubert cried.

"Ah, you will find out soon enough."

There was a resounding smack, followed by a sharp cry of pain.

"Tell me," Hubert demanded.

"For weeks, I have spared you from what your journeyman did to our daughter," Perronelle whimpered, "but I could keep it a secret no longer. Roland dishonored her, according to what Bertine told Clare. No one will marry her now unless you force him to do so. But your beloved journeyman has vanished; even you have given up hope of his return by now, have you not?"

Perronelle paused, and when she resumed her voice was triumphant. "I have also written to the Prioress of Saint Francis Abbey. In a moon, Bertine will become a novice there."

Who had crafted this lie? Fury blazed throughout Roland's body. He turned to Thomas. "I never—"

A piercing scream cut him short.

He and Thomas rushed to the door, which had not yet been barred for the night. Entering the anteroom, they saw Perronelle crouched on her knees, moaning, as blood spewed from her nose.

Hubert seized her by the shoulders and shook her violently. "I will kill you," he growled.

Without thinking, Roland strode into the room. "Let go of her!" he shouted.

Hubert released his grip on his wife's shoulders and stared darkly at Roland. Thomas helped her to her feet. Whimpering in pain, she pointed at Roland. "This is all your fault, vile Catalan!" she seethed as Thomas led her to the stairs.

Once again, after months of being away, Roland was trapped by Hubert's intense gaze. There was a fleeting glimpse of the hurt the man endured when his apprentice abandoned him. But his pale blue eyes quickly narrowed, full of a rage Roland had never before witnessed in him.

"You defiled my Bertine!" Hubert shouted. "You betrayed her . . . and me!"

His words drove deep into Roland's heart as Hubert continued his attack.

"Your lover the countess's daughter disappeared as a just punishment for your betrayal."

He is right. Roland stood there, unable to move, as Thomas stepped between them.

"A punishment that you yourself meted out, Hubert," Thomas growled. "You poisoned her to get revenge on Roland for breaking free from you."

Hubert's eyes widened. "What is this about poison?"

Roland darted forward and grabbed Hubert's shoulders. He had never stood so close to the surgeon before and was surprised to discover that he towered over him. "I found her. She has been poisoned—I have to find out what the poison is and how to counteract it." Roland's words tumbled out. "You must help me!"

Hubert glared at him, his nostrils flaring in defiance. "I don't have to do anything to help you," he shouted. "It is God who is punishing you for your betrayal, Roland, not me."

Still gripping Hubert by the shoulders, Roland groaned. *I did cause Magali to be poisoned.*

As these words echoed within Roland, Thomas thrust the open crock of the white powder toward the surgeon. "You can't deny that you tried to murder Magali with this poison. I found it on your shelf in the shop. Tell us what it is at once."

Hubert bent down to examine it. "I do not know what this is and I did not put it there."

Roland met Hubert's defiant gaze. *Liar! No longer will I let you control me!* "Admit the truth . . . you poisoned Magali," he shouted. He released Hubert's shoulders, about to grab him by the throat, but the surgeon quickly backed out of his reach. His defiance was now stripped away and the color had drained from his face. His forehead was creased with bewilderment.

"No . . . clearly someone is trying to blame—"

Hubert stopped abruptly, interrupted by a fit of coughing. Roland dropped his arms and stared at him—was this another of the man's ruses? Hubert reached for a cup from a side table and lifted it to his lips but before he could drink from it, he started choking. His face was purpling as he continued to choke and his cup crashed to the floor, shattering into pieces. Hubert wobbled, struggling to keep upright. Roland stood rooted in place as Thomas grabbed Hubert by the arm to keep him from falling. Thomas barely had time to lower him to the floor before he vomited profusely. Thomas quickly turned Hubert's head to the side so that the air could flow freely into his lungs.

Hubert's face had now become an even darker purple. Thomas hit him hard on the back, trying to dislodge whatever was blocking his windpipe. When that failed, Thomas reached inside Hubert's mouth and stuck a finger down his throat, continuing his frantic search for the blockage.

Never before had Roland done nothing to help another doctor stave off a person's death. But in this moment he could only stare at Hubert's horribly discolored face and silently hurl the surgeon's words back at him: *This is your just punishment for trying to murder Magali.*

Though it was a hot summer day, he suddenly felt cold. He imagined Magali speaking urgently to him—*Roland! Help them!*

He wasn't strangling Hubert, but neither was he helping Thomas. That was negligence, very close to murder itself, and hardly different from hiring assassins. He had promised her not to take the path of revenge. *You are not a murderer*, Magali's voice insisted. *Do something!*

At once, he sprang to action. While Thomas continued trying to restore Hubert's breath, Roland stooped down and pressed a finger to the surgeon's throat. No heartbeat. "It's his heart too, Thomas!" he shouted. "Help me roll him onto his back."

Roland had no knowledge of how to make a person's heart resume beating. Desperate to take some action, he knelt beside Hubert and, leaning over him, pushed against his chest with both hands. Still no heartbeat. Roland repeated this action several times but to no avail. Thomas and he rolled Hubert back on his side and struck him on his back, trying in vain to unblock his windpipe. Nothing spewed out.

Once Hubert was on his back again, Roland pressed his hands against Hubert's chest several times again. No heartbeat.

"It's no use," Thomas said and rose to his feet.

But Roland kept pushing against Hubert's chest while Thomas went to the surgeon's shop. He soon returned with a looking glass, which he held to Hubert's nose and mouth. There was no mist of breath on its surface.

Roland felt once again for a heartbeat.

Nothing. Hubert was dead.

22 AVRIL

It was still dark when Roland rose from his pallet and splashed water on his face. He had not slept at all, and the water helped revive him a little. It was Easter Monday—an hour or so until the apothecary shops would be open.

There was a knock on the door. It was Thomas, looking just as fatigued as Roland, carrying a loaf of bread and a flask. Hubert's keys jangled from his belt. "We will look for the white powder in Hubert's warehouse," he said, "but then I must go to take his place at the surgery shop."

Roland nodded. "I can walk the streets freely now, since Perronelle will surely spread the word that I have returned."

Thomas's expression was grim. "She probably rejoices that her husband is dead. I too should rejoice, but I do not. I can't help but wonder if by imagining murdering Hubert, I had a hand in his death."

Roland stared wide-eyed at Thomas. Hubert had choked and his face had purpled. This is exactly what would have happened if Thomas or he had strangled him. His heartbeat quickened at this strange similarity.

"No," he said at last, "you did everything you could to save him. At first I did nothing at all."

He told Thomas everything that passed through his mind in Hubert's great room, including hearing Magali's voice from within.

Thomas smiled. "Your love for her saved you from the guilt that surely would have weighed on you for the rest of your days."

"Yes."

They ate quickly and drank cool water that soothed Roland's parched throat before setting out for the warehouse. In the gray light of dawn, they talked about the cause of Hubert's death. Thomas thought it was natural, not the result of poison. After all, Hubert's face had been swollen and he had been having similar fits, though much less severe, for many months. And he had refused to take a remedy for dropsy as he worked tirelessly to heal the droves of patients who came to his shop for his new remedies.

Thomas opened the warehouse door with a key from Hubert's key ring. Inside, they discovered that it was filled with crocks and satchels, all neatly arranged on shelves with parchment labels written in Hubert's cramped script. Clearly, he had been buying copious supplies to make the remedies that Roland sent him.

Roland and Thomas divided the room into two sections, reading the labels and opening any crocks that looked like the one they'd found in Hubert's shop. None were for "angelica" or arsenic or whatever the white powder truly was; nor was there any St. John's wort and valerian, the two herbs that Isaac advised for Magali.

In the months after Roland stopped his apprenticeship, Hubert had been busy working to build his precious reputation. All for naught. Something had probably failed in his own health, in his own body, to cause his death. To Roland's surprise, he felt a momentary pity for the man, but the feeling quickly vanished.

"Even though we find no evidence here, maybe Hubert was indeed the poisoner," Thomas said as they finished their search.

"I am not certain of that." Roland opened his satchel and clasped the crock of the powdery substance. "But the most important task is to find out what this is."

"True, but tell me why you believe Hubert might not be the poisoner."

"His last words . . . He started to say that someone else was trying to make him seem guilty. And something else seems amiss. The white powder was found on Hubert's shelf in his shop, but Jean the apothecary's ledger showed that he had purchased angelica, not arsenic. If the herb recorded there was a lie, could there be other lies in Jean's records?"

"Maybe." Thomas fell silent for a moment. "Who would be so angry at Hubert as to make him seem guilty for their treachery?" he mused.

They reached the warehouse door and stepped outside. It was early morning and already women were carrying long loaves of bread home for their families to break their fast.

Thomas's eyes were fixed on the road ahead. "It could be that

Perronelle wanted to put the blame on Hubert; after all, she opposed several of Hubert's decisions. She did not want Bertine to become Magali's companion or your betrothed. Furthermore, she vehemently opposed the joining of Provence to the French kingdom. And we saw with our own eyes her anger toward her husband."

"Very well, I will add her name to our list."

"I would add Clare's too," Thomas said quietly.

Roland glanced at his friend in surprise. "Why?"

"She purchased Magali's remedy, and she feels bitter toward her father. But other than that, I do not know. It is just a feeling. She keeps many things in her heart."

Or she keeps many secrets from Thomas because she suspects he is unfaithful to her. But Roland kept this thought to himself. He bade Thomas farewell when they reached the street down which Hubert's shop lay in one direction, and the apothecaries in the other.

Wishing to be alone with his thoughts, Roland kept to the shadows of houses and shops and went over the list of names in his mind's eye as he walked: Perronelle, Clare, Hubert, Vincent, Giraud, Solange, and Bertine. Maybe even Père Etienne. The men might all have conspired together. Maybe the women, or some of the women, were also working together. Or was Solange working on Hubert's or all of the men's behalf?

Stop making conjectures! As Roland hurried to the apothecary shop, which was much farther away than he remembered, he imagined Magali in this very moment. Nearly a week had passed since he'd last seen her . . . her mother was surely at her side by now. How was Magali faring? Was the broth working to purify the poison from her blood? Lady Beatrice had promised to send word about her daughter as soon as possible, but the message would likely not reach him until tomorrow.

A memory returned to him. After she found the sketch of the

hanged murderer among his drawings, Magali and he had talked about how a person could be driven to take the life of another.

"I think that anyone could reach that brink of choosing whether or not to commit murder," she'd said thoughtfully. "Even one of us. I would want to be with you to face that dark part of myself."

"And I would want to be with you," he'd said with confidence then. "If we were apart, I would come to your aid, and I know that you would do likewise."

"I would indeed."

Last night, had she kept her promise? No, it was simply his imagination. She was a day's journey away, and very ill. He himself, through his love for her, had been the one to fight against his urge to strangle Hubert. But if he discovered that someone else was Magali's poisoner, he would have to face this dark part of himself again.

At last, he reached the apothecary's shop. Jean, who was seated at his worktable, scowled at him and took his time making a fertility charm for a waif of a woman with a blackened eye.

Roland barely restrained his anger at the man who had hurt her. "I am a doctor and can make you a poultice for your eye," he said gently, remembering his mother's remedy for a black eye.

The woman gave him a grateful look and nodded. After paying the disgruntled apothecary for several herbs, including betony, Roland set to work making the poultice. As he pressed it against the woman's eye, the warm feeling of helping a patient to heal washed over him again, allowing his fear for Magali's life to briefly recede.

After the woman left the shop, clutching the fertility charm and more supplies for making the poultice, Jean narrowed his eyes at Roland. "Leave at once. I have nothing to add to what I already told you."

Roland opened a pouch tied to his belt and showed Jean a handful of gold and silver coins. "I will pay you well if you answer my questions."

Jean hesitated, then approached. "How much will you give me?"

"Fifty livres tournois."

Jean licked his lips as if anticipating a savory meal. "Do you promise not to involve me any further after I answer your questions?"

"Yes," Roland replied. "As long as you promise never to speak of my visit to your shop."

"Of course." Jean bobbed his head. "What do you want to know?"

"In your ledger, you wrote that Hubert the surgeon purchased angelica root. Is that true?"

Jean stared at the coins. "No."

Roland thrust the crock of arsenic close to the apothecary's face. "Did you sell this white powder that day?"

Jean nodded. "It is arsenic, not angelica. I was paid a generous sum of money to mislabel it in my ledger and lie to anyone who asked about it. Though not so generous as the amount you are offering," he added hastily.

Roland leaned closer to the man's swarthy face. "And who was the person who bought it? Was it truly Hubert, as you wrote in your ledger?"

Jean kept his gaze down as he used his sleeve to wipe beads of sweat from his face.

"Tell me who it was," Roland demanded.

Jean glanced up, his gaze fearful. "I cannot or great harm will befall me."

"Tell me the truth." Roland's voice shook as he grabbed the man's arm.

"I cannot!"

"Answer me this, then," Roland pressed. "Was this person connected to Hubert in some way—were they either a family member or a servant?"

Jean hesitated and shifted his gaze from the floor to Roland, who pulled out another handful of coins from the bag.

"It wasn't Hubert," the apothecary admitted as he took the money.

"Then which was it, a servant or a family member?" Roland drew closer to the cowering man.

"A servant."

Not Hubert himself, then—but this servant may well have been working for him.

Try as Roland did in the ensuing minutes, he could not extract Solange's name or the name of another servant from Jean. Nor would the man reveal whether he knew the identity of the person who'd sent the servant.

"What is the remedy for arsenic poisoning?" Roland asked.

"I don't sell it," Jean sneered. "You will have to go to Genevieve's shop."

Before leaving, Roland gave the disgusting man a few more coins. "Tell no one of my visit," he warned again, "or I will be the one to do you great harm."

Roland clutched the two satchels of remedies he'd purchased from Genevieve. One contained a vial of a theriac made of many ingredients, including a venomous snake's flesh, poppy juice, honey, cinnamon, and wine. The apothecary had warned Roland that sometimes the theriac caused the symptoms of the poison to worsen and at other times the theriac seemed to have no effect at all, but it was the best chance Magali would have at surviving the arsenic. The other satchel contained a crock of river clay. The patient was to ingest the clay in the hopes that the arsenic would bind to it.

"I do not know if eating the clay is more effective than taking the theriac," Genevieve admitted, "because all of my customers choose the theriac. But when I was a child, there was an apothecary in Arles who sold clay as a remedy for poison. I never witnessed the effect of the clay, but it seems worth trying. I do not think it can hurt."

It was still early in the day; he could reach Aix-en-Provence by late tonight. He would give Magali the clay—he did not want to risk causing her further harm by giving her the theriac. He hurried toward the stable, where he could secure a carriage.

It was now mid-morning and the streets were crowded with purveyors of food, beggars, and dogs devouring any scraps of food they could find.

Roland encountered a number of former patients on his way to the stable who were eager to greet him and curious to hear the details of Hubert's death.

"It is strange that the surgeons' guild master died on Easter Sunday," one woman remarked. "His remedies have caused many of us to feel as if we too have risen from the dead."

"But Hubert himself will never rise from the dead," another woman wailed. "He died on the same day that the countess and her new husband tried to win our favor with their Easter feast. They cannot fool us . . . we all know the king of France will soon rule over Provence and force us to pay high taxes. God is surely punishing our city. I will pray at the Virgin's altar this very day."

"Roland!" a man called to him from across the street as he attempted to continue onward.

It was a boat captain whose leg Roland had helped save nearly a year ago. Roland greeted the young man, pleased to see that he walked with only a slight limp.

"Thomas told me that you no longer lived in Arles," the captain said.

"Yes, I have returned to the university—I was sorry to hear of Hubert's death. He taught me much about the practice of surgery." Roland replied with the first words that came to his mind—but how did he truly feel about Hubert's demise? He was still too stunned to grasp the finality of it. And still he did not know for certain if the surgeon had poisoned Magali.

"And you served him well as an apprentice," the captain said, putting a hand on his injured leg. "I will never forget the day you helped him set my bones."

"Your leg looks like it has healed well."

The captain grinned broadly. "Yes—thanks to you and Hubert, I can play games of chase with my children."

Magali, I will come to you as soon as I can, he told her silently as soon as he bade farewell to the captain and hurried toward the stable. But he was delayed further as the news of his return spread through the streets. Some of his former patients even asked him to come to their homes and soothe a teething baby or tend to a child with a rash. He quickly advised them without asking for payment.

Most of the patients also tried to persuade him to return to Hubert's shop. "He has taught the other surgeons about many new remedies," one man proclaimed. "You will learn much more in his shop than you will at the university. Many years ago, I nearly died at the hands of a doctor who attended the university in Paris."

How many times had Roland heard similar stories from his patients? With difficulty, he contained his anger. "One day, I hope that doctors will learn only effective remedies at the universities," he said, "but now I must go."

At last, Roland reached the stable. He was securing a carriage and driver when Thomas called to him from across the street.

Roland paid the ostler and told him he would return shortly. What had happened to Thomas in the hour since he last saw his friend? His face was drawn, his lips pressed together in a tight line.

The surgeon motioned for Roland to follow him to a deserted alley.

"What has happened?" Roland whispered. "I have never seen you look so distraught."

"I don't really know," Thomas said. "I am used to tending ailments or wounds that I can see with my own eyes, not invisible ones such as diseases of the spirit. But, Roland, I swear to you that there is some hidden disturbance in Hubert's household, maybe even his ghost. I fear that there will be another attempt to take someone's life."

Roland stared open-mouthed at Thomas, who usually scoffed at superstitions.

"I beg of you," Thomas pleaded, "stay in Arles but one or two more days and help me discover the source of my dread once and for all. Otherwise, I fear yet another innocent person will lose their life. Do you not remember that someone in Arles purchased the deadly belladona only a few days ago?"

Roland had forgotten all about that detail; a queasy feeling came over him as he watched the ostler saddling a horse. "But Thomas, I have to leave forthwith and take the remedy to Magali!"

Thomas clutched his arm. "Then send the remedy ahead of you, along with the instructions about how to give it to Magali! Tell the countess that you yourself will come very soon. But I beg of you, help me to stop this person from attempting to kill someone else. I believe that by working together, we can act before it is too late."

Roland shifted his gaze to Thomas's distraught face. *Magali, what should I do?*

He imagined her looking intently into his eyes and saying in a somber voice, "If someone were harmed, you would regret not trying to stop that for the rest of your days."

She was right. Roland gave Thomas a grim nod. "As you have helped me, I will help you."

That very morning, while Roland was on the street of apothecaries, Thomas had made an important discovery in Hubert's ledger. There was only a record of him paying for the valerian and St. John's wort on March 11. The purchase was from Genevieve's shop, at the same cost that she'd recorded in her ledger. There were no other expenses listed for that day or for the days before or after the eleventh. What Thomas had found was not proof of Hubert's innocence, but it did support their guess that Hubert had not been the one to purchase or mix the poison into Magali's remedy.

Thomas would return the arsenic to its original place, on a shelf in a wooden cabinet with a glass window. If Hubert was not the person who'd killed Magali, the poisoner might need it to poison someone else. Who was this person? Had the same person bought the poison and brought it to Hubert's shop? And who had mixed it with Magali's remedy?

Hidden in the alley, Roland watched the carriage carrying Genevieve's remedy set out toward Aix-en-Provence and considered these questions.

If only there was a way to know by some invisible mark made by the guilty person's hand as he or she grasped the crock and removed it from its place.

23 Avril

It had been eight days since Roland had seen Magali. Lady Beatrice had still not sent word of how she fared, and Roland hoped desperately that this was a good sign.

As the bells of Saint Trophime announced Hubert's funeral Mass, Roland entered the chilly nave, feeling as a soldier must feel as he readied himself for battle.

A crowd of people, everyone dressed in black, was already gathered, and many of them showed surprise when they registered Roland's presence. Others, mostly surgeons and bookshop owners, smiled in greeting. Vincent and Giraud simply avoided looking at him.

Thomas and Roland joined Hubert's family members in their accustomed place, and as Roland knelt at the end of the row, he heard someone gasp. Pretending not to notice, he nodded a cursory greeting to them all.

Throughout the Mass, he was aware that several family members were stealing glances at him. He did not blame them for being curious or angry. Not only had he lied about his intention to marry Bertine, but also, and even worse, they believed he had taken her virginity.

When the Mass ended, Père Etienne led the way to the cemetery, followed by pallbearers carrying Hubert's casket. Roland trailed behind the family, allowing them privacy. Still, he doubted that anyone in the family—other than Bertine and the grandchildren—truly mourned his passing.

Bertine's black clothes and black handkerchief that she used to wipe away her tears brought out the fairness of her skin. Roland wondered if she knew of her father's plan to betroth her to Giraud.

As the guests made their way to the post-burial feast, François approached Roland.

"You are not welcome at our table," he said curtly. "Tell me, why have you suddenly returned to Arles? Surely you are not here simply to attend my father-in-law's funeral."

The previous day, when Roland and Thomas were planning what they would say at the funeral, Thomas had shared that Marie's husband, François, was quickly assuming Hubert's place as the head of the family. Roland had prepared himself for this conversation.

"For several reasons," Roland said. "First, I need to ask Bertine to forgive me for lying to her about my intentions to wed her—"

"But you *must* wed her," François insisted, "now that you have taken her virginity. Surely that is why you are here: to make the honorable choice."

"No, on both counts. I did not harm her, nor do I intend to wed her."

"You are lying!" the vintner seethed, struggling to keep his voice low.

Roland drew himself to his full height and crossed his arms against his chest. "I am not. Have a midwife examine Bertine. Her mother and sisters can be witnesses." But as soon as the words left his lips, he realized what the consequences of this would be. If word spread that Bertine was a virgin, she would likely be forced to marry Giraud.

François tilted his head in confusion. "So, you returned to Arles simply to apologize to my sister-in-law?"

"I am also here to discover a person who attempted the sin of murder."

"What?" François's small eyes appeared to double in size.

"The countess's daughter has been found," Roland said, careful to conceal his worry about her. "She has been poisoned and is very weak. I believe that the person who committed this foul deed lives in Arles. Furthermore, this person may be someone in Hubert's family or one of his servants. There could also be more than one person conspiring to harm the countess's daughter."

François snorted with contempt. "This is a foolish accusation."

"Believe whatever you like," Roland said mildly. "What I need from you is your cooperation as I observe Hubert's household and gather evidence. I also need for you to keep our conversation to yourself."

"I owe you nothing! You have brought only trouble to my wife's family." François abruptly turned away.

"If you do not do as I ask you," Roland said quietly but firmly to his back, "I will inform the countess and she will punish you severely. You see, I am here on her behalf."

François spun around, his mouth agape. "Why has she engaged *you*? You have neither noble nor Provençal blood."

"I served as a doctor to her daughter."

François stared at Roland as he tried to absorb these tidings. "Am I on your list of the people who may have done this terrible deed?" he asked in a wavering voice. "Is my wife?"

"Not given what I know so far."

"Thank God," François breathed out. His face suddenly grew pale. "The person responsible for Lady Marguerite's murder will probably be executed in this very place."

Roland shuddered as he imagined the poisoner hanging from a noose, the head lolling forward, right in this square. "You have no choice but to let me proceed," he said firmly.

"Very well," the vintner said, "as long as you, too, keep your work as discreet as possible."

"I will. You must impress upon your family that no word of this deed is ever to be spread to anyone else. That would cause the French king to punish the people of Arles severely."

"*D'accord*," François said in a resigned voice. "You may join us at our table."

"Roland, I will need your help to learn about the remedies that you collected for Hubert and to sort through the supplies he stored in his warehouse."

Hubert's funeral feast was held under tents in the church square. Thomas had been doing his best to fill the awkward silence at the table where Hubert's family sat, and Roland had been doing his best to help him.

"Certainly," he said quickly. "I hear that more and more people flock to his surgery shop because of his new treatments. It seems that he has become more than a surgeon."

"Yes, that can surely be said of him."

The two men continued the shallow conversation as long as possible, making certain everyone understood that the remedies Roland had discovered had helped to increase Hubert's fame and wealth—and that even after his death, Roland remained loyal to him.

Other than the children, no one at the table had much appetite for the savory meats and pies served at the feast. Roland was glad that he was not seated close to Bertine. The few glimpses he'd gotten of her had revealed that she was more hurt than angry at him. Her mother, on the other hand, had veritable daggers in her eyes pointed directly at him, as did Clare. And at the magistrate's table, Giraud was swilling wine and casting ominous glances in Roland's direction whenever his parents' attention was elsewhere. Maybe the dreadful presence that Thomas sensed was anger—at Roland, the nobility of Provence, and the French king.

Roland was relieved to see François at last rising from his seat to lead his family home.

Roland walked over to him, ignoring the cold stares of the other family members. "With your permission, sir, I wish to visit Hubert's youngest daughter tomorrow afternoon."

"For what purpose?" François asked, playing the part of the suspicious head of the family perfectly.

"I wish to offer her my condolences and my apology."

"Very well," François said. "You may visit her in the great room with the family present."

"As you wish," Roland said with another deep bow. Again, he was grateful that Bertine did not look at him.

24 Avril

It was strange to break his fast at Thomas's house—Roland had never before been inside. His friend's sons had grown quite a bit since Roland had last seen them, and as always wanted to hear his stories about Barcelona and the sea. Clare, however, greeted him coldly, making no effort to hide her dislike of him.

He did not blame her—he still felt ashamed of the lie he had told Bertine.

As they ate, someone knocked on the door. It was Solange, huddled in a dripping wet shawl—scant protection from the heavy rain beating against the windowpanes. Ah, two people on his list of possible poisoners in the same room. Roland grew very alert, casting furtive glances at Clare and Solange and straining to hear every word of their exchange.

"Come, warm yourself by the fire," Clare said briskly.

The girl entered with a grateful smile. "Madame Perronelle bid me to fetch you, Madame Clare," she said, spreading her hands close to the blaze. "She wants your help in sorting through Monsieur Hubert's possessions to decide what to keep in the family and what to give to the poor."

"I will walk there with you after we've finished eating," Clare replied. "Maybe the rain will have lessened by then."

She turned to her boys, who were devouring bread and honey, and smiled. "Before you go to school, wipe that honey off of your faces," she said as she combed the younger one's fair hair.

"Yes, Mama," the older boy, Nicholas, replied dutifully.

"And after school, walk to Grandmama's house. We will have supper with her and spend the night."

"Roland and I will join you there in the late afternoon, *ma femme*," Thomas said.

She frowned but said nothing.

After Solange and Thomas's family left, Thomas and Roland sat in front of the fire. It stirred Roland's memories of sitting with Magali in front of the hearth on rainy days, reading books or playing chess. With difficulty, he shifted his attention to the question Thomas had just asked him.

"No, I don't know what you sensed in Hubert's great room two days ago, other than the anger everyone feels about my despicable treatment of Bertine," Roland replied. "Or maybe you were merely overwrought by Hubert's death."

"No, I truly felt something very disturbing." Thomas sighed as he rose to bank the fire. "How I prefer healing the body to trying to figure out what is in people's minds, including my own. Tell me, did you notice anything amiss as we broke our fast?"

"Not really. Your boys seem sad at their grandfather's passing. I did notice something unspoken pass between Clare and Solange."

Thomas nodded. "Clare taught Solange how to serve in Hubert's household when the girl was only eleven. Ever since, Solange has wanted to please Clare; she has always been quick to do her bidding."

"I have also noticed that Solange has more freedom than the women of Hubert's family," Roland said as they donned their cloaks. "She goes alone on many errands, including to meet Denis at the stable when he journeys to Arles. Solange also accompanied Bertine to the château. I'd wager she knows many things about the inner workings of both households."

"Yes. We will need to find a way to speak alone with her." Thomas stared into the fire. "Now, tell me what you noticed about Clare this morning."

"She is quite angry with me, but she has every right to be." Roland shrugged. "And unlike her boys, she does not seem upset by her father's death." He looked over at Thomas. "Do you think she knows about Lucienne?" He blurted out the question before thinking.

Thomas winced. "I don't know. She has never been to Montpellier, but her wit is very sharp, so she may suspect." His lips pressed together in a tight line. "It has been very difficult not seeing Lucienne these past few months, but now that Hubert is dead, it will be easier to annul my marriage."

It has been very difficult not seeing Magali these last eight days—I can't imagine what many months would feel like, Roland thought. Aloud, he said, "I must risk being bold today. It is the only way to discover who tried to kill Magali."

"*We* must be bold," Thomas corrected him. "Seeing that the two of us are working together may cause the guilty person to act hastily and make a mistake."

"Let us hope for that. Let us hope that I may go to Magali tomorrow."

As they set out for the surgery shop, the rain stopped and a chilly wind pushed gray clouds across the sky.

"Do we confront Solange this morning or wait until after you apologize to Bertine?" Thomas asked quietly.

"I think we should wait so that no one suspects our true purpose."

"*D'accord.*"

They reached the surgery shop where they found a long line of patients, most of them unfamiliar to Roland, waiting to be admitted. It seemed that word of Hubert's wondrous remedies had spread to nearby towns.

"Thank Saint Peter you are both here," one of the other surgeons, Gregoire, greeted them as he tied his apron.

"Will you pay us on Saturday afternoon as Hubert always did?" another surgeon whose name Roland did not remember called from across the room.

"Yes, of course," Thomas replied. "And the surgeons' guild will meet two evenings hence to choose a new guild master."

"No doubt it will be you," Gregoire said with a grin that made him appear boyish despite his wrinkled face.

Thomas said nothing as he strode to his worktable. For the first time, Roland considered whether or not his friend would want to take Hubert's place.

How strange it was to return to the very spot where he had once worked by Hubert's side, where he had taken in every word of his master's teachings. It was even stranger to think that the man was gone forever.

Tears sprang to Roland's eyes. How innocent he had been . . . a boy who basked in the care and attention of a man who treated him as a father would, as his own father should have treated him. And yet at the same time, even from the beginning, there had been another aspect to Hubert, confusing and unsettling. Had the man simply been making use of Roland to further his own plans, entrapping his apprentice in a web that was strong and delicate at the same time?

He would never know for sure.

As he set out remedies and surgical tools for his morning work, he returned to the question of who had poisoned Magali. Both the remedy and the arsenic had been purchased on March 11. Clare had bought the remedy. Where had she stored it, or to whom had she given it when she returned? Similarly, where had Solange or another servant taken the arsenic, or to whom had this servant given it? And where and when had the two purchases been mixed together?

Something else puzzled Roland. If Hubert had indeed arranged for a servant to purchase the arsenic on his behalf, it seemed that the warehouse would be a more secret place to store it than his shop. Yet Thomas and he had searched the warehouse thoroughly and found no trace of it.

It was likely, then, that someone other than Hubert was Magali's poisoner, but that person had intended to make him appear guilty.

"Hubert's keys . . . to whom did he entrust them?" Roland asked when Thomas came to see if he was ready to take a patient.

"As far as I know, only me—unless, of course, someone 'borrowed' them when he was asleep." Thomas clapped Roland on the back. "We are getting closer to discovering the truth."

"Yes," Roland agreed, feeling more hopeful than ever before. If only he could feel as hopeful about Magali's recovery.

Soon every surgeon was hard at work pulling out rotten teeth, stitching up cuts, and lancing boils. Roland was grateful when his first patient, a young fishmonger with a deep cut in his arm, presented himself.

That morning, everyone whom Roland cared for was either relieved to see that he had returned or had heard of his reputation as Hubert's journeyman and treated him with respect. For Roland's part, just as when he made the poultice for the woman with a black eye, the familiar routine of attending his patients settled him and took his mind away from Magali and the terrible discovery Thomas and he might soon make.

In the fleeting moments when the surgery table was unoccupied, Roland searched Hubert's area. He saw the arsenic in a glass-paned cabinet, so innocent-looking in its small pottery crock.

After searching the shelves and chests, Roland found no St. John's wort and valerian mixture. But there was a simple explanation for that: Hubert had brought the mixture to the château. He may or may not have known that someone had added arsenic to it.

In the late morning, Roland tended to a woman clutching her chest and moaning. After asking her about when she first noticed the pain, he gave her a remedy with a small amount of foxglove—the same remedy that could have saved Hubert's life—then covered her with a blanket and bade her to rest while the medicine took effect.

His mind returned to the arsenic. Maybe it had been mixed into the valerian and St. John's wort mixture on this very table. If so, the person who did it would have to have done it at a time when no one was in the shop, and therefore would have had to "borrow" Hubert's key.

The careful steps the murderer had taken to execute their plan were becoming clearer, but Roland still did not know why they had done it—or who they were.

Thirteen

> "See how these men accuse you of so many vices in everything. Make liars of them all by showing forth your virtue, and prove their attacks false by acting well."
> —ADVICE FOR WOMEN FROM FIFTEENTH-CENTURY WRITER CHRISTINE DE PIZAN'S *BOOK OF THE CITY OF LADIES*

Arles, France
24 AVRIL, 1479

As soon as Roland entered Hubert's great room, he sensed the presence of what Thomas had been trying to describe. The children were not there, but everyone else in Hubert's family, except for Bertine, glared at him. And this time it wasn't just their anger he felt; there *was* something else, something cold and dreadful that he could not name. And he could not pin it to any one person present. He fought the urge to flee from whatever it was and go at once to Magali's bedside.

She was still alive! Lady Beatrice's message had arrived not an hour ago. Very weak but alive. For two days now, she had been taking the remedy. *May the poison be binding to the clay!*

François rose to his feet. "Tell us why you have gathered us here, Roland, and be quick about it."

Roland turned to Bertine. Her eyes were downcast and her lower lip trembled as if she were about to cry. How could he have hurt her so? No apology would ever restore her trust in him.

With difficulty, he began. "I-if you please, Monsieur François," he stammered, "I would ask that the family allow me to speak to Bertine without interruptions—except from her, of course."

She started to lift her eyes but quickly returned her gaze to her hands in her lap.

"Certainly," replied François, waving his hand impatiently.

In addition to Bertine's black clothes, something else was different about her: her posture. It had always been upright whenever Roland came for Sunday dinner, but today her shoulders were slumped. He suddenly wanted to clasp her arm and offer her solace. He stopped himself, for that would only make her resent him more.

"Bertine, I made a terrible mistake," he began in a low and unsteady voice. "I misled you into believing that I intended to marry you. I have been sorry since the day I first uttered that lie. I did not want to be dishonest with you, but I feared what your father might do if I did not obey him."

Bertine jerked her head upright, her light blue eyes piercing his. Hubert might as well have come back to life, the resemblance was so strong. "What did he threaten to do to you?"

He swallowed, taken aback by her unexpected question. "It was not an outright threat, but I could not be sure of what he would do."

She crossed her arms against her chest and glowered at him. "I do not believe you. My father always praised your wit and skill as a surgeon. Surely there is another reason that you could not truly commit to marrying me."

"Yes, there was, and I told your father about it. You see, I was not sure that my brother would approve my betrothal to you. He serves at the court of Spain and has often spoken to me of arranging a marriage for me. I needed his permission to wed you." Roland bowed his head. "Regardless of these reasons, I should have been more forthright with you. I beg you to accept my apology."

She rose swiftly to her feet. "Liar!" she cried. "I read Magali's secret book and discovered the true reason you do not wish to marry me. Magali and you love one another."

His face burned in shame and he cast his eyes down again, unable to bear her hurt look. *Magali, what should I do now?*

Suddenly, he knew the answer. Instead of following his rehearsed speech, he must speak from his heart.

He stood up. Her face was flushed with anger, but she had not turned away from him.

"Bertine, I will always regret betraying you," he whispered at last, hoping that she alone could hear him. "I told Magali how much I enjoyed your friendship and later, I told her how I deceived you. She urged me to ask for your forgiveness. Maybe you are not ready today, but I hope one day you will be."

Bertine's eyes filled with tears. "Magali!" she moaned and strode out of the great room.

Roland forced himself to face Hubert's family again at supper that night. None of Hubert's grandchildren were present at the table, nor was Bertine.

In the hours since he'd last seen her, Roland had become convinced that Bertine could not be the one who'd tried to take Magali's life. How could she, since she was clearly bereft at her friend's disappearance?

The dark presence was still among those gathered around the table. Roland's legs trembled as he forced them to remain still. He was relieved that Bertine was not part of whatever haunted him. He fought his desire to spring to his feet and dispel whatever this invisible thing was by demanding to know which one of them had given Magali poison. If he did something so rash, the person responsible would simply retreat into silence, and he would never discover the truth. "Have patience," he imagined Magali whispering in his ear. "The end of our search is drawing nigh."

He pushed his plate away from him and looked at François. "Monsieur, there is no denying what Bertine said before supper.

Again, I am sorry that I was not truthful with her. Regarding another matter: I heard that her betrothal to the magistrate's son was broken on account of my impropriety. I certainly do not wish for her to wed him, but I want the family to know that those rumors about me are not true." He looked around the table and everyone but Thomas avoided his gaze. "I also want to know who spread these rumors."

Clothes rustled as people shifted uncomfortably in their seats.

"I did," Perronelle admitted defiantly. "When Bertine was born, my husband promised me that she would enter the convent of the Franciscans."

"Mama, you know that Bertine does not wish to become a nun," Clare said firmly. "But neither does she want to wed Giraud. He frightens her, especially when he drinks too much."

"I am Bertine's mother, not you," Perronelle replied coldly, "and I will decide her future. Mark my word, within a fortnight she will be cloistered."

Clare's face flushed and she rose to her feet. "And I will do everything in my power to keep her out of the cloister," she said in a low voice.

Thomas put his hand on her arm. "*Ma femme*, you may go to Bertine shortly, but remain here for a few more moments."

Clare reluctantly sat back down, and Thomas turned to Roland. "I am curious about something. Surely you did not return to Arles simply to attend Hubert's funeral; nor does it seem likely that you came only to apologize to Bertine. Tell us, why are you truly here?"

Roland did his best to disguise what lay inside of him and say only what he and Thomas had rehearsed. "For one, to settle my final accounts with Hubert, for he has not paid me in full," he said. "Second, the countess has asked me to make inquiries into the true cause of her daughter's disappearance. But you must swear to never breathe a word about her suspicions to anyone outside of this room. Otherwise, the king of France would take bloody revenge on the people of Arles."

Around the table, everyone grew very still.

"I remember the day a messenger from the château came to Arles and announced that Lady Magali had disappeared," Thomas said, breaking the silence. "The story he told was that she had run away, but immediately there were rumors that something even worse had befallen her."

Marie met Roland's gaze. "Since you are in love with the countess's daughter, I suspect you know if these rumors are true. Tell us what really happened to her."

Roland allowed a few moments to pass before replying, "Lady Beatrice believes that Magali may have been poisoned."

Marie's eyes grew wide. "Bertine and my father visited the château. Does the countess suspect them of poisoning her daughter?"

"Yes."

"Or someone else in the family could have committed the deed and made it seem that my husband or Bertine was guilty instead," Perronelle said grimly, looking around the table. "The poisoner could be one of us."

Almost everyone cast their eyes downward.

"It also seems possible that one of your servants could have been a part of this plot," Roland added. "If anyone knows of details that might be important, please tell me."

"If anyone here knows something," François promised, "it will be brought to your attention immediately."

Roland stood and bowed to him. "*Merci*, monsieur. Now, I wish to speak with the servant Solange in the courtyard. Will you send her out to me?"

François nodded his assent.

Once outside, Roland collapsed onto a stone bench. One or more people gathered around Hubert's oaken table had almost certainly been involved in Magali's poisoning. And now this person or people knew that they were being hunted. Roland had only been hunting a few times, but he knew that animals took desperate measures in order to survive.

He considered the desperate measures that the murderer might take: fleeing Arles, blaming someone else—which the guilty may have already done—or ending their own life. Or—he sprang to his feet—murdering the person hunting for Magali's poisoner!

The door to the courtyard opened and Solange approached him. She was breathless and her face was flushed, as if she had been running. He waited a moment until she caught her breath.

"You serve many people in this household, do you not?" he asked.

"Yes, monsieur."

"Do any of them send you to various shops in Arles?"

"Yes, monsieur."

"Have you been sent within the last month or so to an apothecary?"

Silence.

"Answer my question."

"Yes, monsieur," she replied, her voice barely audible.

"Who sent you?"

Again, silence; Roland resisted the urge to shake her by the shoulders. "You must answer me," he commanded.

"I cannot," she whimpered.

"If you remain silent, you are in danger of being punished for a crime that someone else committed."

Solange bowed her head and started to cry.

"You might well be hanged in the church square if you do not tell me," he threatened.

Tears slid down her cheeks but her lips remained locked together. He felt a wave of rage pass through him—but then he realized he could use her silence to his advantage. "Go now, then," he bade her roughly. "Warn the person who sent you that I am very close to knowing the truth. The countess's wrath might be assuaged a bit if that person came to me and confessed."

Solange fled.

As the sun slipped behind the courtyard wall, Roland's mind sprang to action.

Underneath Hubert's surgery table, the still, warm air smelled of alcohol and the turpentine scent of Isaac's wound-sealing remedy. Blankets that hung to the floor on either side hid Roland and Thomas from view and muffled the sound of Saint Trophime's bells.

They had been here nearly two hours now; Roland's body was stiff and cramped, but his mind was still alert.

After everyone in Hubert's household had gone to bed, Thomas had unlocked the outer door to the shop and Roland had entered. After returning the key to its accustomed drawer in Hubert's desk, Thomas joined Roland under the table.

Another hour crept by in the stifling darkness. The midnight bells rang. As the last stroke faded into silence, there finally came a creaking sound. Someone was opening the door that connected Hubert's house to his shop.

Roland's heartbeat quickened as he heard footsteps approaching. Faint light appeared through the coarse weave of the blankets and he smelled beeswax from a candle.

The person crept closer to the shelf containing the arsenic. Lifting the blanket, Roland saw the hem of a woman's shift and her bare feet. The poisoner! At once, his arm shot out and he grabbed her by the ankle. She screamed and kicked wildly, struggling to get loose. Something thudded to the floor and rolled away. Gripping the woman's ankle tightly, he emerged from his hiding place just as she lost her balance and fell face forward onto the table.

He stood, still gripping her ankle, and grabbed the other one too. He tried to turn her over onto her back to see who she was. She kicked at him fiercely with both legs, but he managed to hold on.

Thomas came out from beneath the other side of the table. Seizing her by the shoulders, he and Roland forced her to turn onto her back. The woman had set her candle on the top shelf, and by its light they saw her eyes darting wildly from one captor to the other. Roland could not move as he stared at her. *You never even met Magali . . . why would you try to murder her?*

"Clare!" Thomas cried out, pinning her shoulders to the table. "What have you done?"

What have you done? Thomas's question echoed in Roland's mind as he stood rooted to the ground.

"There was a noise coming from Papa's shop and I thought it was a thief," she said, panting.

Her lie sickened Roland but also stirred him to action. He stooped down to retrieve the crock of arsenic, then thrust it close to her face. She jerked her head away from it.

"You are the thief," he growled. "You tried to steal Magali's life and my joy."

"No!" She shook her head vehemently.

"You came here tonight for the weapon that you used to murder Magali. You intended to kill me with it."

She grew very still.

"Admit the truth," Roland demanded.

Though Clare bore little resemblance to her father, she stared at Roland as Hubert once had, taking his measure without revealing anything that lay within her. Her gaze kindled the same disquiet, the same helplessness he'd always felt under Hubert's scrutiny. "I did not kill her, nor do I want to kill you," she said, her voice steady and clear, soothing as Hubert's once was. "It was my father's doing."

How Roland wanted to believe her. If he could, it would be as he suspected all along . . . that Hubert had poisoned Magali.

Breathing heavily, Thomas glared at his wife. "Why, then, did you come to take the arsenic away?"

"I wanted to protect my father's good name . . . and our family's."

Thomas laughed bitterly. "You hated him."

"You did too," she retorted.

"True."

Watching this exchange, the truth of the matter became clear to

Roland: Clare was a liar, just like her father. Hubert had duped Roland, but never again would he be deceived. He slammed the crock of arsenic onto the table. "Answer me this—how did you know that this crock was here?"

"I-I was searching for a remedy for Mama's headaches," she stammered. "I hadn't seen this crock before and wanted to find out what it was."

"Now you're changing your story," Roland said. "I don't believe you!" He seized her by the neck with both of his hands. "Tell the truth!"

Choking, she clutched at his hands and tried to pull them away.

"Stop, Roland!" Thomas shouted, grabbing him by the shoulders and trying to break his stranglehold.

But Roland could not let go. He had to know the truth. "Admit that you poisoned Magali!" he shouted.

Clare nodded vigorously. His grip around her neck tightened.

Magali's voice echoed in the core of his being. *You are not a murderer . . . you are not a murderer.* An anguished cry burst out of him as he let go of Clare. His legs were so weak he had to clutch the table to keep from falling to the floor. *I am not a murderer . . . I am not a murderer.*

Clare fell back onto the table, gasping for breath.

"Why did you poison the countess's daughter?" Thomas demanded.

She did not answer. The only sound in the room was her breathing, which gradually slowed.

"You never even met her. Why poison her?" Thomas pressed.

"I thought I could keep one more secret, as I have done for years," Clare replied, her voice dull and low. "I thought everyone would believe that my father poisoned her."

"You wanted your own father to be executed for your vile deed?" Thomas asked.

"Do not judge me, Thomas," she cried. "You too rejoice that he is gone. You would have done so even if he had died by the noose."

A numbness such as Roland had never felt before was creeping through his veins. He had to know the truth before he succumbed to it. "Answer the question," he commanded. "Why did you poison my Magali?"

She sat up on the table, her shoulders hunched over and her hair hanging over her face like a dark curtain. Her short, round figure transformed into that of a child caught in a wrongdoing.

"For Bertine's sake," she cried.

Roland's body tensed. "Did she conspire with you?"

"No one did. Solange did my bidding, as she has done for years, but I alone am to blame."

"I do not understand how killing Magali would benefit Bertine," Thomas said. "She so enjoyed the company of her new friend."

Clare abruptly rose from the table and stood before Roland. She had swept her hair from her face and her eyes burned into his. "Bertine loved you with all of her heart. She wrote poetry about you," she choked out, "and what did you do in return? You lied to her, lulling her into believing that one day she would be your wife."

I am a liar. Roland backed away from Clare, but she stepped closer.

"You hurt Bertine deeply . . . because of you, she lost her innocence. I wanted to hurt you just as deeply." Her words were tumbling out faster. "And your friendship with Thomas hurt me as well—to the quick. He was happy in your company and spent more time with you than he ever has with me."

Clare turned to her husband. "I loved you, Thomas, but you never returned my love."

He bowed his head. "Then I too had a hand in this treachery."

"No, it was only Clare's doing . . . her choice." Bertine's voice, though quiet, startled them all. She stood in the doorway between the house and the shop, wearing a shift and a black shawl draped over her shoulders. Her tears sparkled in the candlelight as she met her sister's gaze. "Clare, I followed you downstairs and have heard everything. And you omitted the most important reason that you wanted Magali dead. Tonight, I realized something I had not considered before. You are jealous of her because I love her too. You poisoned her so that you could have me all to yourself again. Did you not see that there was room in my heart to love you both?"

Clare shook her head, tears streaming down her face. "I beg of you, Bertine, forgive me for what I have done."

She reached for her sister's hand, but Bertine drew back. Clare's piteous cry, like that of a wounded animal, echoed in the candlelit room. She sank to the floor, her face in the shadows.

"Forgive me, Heavenly Father, for what I have done and what I must do now," she whispered.

She arched her head back and lifted something to her lips. A bitter smell filled the air.

Roland had smelled this odor once before, at a shop in Barcelona. In a flash he remembered the belladonna.

"Be quick, Bertine!" he shouted. "She's poisoning herself!"

"Clare, stop!" Bertine flew to her sister, wrenched the vial from her hand, and turned it upside down. Only a drop of poison remained. "No," she moaned as Clare collapsed in her arms.

Clare's face twisted in agony as the poison began to spread through her body. In only a few moments, her body started to convulse violently.

Bertine wept, stroking her sister's hair just as Clare had always done to soothe her.

25 Avril

"Roland, let me go with you!" Bertine cried.

Standing behind her, Thomas had to hold her back from following Roland to the door. He still felt very weak, but he could not wait a moment longer to begin his journey to Magali.

Thomas had made Bertine take a brew made of poppy flowers to put her to sleep, but it hadn't taken effect yet. The sadness in her voice touched Roland and he turned back to her. Behind her, Clare's body, covered with a blanket, lay on the surgery table.

"Bertine," Roland said, his voice hoarse and low, "I promise to tell Magali how much you wanted to come with me. She will understand why you could not. And I promise to read your poem to her."

"Bertine, I need you here . . . Nicholas and Arnaud need you here," Thomas gently repeated what he had already told her. "You alone can help them grieve for their mother's passing. And you must help me convince them and everyone in the family that she died from falling down the stairs, not by taking her own life."

Bertine faced her sister's body again. "Oh, Clare, how could you leave your children of your own will?" she cried out. "How could you do this terrible deed to Magali . . . and to me?"

"We will never know," Thomas said as he held her.

Roland bowed his head. *How could your sister do this to any of us?*

Her energy spent, Bertine collapsed in Thomas's arms. He carried her to his surgery table and laid her down, then returned to the door and embraced Roland, his strong arms providing the same support he had always offered. But Thomas would need just as much support in the coming days, and would have no one to provide it until he could go to Montpellier . . . to Lucienne.

"I will pray for Magali," Thomas said as he released Roland. "May your journey to her be swift and safe."

"And may you be strong for your sons, as you have been strong for me," Roland said. "Thomas, without your help, I could never have discovered the truth. Thanks to you, I will now be able to share it with Magali . . ."

Before she dies? The question hung in the air as Roland turned to the door, hoping he found the strength to reach the stable.

Fourteen

"The distance is great from the firm belief to the realization from concrete experience."
—ISABELLA I, QUEEN OF CASTILE AND LEON (1474-1504)

25 AVRIL

Magali was asleep when Roland reached her bedside in the late afternoon. One look at her hands, which were spotted with reddish brown sores, and he knew that the poison was still coursing through her veins.

Lady Beatrice, dressed simply like a townswoman, sat in a chair next to the bed. She shook her head slightly, her chin trembling as she fought tears. "The sores are all over her body," she whispered as she struggled to her feet. "Come to the hall with me and tell me everything."

"A woman—Bertine's own sister—sought to kill my child?" Beatrice asked when Roland finished telling her what he and Thomas had discovered. "Though you have told me her reasons, I do not understand."

He clasped her shoulders tightly. "It has been less than a day since I learned the truth, and I still don't understand either."

Beatrice bowed her head, her body heaving with fresh tears of sorrow mingled now with rage at the woman who had poisoned her daughter. It was only Roland's hands gripping her shoulders that steadied her, kept her from dissolving completely.

25 Avril

The sun was setting when they returned to Magali's bedside. Roland sank to his knees and clasped Magali's hand. It was light and warm. As he stroked a small place on her palm that had no sore his mind darted about, desperately searching for anything else he could do to keep her alive. And yet deep inside he wondered if she was dying and if there was anything else he could do for her.

"We will keep giving her the clay," he said, "and the cleansing broth. Tomorrow I will send Isaac a message, asking him for advice. He might know of a salve we can put on her sores."

"She doesn't complain about her hands and feet, but she says they are numb," Lady Beatrice said as she threaded her fingers through Magali's hair.

Roland ached to do the same. "We will ask Isaac for a remedy for numbness too."

They took turns watching over Magali all through the night. Every two hours, one of the nuns brought a bowl of the clay mixed with oil and a cup of broth. At midnight, Magali stirred and opened her eyes, and she smiled when she saw Roland. Her smile was just the same as ever! He grinned back at her and leaned down to embrace her gently. The bones of her shoulders protruded noticeably now but her hair smelled, as always, of lavender. How he wanted to collapse onto the bed beside her and hold her through the long night.

With great difficulty, he returned to a sitting position and took her hand in his. "Try to take something to eat and drink," he said, offering her a spoonful of the clay and oil mixture.

She took a mouthful and shuddered before swallowing it. "It's sandy . . . like the mud pie I once ate as a child," she said, her voice faint.

"Did your mother tell you why we are making you eat this clay?"

Magali nodded as she opened her mouth for another spoonful. "Tell me what happened in Arles," she murmured. "Everything."

He shook his head. "You need to rest."

She gripped his hand with surprising strength. "No, there must be no secrets between us. Please, Roland."

Her gaze was so fierce that it frightened him. Against his better judgment, he told her what had come to pass.

"I cannot believe Bertine's own sister would do this," Magali said as tears streamed down her face. "Bertine loved her and often talked about her, and I believe Clare loved her children and Bertine—why would she want to make them suffer by taking her own life?"

She made you suffer too! And me! Roland barely kept these words to himself. Magali was crying harder now as Roland combed his fingers through her hair, wishing he had kept the truth from her.

The bells were ringing the first bells past midnight by the time her tears subsided.

"I must see Bertine," she said in a weak voice as she closed her eyes. "Please, Roland, send for her."

27 AVRIL

Beatrice sat on the edge of the bed and embraced Magali, who had just awakened. "Good morning, Mama." She struggled up to a sitting position. "Is Bertine coming soon?"

"Yes, *ma chérie*, in a few days." Beatrice smiled. This was the first morning since she came to Magali's bedside that her daughter had been wide awake. Beatrice's heart filled with hope, until she remembered Isaac's advice: *I must warn you that, just as with Magali's maladie de l'esprit, there is no guarantee that we can heal her of the poison.*

After breakfast, at which Magali took more of the clay mixture and the broth than she had for the last two days, a young nun came with a bowl of warm lavender water and soft linen rags. Together, she and Beatrice gently undressed Magali and bathed her, something

Beatrice hadn't done since Magali was a child. Even then, her daughter had loved the smell of lavender.

Once Magali's body was dry, Beatrice applied a salve that Isaac had recommended to Magali's sores.

"Thank you, Mama," she said. "That feels good."

"I am glad," Beatrice said.

After helping Magali don a clean shift, Beatrice brushed her daughter's hair.

It was as curly as always, but there were so many strands of hair caught in the brush . . . another sign of the poison in her body. A hot wave of anger pulsed through Beatrice. Clare herself was a mother; how could she have brought such suffering on Beatrice's only child?

Magali moaned and Beatrice suddenly realized that she was brushing her daughter's hair too roughly. Again, she brought herself back simply to the task at hand.

Beatrice and Magali spent the morning reading poetry, including a verse written by Bertine. When Beatrice had first read the poem with Magali the previous day it had seemed simple, easy to understand, a short piece about love and how mutable it was. But this morning the verse seemed deeper in meaning, one that Beatrice found difficult to express in words.

As she read it aloud for a second time at Magali's request, a peaceful look came over her daughter's face.

"It reminds me of the ocean, always changing," she murmured as she drifted back to sleep.

29 AVRIL

Roland was waiting outside the hospital when Thomas's carriage arrived. His friend descended while his sons and Bertine remained inside. In the bright sunlight, Roland could barely see their faces as he greeted them. Never had he seen Nicholas and Arnaud so subdued.

Thomas led him to the shade on the other side of the busy street where the boys could not hear them. "We have laid Clare to rest," he quietly told Roland. "Bertine will visit with Magali but for a short while. Then I am taking my sons and her to the sea—I think it will do them all some good to be away from reminders of Clare."

Roland remembered Magali's fervent wish to go to the sea when he first met her. Maybe she too had simply wanted to escape from something... her illness?

When Thomas asked how Magali was faring, Roland replied, "She is still taking the clay remedy and drinking the broth. All I can say is that her sickness isn't getting worse."

Thomas's gaze was full of compassion. "It must be very difficult not to know what will happen."

Roland nodded somberly. "I will prepare Bertine for Magali's weakness and her sores before she sees her. But first tell me what has come to pass in Arles since I left."

Thomas said that there may have been suspicions in the family about the cause of Clare's death, but no one spoke of them aloud. Thomas had decided not to remain in Arles. Gregoire and his son, who was soon to be a master surgeon, would take charge of Hubert's shop and buy his house. Thomas planned to sell his house and move to Montpellier with his sons and Bertine. Bertine had quickly agreed to this plan. Since her reputation was now ruined, she would neither be forced to wed Giraud nor be allowed to enter the Franciscan convent. Perronelle would join the cloister there in her daughter's place.

"I am glad that Bertine is set free," Roland said.

"So am I," Thomas said. "François has arranged for her to receive an allowance, and she will live with the boys and me. She will have enough money to hire tutors to help her pursue her studies. One day, I believe that she will become a tutor herself."

Roland remembered her beautiful poem. "And continue to write poetry," he added. "I hope that she finds peace in Montpellier. And your boys and you too."

"In time, I feel certain we will." Thomas smiled. "Lucienne and I will be wed after my sons' grief has subsided. I will pray that Magali heals so that you can be married too. Maybe you could live in Montpellier and we could continue to work together and try new remedies that you find in your ancient texts." Thomas's face brightened as he made this suggestion.

Roland bowed his head. "I do not know."

Bertine entered the hospital with Roland beside her. She looked much different than she had at the Easter feast when Beatrice had last seen her. Then she had worn forest green, which had suited her well for it had brought out the rich tones of her skin. In contrast, the black bodice and skirt she wore today almost made her disappear under the weight of her grief.

Again, anger rose within Beatrice at the suffering Clare had caused. She bowed her head, struggling to contain it with a silent prayer to the Virgin.

While Roland waited in the doorway, Bertine rushed to Magali's side and took her hand. "Magali," she said. "Roland tells me that you wanted me to awaken you when I arrived." She gently shook Magali's shoulder until she stirred, then called her name again.

This time Magali turned at once to the sound of her friend's voice, a smile lighting her face. "Bertine, you are here . . ."

Laying her head on the pillow beside Magali, Bertine began to weep. Beatrice ached to console her but knew it was important for the two young women to have this time just with each other. Roland, still standing in the doorway, must have known this too, for he stood silently, looking down at his feet.

"I am so sorry that I never told you, but I read your secret book and found out about your love for Roland and his for you." Bertine drew in a deep breath, then let out an anguished exhale. "If I hadn't told my sister about it . . . she would never have poisoned you!"

Beatrice grew still. She had been so busy preparing for her wedding that she had not known that Magali kept a secret book. Beatrice had already burned hers—she would have to burn Magali's too.

Bertine was crying harder now—the sound filled the hospital and the nun tending to the other few patients in the small room frowned at the disruption. Beatrice quietly rose and gave the nun a pouch filled with coins, and her frown vanished.

By the time Beatrice returned to her chair, Magali had somehow found the strength to face Bertine. "None of this . . . is your doing," she said. "You are . . . like a sister to me. I wanted you to know everything about me . . . that is why I left my secret book open to those pages."

"You are a sister to me too, Magali," Bertine murmured. "I will pray for you to heal."

Magali smiled faintly. "I hope you will keep writing poetry."

"You just reminded me . . ." Bertine sat up and drew two books from her satchel. "I made a copy of all of my poems for you to read," she said through her tears. "I also have that book I borrowed from you—I had a copy of it made to keep. I will never forget reading it with you. You know, the one we enjoyed so much about Jeanne the Maid."

Magali did not answer, for she was already fast asleep.

Beatrice went to Bertine and put a hand on her shoulder. "I will walk with you to your carriage," she whispered.

"And I will stay with Magali," Roland said as he entered the room. He bowed his head to Bertine. "I wish you well in Montpellier, Bertine. Once again, I am sorry for deceiving you."

The pain in his voice surprised Beatrice. Bertine kept her eyes downcast as she gave him a slight curtsy. The two women walked slowly outside, heavy with the uncertainty of what would happen to Magali. In the bright sunshine, Beatrice embraced Bertine. "I too wish you well," she said. "I will never forget you and how you brought happiness to my Magali."

Bertine shook her head, her lips pressed together. "I brought about her suffering."

Beatrice squeezed the young woman's hands and held her gaze. "I know that you feel responsible for what happened to her. Roland does too, but she forgives you both. I forgive you too. Try to release yourself from your guilt. I pray one day that you will."

1 Mai

For the second day, Lady Beatrice and Roland took Magali by carriage to the Arc River. Near the water's edge, they sat on a blanket hidden amidst willow trees. It was a warm day with the smell of apple blossoms wafting toward them from an orchard nearby.

Seated on either side of Magali, Roland and Lady Beatrice exchanged a hopeful smile. The clay remedy seemed to be working! Magali was more alert than she had been since Roland had returned to her bedside nearly a week ago. She was now eating a little meat and bread, along with the remedy and the broth. And instead of sleeping most of the day, she only needed a nap in the afternoon.

Magali sighed in delight as she watched the river tumble over rocks. "How I enjoy the spray on my face," she said, "and the sound of the water's music."

And so Magali's healing continued. Each day her spirits were restored a little more, and in the last two days her sores had begun to form scabs. According to Isaac, it would be weeks, even months, before her healing was complete, but still Roland felt a weight lifting from his shoulders.

Roland visited Isaac late one night at his shop. Never before had he seen the doctor look so relieved, and Isaac made the same observation about Roland as they sipped wine.

"The poisoning was a terrible ordeal for Magali to endure, but at least there is something good that came of it," he said. "Now we will know how to treat patients who have been poisoned with arsenic." He put a warm hand on Roland's shoulder. "I want to thank you again for the other remedies you've shared with me these last months. I am especially interested in finding out if bathing in warm mineral springs will help my patients with mania and melancholia. I think you should try that remedy again the next time Magali suffers from her *maladie de l'esprit*.

"If you one day resume searching for remedies in ancient texts, I would be eager to continue trying them on my patients." Isaac's visage darkened. "But I fear that will not be possible. Soon you and I may no longer be free even to exchange secret messages. I may even be forced to flee with my family."

Anger burned inside Roland at the French king's cruelty. He was also a fool to banish Isaac and his people—people who had once lived among Christians, exchanging knowledge about the body and remedies for illnesses. He reached inside his satchel and drew out a pouch heavy with coins. "Lady Beatrice wanted me to thank you heartily for all you have done for her family. Now that she is part of the French royal family, she will try to do whatever she can to protect the Jewish people of Provence. If you and your family are expelled, however, this money can be used on your journey to a new home."

Tears glistened in Isaac's eyes as he took the pouch. "Please tell Lady Beatrice that I send her many thanks, and also share with her my sorrow that the bond between our two families will be broken after so many years." He set the pouch on a desk and rose to his feet. "Now I must ask you to leave, for I am to perform a new surgery tomorrow and need to be well rested."

Roland stood and together they walked to the door.

"What will the future bring for you and Magali?" Isaac asked.

"Lady Beatrice promised us that we could be wed," Roland said, smiling broadly.

Isaac smiled too and clapped Roland on the back. "May your lives together be full of joy."

Roland's smile faded. "You and I may not see each other again," he said sorrowfully. "I cannot thank you enough for all that you have done for me and for Magali. You have truly been my guide through the labyrinth of the spirit."

As they stood by the door in the shadowy anteroom, Roland embraced Isaac with all his heart.

10 JUIN

I must be strong, Beatrice silently reminded herself as she rose from her bed and dressed in a plain bodice and skirt made of coarse gray wool. In her looking glass, she saw a woman pilgrim with sad eyes and trembling lips as she fought tears yet again.

I must be strong. She threw open the shutters of her room to the dawn, a rosy light bathing the cobblestone streets of Rocamadour. A stone's throw away, the chalky cliffs of the town were also reflecting the light of the rising sun. Carved into those cliffs but not visible from the inn where they lodged was the statue of the Black Virgin and the Child Jesus on her lap. Beatrice closed her eyes and imagined them. *Dear Virgin, you had to surrender your child to death. My child will remain alive, but far away from me. Help me to bear this loss and help Magali too. And help me keep yet another secret from my husband.*

All too soon there came a knock on her door. As soon as she opened it, Magali burst in, followed by Roland, both of them dressed in the simple garb of pilgrims. They each wore wedding bands, for the previous day they had received the sacrament of matrimony, under false names, at a chapel near the statues. Magali was still pale and thin but her eyes . . . they were full of life again. And Roland, who had shaved his beard, looked younger and more carefree than ever before.

Magali threw her arms around her mother. "Mama, I will miss you so much," she said, her tears wetting Beatrice's cheek. "But I rejoice that I may see you again."

If I can figure out a way to keep our visits a secret from the royal guards who are sure to insist upon accompanying me. "Yes, ma chérie," Beatrice said aloud, embracing her daughter tightly, not wanting to let her go—but already the morning bells were ringing. The driver of the carriage that would take Magali and Roland to Spain would be waiting for them at the stable.

Reluctantly, she released Magali, and turned to embrace Roland. "You have taken such good care of my Magali, and I know that you will continue to do so," she said.

"Yes," he said as they drew apart. "And Magali and I will protect you from afar by never revealing who she truly is."

It had taken Beatrice several restless nights, as they traveled north from Aix-en-Provence to the shrine of Rocamadour, to settle upon the lie that she would be forced to tell Philippe. She had finally determined to tell him that Magali had recovered from the ulcer and that Beatrice had arranged for her to enter a Benedictine cloister. She hoped he would be relieved that Magali, with her unpredictable disease of the spirit, would neither live at the château nor attend his uncle at the French court in Toulouse.

Magali and Roland would travel to Spain, and along the way they would search for a place near the border of France and Spain with a Benedictine convent. God willing, Beatrice could secretly meet Magali and Roland there on occasion—at least once a year, she hoped.

"It won't be safe to write directly to you," she said, her voice wavering. "But I have thought of a way for us to communicate indirectly. Roland, I know that you will write to Thomas; I, in turn, will write to Bertine. He will share news of you and Magali with her and I will ask her to share it with me."

"What a clever idea," exclaimed Magali.

"Please know that I won't be able to reveal very much in my letters," Beatrice said bitterly. "My new king has ways of knowing about the correspondence of everyone at court."

As tears rolled down her cheeks, Magali squeezed Beatrice's

hands. "You have sacrificed your freedom for mine," she cried. "How I wish you too could remain free."

Beatrice gently wiped her daughter's tears away. "Knowing that you and Roland are happy will sustain me. And Philippe has been kind to me thus far. I have accepted my new lot, though I will miss you very much."

Beatrice embraced Magali again, unable to restrain her own tears a moment longer.

Mother and daughter held one another for a long time.

Through the open window came the sound of people on the streets, speaking a cacophony of languages. They stepped out into the dawn, Roland and Magali side by side, Magali's opposite arm hooked around Beatrice's. Together, they walked to the stable—where, with a final squeeze of her daughter's hand, Beatrice let go and watched the young couple mount their carriage and join the host of other pilgrims who would travel along the ancient path to Spain.

Epilogue

Tarbes, France
7 JUIN, 1480

Roland and Magali stood so close that their arms were touching. Glancing at her face, which was aglow in the light of the setting sun, Roland felt joy warming his whole body that she was alive and, for the time being, hale. Her *maladie de l'esprit* would always be a part of her—it had already manifested twice in their first year of marriage. But bathing in the warm mineral springs near Salamanca where Roland had completed his medical studies had blunted her melancholia and mania a little.

"Look, Roland, the sun is setting!" she exclaimed now, pointing toward the Pyrenees.

But by the time he shifted his gaze from her to the sun, it had disappeared. "I just missed it."

She grinned at him, her dark curly hair whipping in the wind. "You were probably thinking about the new remedy for the falling sickness that I found for you."

In the last year, while he had attended lectures and assisted surgeons at a shop near the university, Magali had helped him by reading translations of ancient medical texts and taking notes on remedies for the body and mind. After receiving Isaac's permission, Roland had written to Thomas about how he shared remedies with a

Jewish doctor. Now both Isaac and Thomas were observing the effects of remedies that Roland sent to them.

Roland and Magali stood watching the red glow that was fading behind the mountains. As the sky darkened, a multitude of stars appeared, some large and bright and others so small Roland could barely see them.

"Our first stars of the night," he said, remembering that evening in Montpellier when he'd felt so lonely in the company of Thomas and Lucienne. They too had wed in the last year, and she was already with their first child.

Roland tightened his embrace of Magali. They had decided to try to prevent the birth of a child through herbal and other methods, at least until they found a better remedy for Magali's illness. *If we find one*, he reminded himself with sadness.

"I will see Mama on the morrow and meet my baby brother!" Magali said excitedly as they walked along the narrow, curving street to their inn. "How I wish I could see Bertine too."

"As I want to see Thomas," Roland said, "but the time for his child's birth is nigh. Maybe next year, he and Bertine will be able to make the journey here together."

Magali and Lady Beatrice would meet at the Abbey of Saint Savin in Tarbes, which was nestled in the French Pyrenees and on the pilgrimage path from Spain to France. A year earlier, on their way to Spain, Roland and Magali had seen the beautiful abbey for the first time and written to Thomas that it would be a suitable convent for Magali to supposedly become cloistered. As another precaution apart from the circuitous letters, Lady Beatrice had paid a large sum of money for a girl from Tarbes to become a novice in Magali's place. Neither Beatrice's husband nor his uncle the king had ever met Magali, or expressed any interest in meeting her, so the ruse might well work. Still, Roland had misgivings. What would Lady Beatrice's husband or his uncle do if they discovered that Magali wasn't really cloistered there? Would the Spider King send spies to discover her true whereabouts? While Magali, disguised as a beggar, was visiting her mother, Roland was resolved to keep a secret watch on the convent.

He and Magali reached their inn and enjoyed a delicious meal of cassoulet.

"We should try to prepare this dish ourselves," she said as she swallowed a second, delicious bite.

After recovering from the poison, she had needed nearly three months to return to her former girth. Roland and she enjoyed cooking together, learning new recipes and also returning to favorite ones from the past, such as the plum pastry they'd made at her mother's château. They had prepared that treat for Carlos the first time he'd met Magali. In his letters, Carlos had been quite angry with Roland for marrying a French townswoman (yet another deceit about who Magali really was), but after one day of visiting them at their rented house in Salamanca, Carlos had fallen into treating her as if she were his sister, playing chess and debating with her.

Roland was very happy to be reunited with his brother. Magali and he would soon live only a two days' journey away from Carlos's home in Burgos. On their journey to Spain a year earlier, the couple had traveled through San Sebastian on the northern coast. The town had a beautiful beach where they enjoyed walking, as well as a thriving port, which meant there was a great need for doctors to tend to the many sailors gathered there.

Most importantly of all, there was a warm mineral spring halfway between San Sebastian and Burgos.

"I suppose I forgive you for your adventures in France," Carlos said with a smile as he and Roland bade farewell to each other at the end of his visit to Salamanca. "You are the happiest I have seen you in many years."

Roland smiled as he nodded. "Now that I have finished at the university, I can heed my calling as a doctor and a surgeon fully. And I have followed your advice and found a lover and a friend in the same woman."

Carlos grew wistful. "I have not been able to take my own advice. I have not found such a woman as your Magali. I am envious of you, Roland."

As Magali and Roland finished their meal at their inn, Magali opened her satchel and took out the books they had purchased today. The bookshop was owned by Felise and Georges, the elderly couple Roland had met two summers earlier in Arles. Felise's book about her childhood and her friendship with Jeanne the Maid had since become a favorite of Roland, Magali, Bertine, and, more recently, Lady Beatrice. It had been a happy moment when Roland had discovered last summer that Georges and Felise's bookshop was here in Tarbes and he was afforded the opportunity to introduce Magali to the couple.

Earlier today, Roland and Magali had again visited them at their bookshop and searched for books to give as gifts to Lady Beatrice and Bertine. Just as Roland was exchanging remedies with Isaac and Thomas, Magali was exchanging books, especially ones written anonymously by women, with her mother and friend. In turn, they were sharing these books with a widening circle of women—from Bertine's students to Beatrice's ladies-in-waiting and other women at the French court.

Felise had greeted them enthusiastically over the din of the bookshop, which teemed with customers—both townspeople and pilgrims wearing scallop shell-shaped badges indicating that they had traveled far away to the shrine of Saint James in northwestern Spain and were on their way back to their homes in France or Italy—before waving Roland and Magali forward and saying, "Come with me."

She'd led them past a woman guarding a chest of coins and holding firm when customers tried to barter for cheaper prices and through the adjoining scriptorium, where a master scribe taught apprentices, both boys and girls, how to blend the letters of the alphabet into a flowing script. Artists dipped their brushes into paint and added miniatures to pages that had already been copies. A printer wearing an ink-stained apron sang work songs as he tightened the screws of a large wooden printing press.

"As I said a year ago, this shop makes me happy," Magali said loudly over the noise.

"It makes me happy too," Felise said, smiling as she led them up a short staircase to a pair of alcoves on either side of the stairs. It was quieter here, and filled with light that entered through the open lattice windows. Georges was seated at a table in one of the alcoves, etching images onto leather book covers. He looked older than he did last year and the joints of his hands had knotted more noticeably, but he greeted them with great cheer.

In Felise's alcove was a large writing desk and a shelf containing many books. "Here are my favorite books, as well as several new ones I have written," she said proudly. "You may buy as many as you like. There are more copies of these books for sale downstairs."

Magali chose a book called *The Lady and the Unicorn* and two books by Madame Felise. One, called *Pilgrim's Tales*, recounted stories pilgrims had told Felise about their lives and their travels. "Some of the tales are harrowing, such as when an Italian family was beset by thieves," she told Magali. "But other tales are uplifting, like one about a woman pilgrim who found an orphan boy wandering in the forest and embraced him as her own son."

Felise's other book told the story of Jeanne the Maid's mother.

"As an elderly woman she traveled to Rome to have an audience with the pope," Felise explained. "She knew that her daughter was innocent of heresy and witchcraft and convinced the pope that she deserved a retrial. Because of her mother's efforts, Jeanne's name has been cleared."

Magali beamed. "I knew she was innocent!" she said as she paid for the books. "Mama and my friend will enjoy all of these books so much, but especially this one."

After he and Magali bade the couple farewell, Roland started to follow Magali down the stairs. He stopped when he saw Felise going to her husband's alcove and taking his gnarled hands in her own, her right hand grooved with a deep quill mark. How much longer would they be able to work? How much longer would they be alive? The words of his two mentors, Hubert and Isaac, echoed within Roland: *There are no guarantees.*

Magali, there is a guarantee that I will always love you, Roland said silently as he caught up to her and put his arm around her shoulder.

She gave him a quizzical look—they usually didn't show affection for one another in a public place.

"Like Felise and Georges, may we too enjoy a long life together," he whispered.

She nestled into his embrace, smiling, and they descended the stairs together.

Author's Note

This is a work of historical fiction. While I have attempted to adhere to an accurate timeline of events and historical personages, I have taken several liberties. For example, Greek mythology was not widely translated into the vernacular languages of Europe until the early sixteenth century. Furthermore, I have created a bit more drama about the process of Provence being absorbed into the kingdom of France in the late fifteenth century. Lastly, I also invented several fictional characters, who are in keeping with the historical record of the late medieval and early Renaissance period. Lady Beatrice, countess of Provence, is based on my research into women rulers in medieval Europe. Her daughter Magali is based on the historical figure of Juana, daughter of Queen Isabella and King Ferdinand of Spain. I also invented a nephew for the French King Louis XI. The onus for any other discrepancies or factual errors is solely on me.

My background knowledge about the medieval and early Renaissance time period came from my research as the co-author (with Marty Williams) of two nonfiction books about medieval women, *Between Pit and Pedestal: Women in the Middle Ages* and *An Annotated Index of Medieval Women*. I also consulted many sources about medieval medicine, the history of Provence, and Jewish medieval history. A trip to the southwestern part of France helped me immensely to visualize the various settings of the novel.

Selected List of Sources

1. Bailey, Cyril, translator. *Lucretius: On the Nature of Things*. Oxford: At the Clarendon Press, 1948.
2. Bary-Boloré, Clémence. "The History and Culture of Provence." *French Library*. https://frenchlibrary.org/2022/04/12/provence/.
3. Cobban, A. B. *The Medieval Universities: Their Development and Organization*. Harper & Row Publishers Inc, 1975.
4. Gordon, Benjamin. *Medieval and Renaissance Medicine*. New York: Philosophical Library, 1959.
5. "The History of Jewish Provence." *France Today*. https://francetoday.com/culture/the-history-of-jewish-provence/.
6. Lindberg, D. C., ed. *Science in the Middle Ages*. Chicago: University of Chicago Press, 1978.
7. "Provence-Alpes-Côte d'Azur." *Guide Culturel des Juifs d'Europe*. https://jguideeurope.org/en/region/france/provence/
8. Siraisi, Nancy. *Medieval and Early Renaissance Medicine: An Introduction to Knowledge and Practice*. University of Chicago Press, 1990.

SOURCES FOR THE QUOTES AT THE BEGINNING OF THE CHAPTERS:

1. Fisher, Johanna. "Hildegard von Bingen: Celebrating an Early Eco-Feminist." *Europeana*, March 2022. https://www.europeana.eu/en/stories/hildegard-von-bingen-celebrating-an-early-ecofeminist.

2. Kemp, Simon. "Modern Myth and Medieval Madness: Views of Mental Illness in the European Middle Ages and Renaissance." *New Zealand Journal of Psychology* 14, no. 1. June 1985. https://www.psychology.org.nz/journal-archive/NZJP-Vol141-1985-1-Kemp.pdf.

3. Cybulskie, Danièle. "Last Words from a Medieval Mother to Her Son." Medievalists.net. https://www.medievalists.net/2015/11/last-words-from-a-medieval-mother-to-her-son/.

4. "Treatment of Depression by Maimonides (1138–1204): Rabbi, Physician, and Philosopher." *American Journal of Psychiatry* 165, no 4. April 2008. https://psychiatryonline.org/doi/10.1176/appi.ajp.2007.07101575.

5. Thevenet, André. "Guy de Chauliac (1300–1370): The 'Father of Surgery.'" *Annals of Vascular Surgery* 7, no. 2, pgs. 208–12. 1993. https://www.annalsofvascularsurgery.com/article/S0890-5096(06)60593-1/abstract.

6. "25 Great Medieval Quotes." Medievalists.net. https://www.medievalists.net/2023/05/25-great-medieval-quotes/.

7. Libquotes. https://libquotes.com/marie-de-france/quote/lbh7u3l.

8. Halsall, Paul, ed. "Internet Jewish History Sourcebook: The Expulsion of the Jews from France, 1182 CE." Fordham University, 1998. https://origin-rh.web.fordham.edu/Halsall/index.asp.

9. Anderson, Bonnie S. and Judith P. Zinsser. *A History of Their Own: Women in Europe from Prehistory to the* Present, vol. 1, pg. 346. Harper & Row, 1988.

10. McCleery, Iona. "Both 'illness and temptation of the enemy': Melancholy, the Medieval Patient and the Writings of King Duarte of Portugal (r. 1433–38)." *Journal of Medieval Iberian Studies* 1, no. 2, pgs. 163–178. June 2009. https://pmc.ncbi.nlm.nih.gov/articles/PMC3158133/

11. Withey, Alison. "Medieval Anti-Poisons." *Jewelpedia*, July 2015. https://www.jewelpedia.net/medieval-anti-poisons/.
12. Williams, Marty and Anne Echols. *Between Pit and Pedestal: Women in the Middle Ages*, pg. 7. Princeton: Markus Wiener Publishers, 1994.
13. Williams, Marty and Anne Echols. *Between Pit and Pedestal: Women in the Middle Ages*, pg. 9. Princeton: Markus Wiener Publishers, 1994.
14. "15 Quotes from Medieval Kings and Queens." Medievalists.net. https://www.medievalists.net/2023/08/quotes-medieval-kings-queens/.

Discussion Questions

Characters and Relationships

1. Which characters did you relate to on a personal level? Why?
2. How did Roland change over the course of the novel?
3. What were the societal beliefs about women in the late Middle Ages? How did Roland's views about women change?
4. Compare the women characters to stereotypes about women during that time period.
5. Discuss the parent/children relationships in the novel.
6. What were the prevailing ideas about marriage in the late fifteenth century?

Life in Fifteenth-Century Provence

1. Imagine time traveling to fifteenth-century Provence. What would be some of the biggest differences between your everyday life then and now?
2. What did the novel reveal about prejudice and discrimination at that time period?
3. What did you notice about the political atmosphere at this time period? Does it remind you of politics today?
4. What did you learn about the prevalent religious beliefs of the time period?

5. The novel takes place in the late Middle Ages/early Renaissance. What changes were taking place at that time?

History of Mental Health

1. How has our understanding of mental health and illnesses changed since the fifteenth century? Have any of our ideas remained similar?
2. If Lady Beatrice joined a NAMI (National Alliance on Mental Illness) support group, what advice would other loved ones of people suffering from mental illnesses give her?
3. What stigmas/prejudices about mental illnesses were addressed in the novel?
4. What do you predict about the future of Magali's illness and how it will affect her life?

History of Medicine

1. Did any of the medical/surgical practices mentioned in the novel surprise you?
2. How did Roland's understanding of the body and his vocation change over the course of the novel?
3. Think of at least one of your personal medical issues. How would it likely be treated in the fifteenth century?
4. Do we still have superstitions in our modern medical belief systems?

Acknowledgments

I am very grateful to everyone who helped me on my journey to publish *Roland's Labyrinth*. My apologies if I have accidentally omitted anyone. Know that you too are much appreciated!

My friends Patricia Hurd and Sharon Saxton have been faithful readers since the inception of this book. I am forever grateful to them for their perceptive comments, humor, constructive criticism, and above all, their willingness to read so many different versions of the manuscript! Other insightful readers include my sister Marcella Wilson, neighbor and friend Katie Smiley, and writer friends Liza Nelson Brown and Kathryn Legan. My friends Kim Papastavridis and Sandra Kleinman, who have a deep understanding of language and its nuances, proved invaluable as editors. Terry Repak, my friend and fellow writer, trained her "eagle eyes" on the completed manuscript and spotted important edits and revisions. Horticulturalist and garden historian Lesley Parness gave me "sage" advice on medicinal plants and poisons used in the late Middle Ages. Writer and dream researcher Ryan Hurd was my guide in exploring creative and innovative platforms to connect with readers. Thank you all for helping me create a richer novel that is ultimately more satisfying and understandable to readers.

My family has always been such a wonderful and loving support group, especially my husband Russ Echols who died in February 2025. This book is dedicated to the wonderful man who was my life partner for fifty-one years. Not only was Russ my best friend and the father of our children, but he was also the builder of my writer's shed, my personal chef, my comic relief, my muse, and a self-professed "book widower." I also want to thank my daughter Melissa Moynahan, my son-in-law Patrick Moynahan, and my son Jarrett Echols. Melissa also serves as a publicist extraordinaire, guiding me through the web of social media and giving me practical advice on which publicity avenues to pursue. A big thanks to my siblings, their spouses, and their children (Tamar June and Conor Bean, Emmett Wilson, Drew Schmidt, Daniel Schmidt, Gavin Bowen, Kevin Schmidt, Willa Bowen, and Finley Bowen) as well. Michael Schmidt, Emily Schmidt, Marcella and Ray Wilson, Eric and Annette Schmidt, John Schmidt, Debbie Schmidt, and Mary Pat and Mike Bowen, thanks for helping me arrange book events in Georgia, Texas, and Colorado, as well as spreading the word about my books to friends and neighbors. And of course, I can't forget my grandchildren, Hannah, Adalise, and Loukas, who bring joy to my life and remind me to balance work with play.

Another wonderful support group for me has been my group of "college" friends. It has been an incredible experience to share over fifty years of my life with Nada Carey, Lynn Frank, Patti Schropp, Rita Sislen, Vicki Tauxe, Kathy Zilberman, and posthumously Susan Hollingshead. I can't thank each of you enough for your support, not just about writing but about life! A shout-out to Patti's husband John Dunn as well. A talented sign painter, John created a lovely poster board for me to display at book talks and signings.

Many thanks again to Terry Repak, who has supported me as a writer since we formed a writers' group with several other writers almost a quarter of a century ago. Terry guided me to establish a relationship with an incredible publishing company, She Writes Press. Brooke Warner and her team did amazing work on publishing *A Tale of Two Maidens* in 2023 and now they have outdone themselves in publishing *Roland's Labyrinth*. I am so grateful to project managers Lauren Wise and Shannon Green, astute editor Krissa Lagos, and creative cover designer Julie Metz. You all have exceeded my expectations for a finished product.

About the Author

Photo credit: Karen Varsha

ANNE ECHOLS is the coauthor (with Marty Williams) of two nonfiction books, *Between Pit and Pedestal: Women in the Middle Ages* and *An Annotated Index of Medieval Women*. Her research for those projects inspired her to go beyond historical facts and imagine the fictional stories of ordinary women from the Middle Ages. Her first historical fiction book was *A Tale of Two Maidens: A Novel* (She Writes Press, 2023). After earning a BA and master's degree from Emory University in Atlanta, Anne enjoyed a long career of teaching English to high school students with language learning disabilities. Her husband, Russ, and she have two adult children. Recently retired, she is grateful for the opportunity to divide her time between Silver Spring, Maryland, where her grandchildren live, and Atlanta, Georgia.

Looking for your next great read?

We can help!

Visit www.shewritespress.com/next-read
or scan the QR code below for a list
of our recommended titles.

She Writes Press is an award-winning
independent publishing company founded to
serve women writers everywhere.